The Comancheros

THE

Comancheros

BY PAUL I. WELLMAN

DOUBLEDAY & COMPANY, INC.

Garden City, New York

Library of Congress Catalog Card Number: 52-11616

COPYRIGHT, 1952, BY PAUL I. WELLMAN

To J. Robert Tolle

physician, cattle rancher, and my friend, who
subscribes with me to the excellent axiom: *If
you're too busy to go fishing, you're too busy.*

CONTENTS

ONE: "The Sickening Conceit of Men!"   13

TWO: "To Waste on the Gallows . . ."   30

THREE: "Absolute Courage, Absolute Loyalty . . ." 49

FOUR: "Them Moccasins Was Never Comanche!"   68

FIVE: "By the Same Token, You Stay Out of My
           Country . . ."   80

SIX: "Give Houston Only One Year of Peace
           on the Border . . ."   99

SEVEN: "It Must Be Old Iron Shirt Himself!"   110

EIGHT: "I Am Musketoon, the Chief of These
           People . . ."   125

NINE: "It Adds Up to Worse Than I Thought . . ." 142

TEN: "Without Regard to Any Personal
           Consideration . . ."   162

ELEVEN: "I Think They're the Bravest Men I Ever
           Knew!"   180

TWELVE: "Tapworth Cobb Wasn't No Better . . ."   200

THIRTEEN: "Invulnerable and Invincible . . ."   211

Historical Note

THE WORD *Comancheros* has almost no recognition in formal history. Yet it was a word once excessively well known to the unprotected ranchers on the scantily settled borders of Texas, and there are numerous records of the existence of that strange, shifting, gypsy-like people, in the writings of the earliest explorers of the western plains.

In 1832 Zebulon Pike reported seeing the deep trails made by the Comanchero *carretas* across the plains toward the Comanche country, carrying out goods to be exchanged for Indian loot. Notice was taken of the trails, campsites, and the slinking traders themselves, by Josiah Gregg in 1839, George Wilkins Kendall in 1841, and Captain R. B. Marcy in 1849.

Apparently the inception of the nefarious trade with the Comanches, in which the settlements and ranches of Texas were the victims and prey, began innocently enough. Mexican buffalo hunters from the settlements of New Mexico went out on the Staked Plains to hunt bison. They called themselves *Ciboleros*, and butchered and dried the meat they killed, packed it in rawhide sacks, and carried it to the Mexican settlements, where as *carne seco*—jerked beef —it was an important article of commerce.

Gradually these hunters established trade relations with the Comanche Indians, who at first exchanged with them peltries and other products of the chase, for goods. But presently a new direction was given Comanche war activities by the type of trade in which the greatest interest was shown by their visitors, who became known as Comancheros—those having to do with the Comanches. Because they furnished an avid market for stolen cattle, horses, and other plunder, they were a tremendous spur, virtually a directing force, to the Indians in making continuous raids on the Texas frontier.

By no means were the Comancheros all Mexicans. Unscrupulous Americans and persons of other nationalities participated in the trade. At first the Comancheros made their expeditions out in the Staked Plains in a haphazard manner, with no definite destination, and trusting to accidental meetings with wandering Comanche bands. But later, regular rendezvous were appointed, where the Comancheros with their goods and the Comanches with their plunder met and exchanged commodities. Sometimes the Indians brought not only livestock and goods, but captives, whom the Comancheros often cynically held until they were ransomed by the Texas families to whom they belonged.

But chiefly the trade was in cattle and horses. Live Texas cattle on the hoof were more profitable and easier to handle than jerked buffalo meat in sacks. Horses and mules always found a brisk market beyond the Pecos. Not fewer than three hundred thousand cattle and a hundred thousand horses and mules were, over the years, bartered to the Comancheros by the Indians, and all of that livestock came from Texas, to the accompaniment of bloodshed.

Names of Comanchero rendezvous still stick to some localities on the plains, and they are revealing. There is, for example, Rio de Las Lenguas—the Tongue River. Here often gathered a hodgepodge of Indian tribes—Comanches, Kiowas, Lipans, and the like—with Mexicans and renegade whites, in a native American Babel of the plains, the varied jargons of which gave the name River of Tongues. Near Quitaque, Texas, is a valley called Valle de Las Lágrimas—Vale of Tears—where the Comanches, on occasion, tore weeping kidnaped white mothers and their children apart, as the captives were apportioned to different bands. The tragedy of these unfortunates left its impression even on the callous Comancheros, who witnessed it. Hence the name.

The Palo Duro canyon—that titanic crack in the surface of the plains—was a natural location for such a rendezvous, and traces of what undoubtedly were once Comanchero dwellings existed in it until comparatively recent times, before the elements obliterated them. The canyon, one of the natural wonders of America, was always a favorite visiting place of the plains tribes.

Concerning the chief, Iron Shirt, and his fabulous chain mail, both name and character are based on solid fact. The name, as recorded by George Bird Grinnell, frequently occurred among the plains Indians, and there are traditions of several coats of mail, brought to the southern United States by the Spaniards in the very early days, which fell into the hands of the savages and were worn by them. Fragments of these shirts have since been found.

The Comanches, in particular, had a series of chiefs named Iron Shirt, each of whom wore the chain mail— possibly the same coat, which was passed on from one to the next. The last of this line was killed by the Texas Rangers in the Staked Plains.

With these remarks, the reader is invited to consider this book as a novel, all the major personages in it with the exception of Sam Houston the product of the author's imagination, and save for background and historical actualities, all the adventures described herein purely fictional —although they *might* have happened just this way.

PAUL I. WELLMAN
August, 1952.

ONE:

"The Sickening Conceit of Men!"

1

A BAYOU mist filled the oak grove, so that in the uncertain early light objects even relatively close seemed distorted or mysterious. That, perhaps, was what gave Paul Regret the momentary feeling of unreality, as if the whole thing had never happened.

With a feeling of weariness and distaste, if not of actual remorse, he looked at the youth whom he had just shot, stretched on the wet grass twelve paces away, his young face, with eyes half closed, a glimmering paleness; the ruffled front of his white shirt already staining with blood. Then at least a dozen were kneeling about the fallen figure, Regret's seconds as well as his, the witnesses, even Perigord, who as referee had given the signal for fire. It took only a few moments for the surgeon to make his examination, and they rose as if by concert.

In their faces Regret saw anger, accusation. One muttered, "Assassin!" Another, "Butcher!"

At that selfsame moment they all heard the rapid tattoo of a galloping horse, and through the cottony lather of fog a rider burst.

Paul Regret, seasoned gambler, was not a man easily dismayed, yet his heart sank, somewhat, as he recognized Judge Beaubien.

For all his sixty years the judge was still a horseman; and he sat his saddle like a furious gray-haired centaur as he wheeled his tall hunter into the grove.

They heard his shout, "My son?"

It was half question, half exclamation. Then he saw the prostrate form, half supported by one of the seconds, and threw himself from the saddle to the ground. For a moment he bent over the young face, then stood erect.

"Too late! I am too late!" he groaned.

Regret remained where he had placed himself at first, a slender and not inelegant figure, feet together, coatless, the pistol hanging heavy in his hand and the sharp tang of powder smoke still prickling his nostrils. He was twenty-nine, with a face lean and dark, and a narrow black mustache of which he was a little vain. And he had a reputation for being lucky, but at this moment it appeared to him that he was the unluckiest man in all New Orleans.

Toward him Judge Beaubien turned, a portly but vigorous figure, dressed richly as usual. Regret had always respected, even admired him, but now the older man's face was bitter with fury.

"Paul Regret!" he cried, in a voice almost choked. "Paul Regret, my son's death is on your head!"

He said it with solemn portent, as if he were pronouncing the death sentence in his own courtroom, where he ruled, as everyone knew, like an autocrat, virtually a king.

Regret inclined his head slightly. The judge's feeling, the feeling of all those angry persons about him, was after all understandable. It was, he reflected, one of those inevitable moments in life when a man is not popular with anyone, however little he may be to blame for it.

The youth lying there, with his cambric ruffles dabbled with his blood, was Emile Adrien de Rieux Beaubien. And Regret thought of Eloise Grailhe, the fair and fickle.

Women, he sometimes believed, were at the bottom of almost all the trouble in the world. It was the misfortune of Emile Beaubien that he loved Eloise Grailhe, or thought he did, which came to much the same thing. She was *chanteuse légère* in the French Opera, where her voice and beauty had won her remarkable popularity. She had her legions of suitors, her baskets of flowers, her jewels, her banquets, her universal adulation. To be sure she was an

14

actress: and of all the adorers who pursued her, none had any thought of marriage, save perhaps one. And she smiled upon all of them: but with no particular favor on any, save perhaps one. The man who would have married her was young Emile; the man she may have favored was Paul Regret.

Some whisper of this favor must have reached Emile's ears. He did not mention her name in the quarrel, but chose to act as if he did not know how to lose at *lansquenet*, cursing, and flinging down the cards, and finally casting the word "Cheat" in Regret's teeth.

An epithet most unjust. Though Regret had for years made his living by gambling, he had his own code of honor, and took a pride in honest dealing. Still, he had no wish to fight Emile. That unlicked cub, hardly twenty, pampered, perfumed, and pomaded, had connections too important, and the disparity between them was too evident when it came to a meeting with arms. Regret would have passed over the incident, save for the fact that the youth cast his insult openly, in the presence of a full dozen gentlemen in the Salle St. Philippe.

In New Orleans, in that year of 1843, two fatal things could happen to a man in Paul Regret's position. One was to become a laughingstock. The other was to accept an insult openly, without proper retaliation. A gambler had to keep his pistols in practice.

For the matter of that, Regret's skill with weapons was not unknown. A marksman, particularly with the pistol, must be born with a certain flair, an instinct too delicate to be described, without which any amount of practice achieves little more than mediocrity. Regret was fortunate —or unfortunate—enough to possess that flair, and had perfected it. Habitués of the gallery at the Salle St. Philippe unanimously testified to his shooting, which some of them described as almost uncanny.

Had Emile been less drunk, or less blinded by his jealousy, he might have held his words. He was a fool: but that did not alter the fact that he was a sprig of one of the great families of New Orleans. His mother was a De Rieux, with the blood of the Bourbons in her veins: but that was not even important beside the fact that he was the only son of Judge Beaubien, the most powerful man in Louisiana, a political autocrat who made and unmade governors at his whim, who dictated the policies of the state, and whose decisions in his court nobody dared to challenge. Vengeance was very certain to be directed at the man who had shot Emile Beaubien.

Paul Regret did not reply to Judge Beaubien. He saw no reason to justify himself. He might have urged that this duel was not of his seeking; that he was the aggrieved party; that Emile had been given the choice of place and weapons. These arguments would have had little effect, however, on a man like Judge Beaubien, grief-stricken as he was, and almost mad with pain and fury.

Besides, Regret's reputation was too well known to all those present. They would remember Colonel Rust, Adam Littleton, the river gambler, and Honoré Brisseul, all of whose deaths under these very dueling oaks were charged to him. And that was saying nothing of other affairs which ended without fatalities, although each of his antagonists carried from the field the mark of Paul Regret.

He shrugged. Public opinion always was against a gambler, he thought wearily. From the second who now stiffly brought up his coat, he took the garment and put it on. Then he mounted his horse, lifted his hat to the assemblage, and rode away into the mist.

2

Weapons, cards, and women. They were the three focuses of Paul Regret's life. He had been measurably successful with all three of them, and though all three had somewhat stained his reputation, he thought little of that in the lightheaded way of young men.

Through the fog he rode, his face still and thoughtful.

It was a face which had the gambler's trick of icy control at the card table, and yet could relax into charm and warmth, with reckless black eyes and a flashing white smile under his narrow mustache. And he had an engaging way about him, so that men usually, and women almost always, excused whatever he did. But there would be, he realized, no excuse for him this time.

As he trotted his horse into the town, the fog began to lift so that he could see the streets and buildings. All his life he had lived here: his ancestors had come to New Orleans with Bienville, and once had possessed some wealth, although the family fortunes were reduced now until he, the last of the line, was forced to the cards and the dice for a living. Still, he had managed not too badly in the gay, reckless, gaming life of young men of fashion, to whom wine, profligacy, and the ladies were all that mattered.

With keenest regret, as he rode along, he noted favorite resorts like the Café Rouge, Victor's, the old Opera, and the Salle St. Philippe, where he practiced with weapons, since he must be quitting them all. For he was realistic with himself. Judge Beaubien and the whole De Rieux family were now his deadly enemies. The police and courts were at their command. And while he thought sadly that New Orleans was of all cities the most pleasant in which to live, he must leave it at least for a time, until things changed.

It seemed particularly hard to him, for the practice of dueling was strongly rooted in New Orleans in spite of the law against it. The very presence of that statute, indeed, only served to add a sort of glamour to the other fascinations of the deadly game, and the numbers of famous *maîtres d'armes*—men like Baudoin, Thimecourt, and L'Allouette, all making their living by teaching the trade of death—were an advertisement of the desuetude of the prohibition.

Yet he knew how even a moribund law can be revived and made murderously effective in the hands of those with the will and power to do so. Prosecuted with the De Rieux

17

money, facing Judge Beaubien in his own court, he could expect only a quick, short journey to the gallows.

3

     Regret tethered his horse before his lodgings, which were above a tavern near the French Market, and gloomily mounted the stairs to his rooms. A calendar on the wall told him the date:

May 6, 1843

It was a date he never forgot.

Frowning, he began to gather his effects, putting them into the two trunks and the portmanteau with which he intended to travel. An uncongenial task. But hardly had he begun it, when he heard a step on the stair; and by the quick stab of high heels, the step of a woman.

A knock, now, at the door. With some annoyance he opened it, for a woman, just at this time, was the last creature he wished to see.

But his annoyance changed to something else. In the hall he found Eloise Grailhe.

She stood regarding him with her graceful head balanced a little on one side, and a question in her magnificent gray eyes. Once more he was struck by the richness of her dark hair, the brightness of her lips, and the odd, almost gypsy quality in her. A pretty girl, he had always said. Damned pretty. *Too* damned pretty.

"Eloise!" he exclaimed. "What are you doing here? Isn't the French Opera troupe in rehearsal?"

"It's much too early for rehearsal," she replied, giving him both her hands, and carrying him, as it were, into his room with her, whereat she closed the door behind her.

This boldness he rather disliked. It is one thing to meet a charming young woman clandestinely, with sufficient safeguards, and so make love to her: it is quite another to have her come bolting into your rooms in broad day and in full view of the whole street. His reputation perhaps was not such that it would suffer, but he still had some feeling for discretion. As for Eloise, this might well set going a scandal that would ruin her.

Yet it is flattering to any man to have a pretty and talented young woman so aflame with ardor for him that she is blind to every risk, and there is a consideration which a gentleman owes to the ladies always. To be less than gallant would be disgraceful, especially in view of the sacrifice she seemed bent on making. So he summoned his best smile and raised to his lips the fingers of this girl who, he believed, was engaged in the act of throwing herself at his head.

"Whatever your reason for coming at this hour," he said, "you bring heaven with you." Retaining her hand, and with the smile of a confident lover, he drew her toward him, expecting that she would come to his arms. Instead, she wrenched herself away.

"You fool!" she cried.

The epithet, as well as her sharp voice in uttering it, and the displeasure on her pretty face, set him back.

"Fool?" he echoed, rather stupidly.

"Yes, fool! You've been described to me as a charming scoundrel, Paul—but never has anyone told me you were a fool!"

"Mademoiselle, I fail to follow," he said stiffly.

After all, women do not ordinarily rush to a man's rooms to call him a fool. Particularly to the rooms of a man like Paul Regret.

"Then attend!" she said rapidly. "I'm not here for gallantries or caresses—I'm here to warn you!"

"As to what?"

"Judge Beaubien."

"Oh, that." His voice was careless. "I know of it. Unfortunately I had to meet his son at the Oaks of Allard this morning. See—I'm packing already." He indicated the two trunks and the portmanteau.

"Pack?" she cried. "You've no time to pack!"

19

"Why? A man must take some clothes when he travels——"

"Not a man in your case!"

"My dear, you make too much of the situation——"

"Believe me, Paul, I didn't come here without good reason!" She sounded as if she were straining to keep her patience. "I have my own problems——"

"What problems, little Eloise?" He was half amused. Women's problems usually had to do with what gown to wear, or the kind of perfume to use, or some other triviality.

"Personal problems!" she said. "Family problems——"

She broke off, and he stared at her. Always there had been a certain mystery about this girl's antecedents, although she was accepted as of good blood. Still, he had thought her alone in the world. If she had a family, he had never heard of it. She intrigued him, and he had it on his tongue to question her further, but she interrupted him.

"They're on their way up here now!" she said.

It jarred the smile off his face. "Who?"

"The authorities—to arrest you!"

"How do you know this?" A very different complexion to matters now.

"Judge Beaubien's offices are across the street from the Opera. He arrived foaming, to draw up a warrant and summon the sheriff. It was all over the street, he shouted so! I came as fast as a carriage would bring me——"

She stopped. Both of them distinctly heard the clatter of ironshod hoofs on the cobbles below. A voice in the street said, "He's here. That's his horse."

It was Regret's horse that was tethered in front. He glanced from the window. Judge Beaubien had made his rendezvous quickly, and with him were the sheriff and two or three deputies.

"Oh . . . what will you do now?" The girl's voice sank suddenly to a whisper.

"I'm more concerned for you," he said. "What if—they find you here in my rooms?"

20

"It doesn't matter!" She was almost tearful. "I only want you to go—please——"

To Regret it was evident that this beautiful girl was in love with him. An attractive situation . . . If events just now were not so crowded . . .

"I can't leave you——" he began, indecisively.

She turned on him a face so impatient, so angry, that he stepped back from it.

"You idiot! Can't you understand that I'm doing this for *myself*—not for you? Do you realize what the notoriety of your trial and execution, with my name drawn into it, would do to me? Being found in your rooms I can survive —but *that*, never!"

The change in her so bewildered him that he uttered a stumbling, blundering remark. "But I—I thought—you loved me——"

It left him wide open to withering feminine scorn. "*Love* you? The sickening conceit of men! Because I've flirted with you once in a while—you've built on that? I merely amused myself! This is too ridiculous—it's infuriating, if it weren't so laughable!"

On the mantel lay his riding whip, which he had placed there when he came up to the room. She snatched it, and turned on him with a face so tense he thought she would strike him.

That was not, however, what made him move with such alacrity. It was the thunder of the sheriff's fist on the door.

To give him due credit, Regret could think and act quickly. His front windows looked down on the street: those on the side opened on an enclosed courtyard, and were framed by a huge bougainvillaea vine, a mass of magenta flowers which grew on the tavern wall. Light as any canebrake panther, he was out of the side window, hanging against the wall, supported precariously by this growth. Even as he trusted himself to the knotted vine, he heard the door within fly open, and the conversation that followed came clearly to him as he clung just outside the window.

21

"Where is Regret?" It was Judge Beaubien's voice.

"He's gone—he fled," Eloise said.

"You're Mademoiselle Grailhe, aren't you? I recognize you from the Opera stage. What are you doing here?"

"I came to do what a woman could do—for vengeance!"

"How, mademoiselle?"

"He—that man Regret—shot down my—the man I loved ——" A sob in her voice. "Emile and I——" She hesitated. "Oh, your honor——"

"You—and my son?" the judge marveled.

"Y-yes——"

"In that case"—his voice grew stern—"explain your presence here!"

"A woman can't call a man out and shoot him," said Eloise clearly. The sob had left her tones, and her voice grew stronger as with the fury of hatred. Regret, listening, silently applauded such consummate acting. "But a woman can take a whip to a man—like the cur he is!" she went on.

Now Regret understood why she had seized his whip from the mantel. He heard her lash a chair with it, slap it against her dress. Quick-witted—very quick-witted—that touch.

"You *horsewhipped* Paul Regret?" asked a new voice, the sheriff's.

"Like a dog!" she said. "And like a dog he ran!"

A moment of surprised silence, then a roar of laughter burst out of the room. Regret heard exclamations.

"Paul Regret whipped!"

"Driven from his own lodgings by a girl!"

"Oh, this is rare! Wait till they hear it at Victor's!"

"Or the Café Rouge! Or the Salle St. Philippe!"

The laughter grew. On his vine outside, Regret winced, he cringed. Women, even actresses, he said to himself, sometimes have their moments of sublimity—but Eloise was overdoing matters. She loved him, in spite of her words, he told himself. But he could almost have wished that she had given him up to the sheriff, rather than using this method of saving him.

Then a new thought came. Was he so very sure after all that the girl *did* love him? Perhaps she had spoken the truth as to her anxiety to get him out of New Orleans, when he thought she was only sacrificing herself for him.

Suddenly many things seemed clear which had not been clear before. Regret had never considered marriage with Eloise. He did not regard himself as the marrying type. His was the usual viewpoint of the reckless and pleasure-loving young men of his coterie toward pretty women in general, and actresses in particular. A boudoir affair—another little conquest—a charming interlude of love-making —these were all he contemplated.

Now it appeared she had seen through him. With all his callowness and stupidity, Emile Beaubien at least offered her honest marriage. Regret could hardly blame the girl for choosing that security. Yet it came to him as a shock.

He had been so sure of her adoration. And now he discovered how numbing to a man's vanity it is to find that a woman has been toying with him, while her real affections belong to another. It was, for him, a rather new experience, and not a pleasant one. He was furious with Eloise, at her faithlessness and selfishness, and at his own folly.

Meantime the laughter continued to come through the window with the cruelty of the cry of a wolf pack. In an hour it would be all over New Orleans that Paul Regret had been trounced like a schoolboy, forced to flee the anger of a girl. Endless mirth would resound in every café, every gaming room: and he, his brow already reddening with humiliation as he clung like a monkey to the vine, could not even deny it.

As has been said, one of the fatal things that could happen to a man in his position was to become a laughing-stock. Thanks to Eloise Grailhe, he knew that he was through forever in New Orleans.

"Mademoiselle," he heard the judge say as the laughter within the room quieted somewhat, "I'm sorry it had to be left to a lady to retaliate on the scoundrel. But you'll have a fuller revenge, I give you my solemn word. You'll see him on the gallows!" Then he said, in a different voice, "Now, may I have the honor of escorting you back whence you came?"

"With all my gratitude," she said prettily.

The sheriff interjected, "Mademoiselle evidently interrupted Regret in the act of packing. See his clothes all strewn around——"

"True enough," agreed the judge. "He may return. Post men here to intercept him if he does."

For Regret, that was sufficient. Silently he climbed down the bougainvillaea into the empty courtyard, and thence quickly lost himself among the crowded buildings of the market quarter.

4

Eloise Grailhe came out of the tavern on Judge Beaubien's arm, and was assisted into her carriage. The judge mounted his horse and rode beside her equipage back toward the French Opera. It was the custom in New Orleans—the gentleman in the saddle and the lady in the vehicle—but it hardly led to intimacy.

Not that there would have been much intimacy in any case. The judge was moodily silent, and Eloise was glad of it. She had hardly spoken the truth when she told him that she loved Emile, his son. But for the matter of that, if all women spoke with full candor of their love affairs, this world would be plunged at once into a state of anarchy worse than war. Eloise merely was observing discretion, and she hoped the judge would not cross-examine her too severely.

Once she stole a glance at his face, and noticed again its texture: the mature, burdened lines; the gray hair and florid skin; the sagging lower lids of the level, assured eyes; the uncompromising, self-willed mouth.

It was only seven or eight squares to the French Opera House. The last of the shreds of fog had gone, and the morning was fine and clear, but Eloise, riding demurely, with her hands folded in her lap, took less pleasure than common in the sun-brightened streets and the changing scenes of the old city. A heavy depression seemed to be weighting her.

After they had passed the Cathedral of St. Louis, the judge spoke for the first time.

"May I ask, mademoiselle, how long you have known my son?"

"About six months," she replied.

He frowned slightly, turning it over in his mind. At last he said, "You knew, of course, his station and expectations?"

"Yes, your honor."

He let it go at that, but she could read his mind. Between Emile Beaubien, the heir of two great families, and an actress like herself, existed an enormous gulf. As well might the judge have rasped out, "My dear young woman, don't you think your ambitions fly rather high?"

She was accustomed to this sort of snobbery. One accepted it, if one chose the stage as a profession—even the opera stage. An actress was condemned in advance to the *demimonde*, her reputation considered at least doubtful. She hardly minded it, except that she felt that as an operatic soprano she should hardly have been lumped with other female public entertainers by this intolerant old man. The opera, after all, had dignity, required talents of a high order.

Yet to arrogant aristocrats like Judge Beaubien, it was only a stage. Of another sort, perhaps, but still a stage, employing grease paint and footlights, and—most damning—sometimes flaunting its shapely feminine performers in tights.

And this in spite of the fact that people like Judge Beaubien crowded the French Opera to see the twinkling legs of the *corps de ballet* in some of the operas. Eloise herself had worn tights—when she played Jemmy in *William Tell*, and the Naide in *Armide*—and saw nothing very sinful about it, provided one had legs that were worth looking at.

Her own legs, as she recalled, had been tumultuously applauded.

No accounting for people. Men like Judge Beaubien, who paid money to look, then were scornful of what they looked at, were beyond Eloise. But she did not say so. Not to the judge, at least.

Instead, she sat straight up in the carriage, and contemplated her slim hands folded together in her lap. Since she left the convent, where she was brought up, the opera had been her life. She was accustomed to the thought of being an orphan: her mother dead while she was a baby, her father also, as the nuns said—and with some sort of a cloud hanging over him, she did not know exactly what. A sum of money was held in trust for her by Colonel Grymes, that cold-faced, white-haired lawyer, who was said once to have had connections with the piratical Lafitte brothers, and from this she was paid an allowance. It was Colonel Grymes who, when the sisters at the convent said she had a better than good soprano voice, suggested she should try for the French Opera troupe, and continue her studies in music, especially since her trust fund was getting low.

That was when she was fifteen. She thought back on it: her presentation to the manager of the Opera by Colonel Grymes, and the manager's rather reluctant acceptance of the responsibility of schooling her—which he undertook, as he said, only because of his devotion for his dear friend, the colonel.

She sang in choruses, and held torches in spectacle scenes, and had a bed in the girls' dormitory, and a place at the table with the ballet, and a constant running of vocal scales under the iron discipline of Monsieur Doumic, the broken-down concert master.

That lasted a year. In the year she grew from long-legged adolescence into the fulfillment of young womanhood. It is wonderful how important are looks in a girl.

Eloise, the management suddenly discovered, was very pretty, with a voice both sweet and flexible, who could reach high C without straining for it. And, of course, the legs . . .

Often she wondered how she would have fared had she possessed bad teeth, or a muddy complexion. But as it happened, she did not have these or any other serious flaws, and since feminine beauty is always a boon to the box office, she began to receive much attention from the management.

She learned prodigiously about music, the mechanics of the theater, the methods of acting, the repertoire, and the odd backstage politics which always occur where play folk gather.

Then she made her debut, when she was seventeen, in *Armide,* as the wood nymph, the role for which her legs qualified her. Shortly after she sang Adina in *L'Elisire d'Amore,* in which she rendered the arias of that outrageous flirt with such happy charm that she received an ovation, her first.

Afterward, there was a dinner, and now she learned a number of other things.

Chief in importance among these were the following: that while men are delightful, they are continuously and forever dangerous to a woman; that one must never believe anything they say; that an actress is considered fair game by them, her seduction becoming in measure a joint enterprise, the lucky winner to be toasted by his fellows; and above all, that a girl who has charming legs, and has not scrupled to display them, is a particular prize for conquest by all of them.

Fortunately, Eloise Grailhe had a level little head, and her convent training helped her. None of her suitors had been toasted by his friends—thus far. Three years had passed since then, she was now twenty, and she had not done badly for a lone wench, on the defensive continually against every man, although sometimes, most inconveniently, men were not on the defensive against her.

Emile Beaubien, for example.

Before God, she had never made the slightest conscious effort to captivate him. He was, for one thing, not appealing to her, callow to the point of being pinfeathered, with distressingly clammy hands, and pimples on the face which she found unpleasant. He was given to the kind of bleating, furthermore, that a girl could hardly respect, when he pleaded with her. He was her own age, twenty, but she felt years older and wiser than he. Yet Emile had fallen in love with her, so precipitately and blunderingly that she was half amused and more than half chagrined by the whole thing.

To be sure, he was heir to the De Rieux and Beaubien fortunes . . .

But she shrugged her slim shoulders at that thought, a little impatiently. Emile was such a fool! It astonished her that he had enough gumption to get into a duel. With a man like Paul Regret, of all people . . .

She considered Paul. He, at least, was not pinfeathered.

A charming scoundrel. She had told him that, and it was the truth. She had been warned against him from the first, and there were enough bad stories about him to condemn him completely.

And yet . . . Paul Regret was handsome, and supple, and he gave you the idea, somehow, that under everything superficial he was a *man*. She remembered with a little, helpless quiver the flash of his reckless black eyes and the flash of his reckless white smile beneath that little neat mustache.

If things were a little different, now . . . But Paul was what he was, a deceiver of women, constantly on the prowl, and not even ashamed of it. The whispers about him—when they were brought to his ears, he just laughed, or confessed them quite blandly. He ought not be given a minute's time by any young woman with her own welfare to consider!

She fortified herself with that last thought, and sat up with her red lips in a firm straight line.

Then she sighed, and her lips softened. After all, Paul

was the most entertaining man in New Orleans. And when he asked her to go to Victor's for a late supper after the performance, it took superhuman will power to refuse him. And when he invited her to ride with him in the park on Sunday morning, she usually went.

He made love to her, gaily, with a mingled grace and gentleness, but never seriously. She could picture in her mind now the strong angle of his jaw, and the way his black hair curled on the neck just behind his ear. Once or twice she had almost succumbed to the temptation to snuggle her face in the hollow of that neck . . .

But she had never succumbed. Never quite. She kept matters on a flirt-and-laughter basis, which was the only way a girl could possibly handle a man like Paul Regret.

Or had she, quite? She colored a little. No doubt about his conclusions when she went to his rooms that morning. His eyes: surprised, then pleased, then smilingly possessive. His voice: warm, and sure. He thought she was so much in love with him that she had come to him like a common hussy.

A large assumption! And she had told him so, roundly. But that did not altogether cure her embarrassment.

Oh, *why* did Paul Regret have to be like Paul Regret?

Or rather, why couldn't Paul Regret be like Paul Regret —but with some important differences?

Well, no use concerning herself. She was *not* in love with him, whatever he thought. And even if she *were,* she told herself primly, millions of women had found men attractive and not to be believed—and wiped those men, wisely, off the slate. As for Paul Regret, he was false, false, to every woman . . .

Just the same, she found herself wondering a little tremulously where he was now, and if he had gotten away from those sheriff's deputies. She hoped very much he had, if only through motives of charity.

Sincerely, she hoped it *was* charity . . .

The carriage came to a stop. They were before the French Opera.

"I must apologize, mademoiselle," the judge was saying. He had taken off his hat. "I haven't been very good company. You must pardon me."

Belatedly, he seemed concerned at his own lack of conversational manners.

As women can do, she gave him a brilliant smile which in no way suggested that she had been as abstracted as he.

"I gladly pardon—a gentleman with grave worries and griefs on his mind," she said. "And I thank you for escorting me."

He looked at her. "You *are* a charming creature," he said as if to himself, and as if in his mind excusing his son, Emile, for the indiscretion of falling in love with her.

Very stately, Judge Beaubien rode away, while the doorman of the Opera House assisted her from the carriage.

TWO:

"To Waste on the Gallows . . ."

1

As FOR Paul Regret, it still remained for him to learn how little a man can understand a woman, no matter how he prides himself on his ability to do so; and how, when he thinks his way around a circle concerning her, she has often completed the circle and is halfway around it again in her thinking concerning him.

When he climbed down the vine on the tavern wall, and slipped away through the courtyard to the street beyond, his most important emotion was bitterness at what he considered Eloise's feminine treachery.

Then he stopped to take stock of himself. He had the clothes in which he stood, and the money in his wallet. Like most gamblers, it was his practice to carry considerable sums, and on this day he had on his person perhaps five hundred dollars—not enough to take him any great distance, or support him for any reasonable period of time, since his tastes and habits had never been inexpensive.

He wondered where to turn, and for a moment, with the injustice and futility of his position, he was near to despair. But presently he rallied himself to think out his first step.

One thing was evident: he was too well known to lurk in the streets, or even the alleys, of New Orleans in daylight, without courting recognition every minute.

By a sort of desperate inspiration he stepped into a tiny hole-in-the-wall coffeehouse, which he never before had given a second glance, much less entered. A fat Italian, smelling villainously of garlic, and a too buxom girl— who, however, he noticed, had fine eyes—were alone in the place. They stared, openmouthed, as he closed the door and turned the key on the lock inside.

"Your name?" he said to the Italian.

"Niccolo Sabetti," the man answered.

"And this young lady?"

"My daughter, who waits on the tables."

Regret surveyed them grimly. "How much does a place like this take in during a day's business?"

Obviously they believed he intended to rob them, perhaps commit other violences, for they saw in him a certain desperation.

"Not—not very much, monsieur," the Italian faltered. "My daughter and I—only enough for a bare living—a few dollars——"

"Twenty dollars?"

"H-hardly, monsieur."

"Ten?"

"Perhaps—on a very good day——"

"Then attend, Monsieur Sabetti, and you too, mademoiselle. It is my whim to be a solitary customer for all of this day. Never mind my reason. For you, it's enough that it is so. Lock the door with a sign on the outside, 'Closed.' I won't molest you, so long as you do as I say. At dark, I'll depart, and for this service I will pay you—fifty dollars. Is that satisfactory?"

They seemed profoundly relieved, and the man nodded. The girl so far recovered from her first fright as to simper at him.

Thereafter, all that day, Regret drank bitter chicory coffee and stared out of a dirty window on the street. The Italian and his daughter did not venture to come near him unless summoned, but watched him half fearfully from the rear of their establishment.

Twice during the afternoon he saw patrols pass—part of the dragnet set out for him by Judge Beaubien. But customers for the coffeehouse were few at best, and the sign on the door discouraged investigation, so they were undisturbed. When darkness came at last, he paid the Italian, gave a handsome tip to the plump girl, and slipped out into the shadowy street.

Which way to go? Upriver to Natchez or Vicksburg? By sea to Charleston or New York? Down the gulf to some Mexican port? He could not decide. But escape from New Orleans he must—and that immediately.

Humiliating as it was, he sneaked furtively through dark alleys and side streets. It is an eerie and mysterious experience for one accustomed only to the brightest lights to find himself thus submerged in opaque blackness in unfamiliar byways. The silence seems to brood, the touch of the cold stone wall to the exploring hand startles like the touch of a reptile, inequalities underfoot seem like pits into which one may fall. The clouded sky of the night increased the blackness of the intricate lanes with which he was so ill acquainted.

After a time he saw a leaping fire ahead of him, and heard the sound of drumming and voices chanting some weird rhythmic chorus. That would be the Congo Square, an open space surrounded by a picket fence, with a few large sycamore trees in it, which was reserved for Negro slaves and never entered by white men, except when the police each evening at nine o'clock went in to fire off a cannon in the center as a curfew. He advanced toward it. About the bonfire were many black figures, and a dance was in progress—perhaps the Calinda or Bamboula, favorites with the slaves, and connected with their voodoo practices.

Regret stopped in the darkness. The spectacle reminded him of something of which he had not thought before. Just across the river from New Orleans was the village of Algiers, a huddle of mean huts and shacks, occupied almost wholly by Negroes, so that white men usually gave it a wide berth at night. What safer place could exist for a man like Paul Regret, since nobody who knew his tastes and habits could by the widest stretch of the imagination picture him as going there?

At once he began a detour, which took him, after an hour of groping, to the river front. For a dollar, a Negro boatman rowed him across the Mississippi. And hardly had he landed on the other shore, when he discovered that from the ferry head a stagecoach was departing for—of all places—the new and raw Republic of Texas, which lay somewhere in the far hinterlands west of all civilization.

Texas? It was the one destination Regret had not considered. For one hundred and fifty dollars he bought passage to some outlandish place called Washington-on-the-Brazos. It was the end of the stage line, and it sounded like the end of the world: and the end of the world, where he might be as far as possible from Judge Beaubien—and the mocking laughter of New Orleans—was exactly where Paul Regret craved to be.

2

He remembered that journey as an eternity of wetness and mud, for it rained incessantly the entire time. The passengers slept where darkness overtook them—in filthy taverns, private homes, even stables—and swore at the fleas that made their sleeping hideous.

All the creeks ran bankfull, and these they forded with great lurchings of their vehicle, and whip crackings and profanity from the driver. At the larger rivers, crude ferries assisted their crossing.

Days which seemed months passed before at length they mounted some low rocky hills and descended into the valley of a yellow, muddy river called the Brazos. On the opposite bank, the houses of the capital of Texas—Washington-on-the-Brazos—were visible.

A ferry, operating on the power of the current pulling against its slanted side, and pushing it on pulleys along a cable, eventually conveyed the stagecoach across, and they got down from the equipage in what might be called —but only in derision—the main street of the town. Mercifully, the rain had ceased for the moment, and Regret, so weary of the coach as to be happy at arriving even in such a destination as this, splashed across the miry road, where currents of water still ran in the wheel ruts, to the shelter of a wooden "portico" supported by a few rickety posts in front of a store.

There he stood for a moment, ruefully examining his mud-smeared, wrinkled clothes. This did nothing to lift his spirits, but when he raised his eyes to the squalid hamlet in which he had arrived, he almost shuddered.

As every gambler is aware, fate at times works stunning reverses. Today, a man may be living at Fracasse's in something like splendor, with gay companions, the best tables and the best wines, the finest tailors, and the prettiest women to make life worth living. And tomorrow the same man may be pawning the coat off his back and wondering where his next breakfast is to come from, while his associates of the day before yawn and look in another direction when he passes.

It requires jauntiness and courage to overcome such vicissitudes. More than once Regret had done so: but now he was confronted by a change in fortune so prodigious that it shook him. That he, to whom the smartest cafés and theaters on the continent, the latest trick of dress, the

34

newest *bon mot* were as familiar as his own mustache, should be reduced to—*this!*

Now he did shudder—visibly. Never had he seen such bleakness, such crudity, such ugliness.

Under the gray sky, which commenced now to weep again, was a scattering of mean log cabins and shacks of clapboard style. Unpainted stores with false fronts straggled down the quagmire of a street. At the hitchracks gaunt horses stood, their flanks and sides streaming with rain water, their heads bowed as if in silent shame at their surroundings. Here and there, where shelter offered, a few lean, sallow men lounged, prodigious as to face hair, and without exception chewing tobacco in the atrocious manner of the frontier.

For a moment despair and homesickness rushed over Regret like a nausea. Then he thought of Judge Beaubien—and the nostalgia left him. Even Washington-on-the-Brazos, with its squalor, was preferable at that moment to New Orleans, and Judge Beaubien.

He was just beginning to feel better at this thought, when he became conscious of a man who was staring at him intently—a very tall and long-legged man, in age perhaps thirty, with a face clean-shaved but of a mahogany color from sunburn, out of which a pair of extremely light blue eyes gleamed in startling contrast. Regret had seen such eyes in a born killer more than once. His own eyes were jet black, and he could kill too. But eyes of this peculiar pale blue invariably set him on his guard.

At first he ignored the fellow's stare. But as the scrutiny continued, it became distasteful. So he turned, and deliberately looked the man up and down. Perhaps, he reflected, the journey on the coach had done little to make him prepossessing, but after all this person's appearance was no better than his own. Its chief features were immense mule-eared boots, a heavy pistol holstered at the hip, a blue flannel shirt, and the wide hat which seemed to characterize all males in this country, the whole indescribably splashed with mire.

35

Regret cocked his hat aggressively, with a warning gleam in his eye. "Is there something about me that is amiss?" he asked sharply. "Something, monsieur, that perhaps does not appeal to you?"

The other's light blue eyes ceased their minute inspection of his costume, his features, the very hairs of his mustache, and for an instant their gazes met and locked.

In that moment a strange thing was born. There is such a thing as love at first sight, in which one look weds two souls in everlasting devotion. This was exactly the opposite —hate at first sight. But it wedded their two souls as indissolubly as the opposite emotion ever joined two lovers. For good or ill, an instinct taught Paul Regret, he was fated to see very much of this man until the end came for one or the other of them.

"*M'soo*," said the Texan in a ridiculous mincing imitation of Regret's "monsieur." Then he added, in a curious flat drawl, "That's French, ain't it? Then you'll be Paul Regret."

"You have the advantage of knowing my name," Regret said coldly, "while I don't enjoy the dubious honor of knowing yours."

His manner was challenging, but it left the other indifferent. In the same negligent drawl, he said, "I'm Tom Gatling, Texas Rangers."

Regret's complete astonishment showed. New Orleans had heard much of the redoubtable corps of men that patrolled the far frontiers of Texas, but he was little prepared to find in this slovenly figure a member of that famous fighting force.

"You got any weepons?" the Ranger now said.

"No."

"Then come along with me."

Regret drew himself up. "May I inquire why?"

"The Big Mingo wants to see you."

Regret understood that this was the Ranger's odd way of taking him into custody, and for a moment hesitated. But among other things he was a good judge of men. He

36

observed the revolver, and a menacing glint in the blue eyes.

"As you wish, my friend," he said lightly.

"Git this straight," the other retorted. "I ain't your friend."

Regret bowed ironically. "It gives me pleasure, monsieur, to return the compliment in kind."

Then he flicked a spot of mud from his sleeve, and disdaining to inquire who the "Big Mingo" might be, fell into step with him.

At once he found this required some effort, for the man's legs were inordinately long, and his strides immense. Nevertheless he managed to walk, so he flattered himself, with something of a swagger, ignoring the stares of the yokels loafing under the porticos. At the same time he took note that Gatling had not even bothered to search him for weapons, taking his bare word that he was unarmed, which argued either for exceptional naïveté or exceptional self-confidence, he hardly knew which.

A moment later it became difficult even to swagger successfully, for they began crossing the atrocious morass which passed for a street. His varnished French shoes now sustained their final ruin, although he endeavored as much as possible to hop from one spot that looked moderately firm to the next, his discomfort adding to his anger. Behind him his companion strode stolidly, his high boots making nothing of the execrable mud. Neither spoke, but when they were across the Ranger jerked his thumb toward the left.

Fuming but silent, Regret waded in the rain with him past a succession of log houses. One of these, slightly larger than the others, was of two sections, with a roofed passage between, known in this country as a "turkey walk." On this open porch Regret noticed a big man with brindle side whiskers, shaving by the poor light, crouching forward at it, but using no mirror, from which he reasoned he was an old soldier accustomed to campaigning, for it is a trick that is learned in the bivouac.

37

"Turn in here," Gatling said.

"Here?"

"Yep. This here's the execootive mansion."

In spite of himself Regret gave a quick glance to see if, for some weird reason, Gatling was joking. Then he saw the man in the passageway glance over toward them, toss the contents of his tin basin on the ground, wipe his face and hands on some kind of huck towel, and go within.

The dazed realization came over him that it was no joke. This mean hovel was actually the "executive mansion" of Texas, and the stark figure he had just seen, shaving in cold water and without even a mirror, must be none other than the celebrated soldier, statesman, and adventurer—General Sam Houston, president of the Republic of Texas.

3

A wizened old Negro in a long-tailed coat of rusty green opened the door and grinned.

"Howdy, Marse Tom," he said with easy familiarity.

"Howdy, Esau," returned Gatling. "The gen'ral's expectin' us."

The servant ushered them into what passed for the office of the rude abode, and disappeared. Regret looked about him. In a stone hearth a fire crackled. The puncheon floors were muddy and filthy, a table covered with papers and writing materials stood in the center, and about the room in epic disarray were stools, chairs, and trunks, with a whiskey barrel, complete with spigot and dipper, in one corner. Beside the table, the steady, measured drip of a leak from the roof created a round splash of wetness.

A door opened, and Sam Houston entered.

Heavens, what a man! Regret's impression, from the glimpse of him outside, that he was big did not do him justice. He was gigantic.

Six feet, six inches tall he might have stood, with a great arching chest and immense shoulders. He was, at this time, in his fifty-second year, and the shaggy hair was thinning on top of his skull, but from his hard cheeks sprouted a tangle of reddish sideburns—roan or brindle, rather, for they were shot liberally with gray—which gave him the maned appearance of a lion. To this the flat glare of his pin-pupiled eyes added a touch of malevolence. A vest of puma skin, an untidy stock of black silk shot with gold threads, a coat of dark blue velveteen, and black-and-white-checkered trousers thrust into the tops of immense boots were the important items in his costume.

Houston halted behind his table, glancing at his visitors from under his prodigious eyebrows.

"Howdy, Tom," he said to Gatling, in a deep rumble.

"Howdy, Gen'ral," the Ranger said. "I brung your rooster."

They both glanced at Regret.

"Sit down, gentlemen," said Houston, taking a chair at the littered table. "Your name is Paul Regret?"

"It is."

His cold glance roved over Regret, as if he regarded him not as a man, but as an item. With a glint of almost cruel satisfaction, he nodded at Gatling.

"Good catch, Tom."

"I demand to know the meaning of this outrage!" Regret exclaimed angrily. "Why am I seized like a common criminal in the moment I arrive in this—this bivouac capital—and haled before you——"

His outburst, which began with such spirit, died off. He perceived that he might better have said nothing at all, for this man was without bowels.

The room was barren, but Houston needed no surroundings. His face, with its lines of force and intelligence, his herculean figure, his majestic presence were enough to awe the boldest. Regret remembered stories of his heroisms, his greatness of mind, and also his surprising pettinesses and how he was capable of almost irresponsible violence when in one of his leonine furies. Sam Houston was such a creature of tumbling passions and sublime achievements as comes not once in a generation, but perhaps once in a people's history.

"Yes?" the president said, as if inviting his prisoner to go on.

His worst enemies would hardly have said that cowardice was a weakness of Paul Regret: yet now the man who had faced the pistols of a dozen antagonists on the dueling field without a tremor felt a qualm—a chill to the bone—under Houston's strange opalescent glare.

When he could not reply, His Excellency laughed with cruel cynicism. "How should you be treated except as a common criminal?" From the table he lifted a paper. "This letter, which arrived by fast express ahead of your coach, is from the New Orleans authorities who learned from the stage company of the destination for which you bought your ticket. It requests your arrest and extradition. I am honoring the request. You start back to New Orleans tomorrow—under guard."

Regret was stunned. Judge Beaubien's arm was longer, his action prompter, than seemed possible. The implacable visage of that terrible old man came before his eyes. In imagination he saw the gallows, almost felt the rope about his neck. Drops of cold sweat stood on his forehead.

"But I'm not—a criminal—Your Excellency," he gasped.

For answer Houston read from the paper. " 'Paul Regret. Gambler and professional duelist. Twelve duels. Four deaths——' "

"Only three, monsieur!"

Houston glanced up with a little frown. "Four. Named here are Rust, Littleton, and Brisseul. Besides which this letter states that you mortally wounded Emile Beaubien."

"Does it say he's dead?" Regret asked desperately.

"No, it was written before he died."

"Emile Beaubien did not die! He is living!"

Houston's look grew indescribably keen. "Your reason for that statement?"

"He has a ball high in the shoulder. He will recover."

"How are you so sure?"

"I don't make mistakes in such matters, Your Excellency! When I kill a man, I kill him. And when I go to pains—as I did with that young fool—not to kill a man, he lives!"

His assurance seemed to amaze the man whom almost nothing could amaze. For a moment Houston was silent, rubbing his craggy chin with his huge paw. Regret grew bolder.

"Your Excellency has himself handled a dueling pistol?" he ventured.

"And if I have?"

"Will not be too hard on another poor gentleman who has defended his honor?"

For a moment Houston brooded. Then he shook his head. "You're described here as a gamester and a common bravo. Texas has too many of such already."

Regret's heart sank. "Excellency," he cried hoarsely, "that letter—it is signed by Judge Beaubien?"

Houston nodded.

"Do you chance to know him?"

"For fifteen years," said His Excellency. "A remarkable man, a most recondite jurist, a very high-toned gentleman."

In spite of this tribute to Judge Beaubien, Regret pursued his appeal. "If you're acquainted with him, monsieur, then you must be aware that of all men he is the most implacable——"

"Perhaps so. But Houston was never of so forgiving a disposition himself." He loved to fall into the third person, like Caesar, when speaking of himself, a habit he derived, it was said, from the Indians among whom he once lived.

"It makes no difference to you that I should be hanged out of mere malice?" said Regret.

Houston glanced at him sharply, his scowl returning.

"Malice," Regret repeated, gaining the courage of desperation. "Because an old man's family pride in a weakling son is affronted, you'd see me hanged on a charge trumped up out of a former duel, long forgotten?"

"Explain that!"

"If I'm returned to New Orleans, Your Excellency, it won't be to face charges connected with Emile Beaubien—who will recover—for such charges would involve him also. It will be for one of the old duels I must answer. Is there justice in that?"

"Hum," Houston said, and pulled a side whisker. "Perhaps there's a certain merit in what you urge." Surprisingly, he spoke now in a tone of consideration. "Perhaps there is," he repeated.

He rose, and Regret rose with him. As the president strode twice or thrice back and forth, with the puncheons of the floor creaking under his weight, Regret grasped the edge of the table to steady himself—so dark had the shadow of Judge Beaubien and the gallows fallen across him.

"Beaubien . . . Beaubien," Houston rumbled, as if to himself. "A notable gentleman, certainly, but he does busy himself too much in Texas affairs. I recollect now, New Orleans money—nay, Beaubien money—had a lot to do with making that afflorescent ass, Mirabeau Buonaparte Lamar, president of Texas." His lip curled over the flamboyant name. "I took Lamar as a high private in the rear rank, and made him a colonel just before San Jacinto. Upon that he erected his career—devoted to the destruction of my principles! Where treachery and dishonesty are requisites, Lamar can hold his own with Judas. And to these he can add a quality the Iscariot lacked—stupidity!"

He spat into a huge brass spittoon. "Two years of Lamar bankrupted the nation which Houston left solvent, strong and hopeful. Lamar ineptitude brought a new strain to our relations with Mexico, while his policies left us less able to defend ourselves. Lamar treachery intensified the enmity of the Comanche Indians and their attacks on our frontiers——"

He stopped his tramping to and fro, and gazed at Gatling as if a new thought had just come into his mind. "Tom," he said, "do you know that I've just had word that the red scourge has struck again?"

"Where, Gen'ral?" The Ranger now rose also, in excitement and horror.

"The upper Trinity. Luke Silvers rode a good horse to death bringing the news. Hot ashes where a dozen homes had been. Fourteen unburied, mutilated bodies. And not a single Comanche carcass to show for it!"

"What was the Rangers doin'?"

"God forgive me, Tom! I'd transferred Cameron's company two weeks before from the Novasota to the Neches. The raiders came through the gap as if they knew it. Last month it was the Rio Frio, six hundred miles southwest. And again just a fortnight after I'd shifted a company. You think that's a coincidence? By the Eternal, it *was* no coincidence!"

Gatling gulped. "What—was it?"

"I don't know. How should I know? I'm only human, God help me. And this—sometimes I think it's inhuman. There's something—out there—back of everything"— Houston waved his hand in an odd, vague gesture toward the west—"more terrible, more mysterious, than any savage tribe—or combination of savage tribes——"

"I—I jest don't follow you—Gen'ral——"

"Something as baffling, evil, and hellishly intelligent as —as the vampires who live on the blood of human victims —the best blood of Texas, may the Almighty have mercy on us!"

Houston's eyes were on the floor, his face lined as if by agony, his shoulders for the moment bowed under such a weight of despair that Regret forgot his own fate in the sudden thrill of horror at an unknown dread.

4

Intense silence, broken only by the drip on the floor from the leak in the roof. Houston was the first to stir. He raised his eyes and they fell on Regret. The sight seemed to recall him from his terrible abstraction.

"You! Can you prove you didn't kill Emile Beaubien?" he said almost savagely.

Regret suddenly remembered his own peril. At the same time his growing hope faded. Furnish such a proof—how could he?

"Only what I said before——" he faltered.

"A man who can know with certainty where his lead will strike in the tense moment of the word for fire must be able to display a skill with weapons more than common!" Houston growled.

He pulled open a drawer in the table and from it took one of the new revolvers of the Colt model, such as had become very popular in Texas during the last two years. This was an extraordinary weapon, silver-mounted, chased, with a handle of pearl. Even in his agitation Regret eyed it lovingly. The Colt revolver, although an invention newly perfected, was familiar to those who practiced arms at the Salle St. Philippe in New Orleans, and he had some knowledge of its possibilities.

"Given me by Sam Colt himself," rumbled Houston. "Gentlemen, if you'll be so good, follow me."

Through a rear door they passed out to the open but roofed passage on which the president had been shaving. Rain still fell dismally, but from the back wing of the log edifice Regret heard the sound of a piano played not unskillfully.

"That's Mrs. Houston," said His Excellency. "Her piano is one of her few refuges in this somewhat primitive land. It is," he added, "the only one west of the Brazos." He began to glance keenly about. "What kind of a target do you like? A cross? A circle?"

At this talk of shooting, confidence flowed back into Regret.

"What distance, monsieur?" he asked.

"That hackberry? It's fifty paces."

"You offer me a target like that? By your leave, it's child's play."

"Then what do you suggest?"

Regret looked around. On a rough plank table lay a heap of miscellany, including rusty spurs, a few tools, a broken snaffle, a saddle skirt, and a small pail half filled with lead musket balls, such as were used in trade with the Indians. Stepping over, conscious of their puzzled looks, he selected one of the balls.

"Your knife," he said to Gatling.

The Ranger glanced at Houston, who nodded; then drew from its sheath the long-bladed bowie knife and handed it over, though with obvious suspicion.

Quickly Regret cut two slivers on opposite sides of the round bullet, leaving them attached so that he could bend them down over a piece of string, thus fastening it to the leaden ball. With a mocking bow, he returned the knife to its owner, and taking his contraption to the dripping eaves which sloped conveniently low at the side of the passage, fastened the loose end of the string there so that the bullet dangled three feet or so below. Having accomplished this, with a push of his finger he set the ball swinging back and forth like a pendulum.

"That," said he, stepping to the opposite side of the porch, a distance of twenty feet, "might perhaps be considered some slight challenge to a marksman. Will you try it?" He bowed again to Gatling.

The Ranger stared. "Hit that swingin' bullet? It's crazy!"

"I had heard," Regret said icily, "that Texas Rangers are very adept with weapons and willing to accept any challenge."

"Go ahead, Tom," Houston grinned. "Teach him a lesson."

Gatling did not like it, but he stepped back to the edge of the porch, drew his revolver, and after aiming back and forth, following the bullet's swing, fired. The musket ball continued its pendulum motion untouched. Again he fired. Again he missed.

Regret noticed that the piano inside the house had ceased playing.

"By the Eternal!" exclaimed Houston. "I'll have a try at that myself!" With his own silver-and-pearl revolver, he fired twice. The pendulum did not even hesitate in its rhythm.

He handed the weapon to Regret. "You actually propose to hit that musket ball?" he demanded.

"I'll try to do something slightly more difficult, Your Excellency—cut the string above it!"

"Impossible!"

"Perhaps. But I'll at least try."

Raising the revolver, he fired. The trick was possible—with a little luck—if one could shoot. They used to practice it for sport in the gallery at the Salle St. Philippe, although it was admitted there that Regret was the only one who had much success with it. There is an instant at the end of the pendulum's swing when bullet and cord are motionless before starting in the opposite direction.

The lead from the revolver cut the string and the falling musket ball bounced off the porch.

Houston stared with almost ludicrous astonishment. But the Ranger's face showed quick disbelief.

"Luck!" he said. "He can't do it again!"

"I think he can," said Houston. "Try it again, Regret."

As has been mentioned, there is necessarily an element of luck in all such shots, and Regret had been congratulating himself on bringing it off. To be expected to duplicate it—on order—was, he felt, rather too much.

There was, however, no way of avoiding it. With misgivings he took his position while the musket ball was suspended and once more set swinging. But as he raised the revolver, the door to the rear wing of the house flew open, and a woman stepped out.

She was tall, quite young, and the look of strong displeasure on her face did not hide the fact that she was pretty.

"Sam Houston!" she cried, in a voice both sharp and petulant. "How often do I have to tell you that the porch of this house is no place for your artillery practice!"

"Margaret, my love!" exclaimed the president, with an expression on his vast visage exactly like a small boy caught stealing jam.

"Grown men!" she continued bitterly. "Indulging in such childish horseplay! Waking the baby and startling me nearly out of my wits——"

"We were only——"

"I'll have no excuses, sir! If Sam Junior grows up to be one of those awful people who twitch out of nervousness, you'll have only yourself to thank! Now take your—your cannons—and these men—and go away!"

The gigantic president bowed in a manner most humble. "Thy wish is ever Houston's command," he said meekly, and led a hasty retreat.

In his office he gazed at them with an uneasy hint of embarrassment. "I trust you gentlemen will—ah—pardon Mrs. Houston," he said. "She's the soul of sweetness and dutiful obedience. But she does fire up a little when she gets rattled——" He hesitated sheepishly. "After all, gunfire *is* a bit rich, I suppose, for the blood of a teething infant——"

He cleared his throat and hastened to change the subject. "Well, we have business, don't we? I must say, Regret, that it goes against my grain to waste on the gallows a man who can shoot as you can."

"In that case, Your Excellency——"

"But there's a problem." Houston ruminated. "A request for extradition from a friendly government—it's awkward to refuse it. If you were a citizen of Texas, now—but naturalization requires months." Suddenly his eye lit. "I have it! If I enlist you in the Rangers—it will make you a citizen automatically and instantly!" He paused at Gatling's scowl. "You have some rebuttal, Tom?"

The Ranger spoke freely. "This jaybird ain't got the makin's of a Ranger, Gen'ral!"

"He can shoot."

"Mebbe. But there's a lot beside shootin'. A Comanche warrior's a thought different in handlin' from a Creole gal.

An' it's a leetle harder ridin' after outlaws than makin' a figger in a cotillion."

"Never imagine," said Regret, "that I can't do anything you can—and better—my horse-faced friend!"

The "horse-faced," admittedly, was not courteous. But then neither was the "jaybird." Again the men locked glances, and the hard dislike grew in both pairs of eyes.

"Well, Regret?" said Houston.

Regret hesitated. With the greatest force it came over him that he had no desire to be a Texas Ranger. The life of those people was hard and dangerous, and he had other plans.

"Yes, or no?" Houston asked sharply.

The Rangers . . . or the gallows? There really was no choice.

"Yes, Your Excellency," said Regret.

"One leetle thing," said Gatling, with the cunning expression of a man who has just thought of an unanswerable objection. "A Ranger has to have a certificate of character."

Houston grunted. "That's true. I'd forgot. Yes, he must have a recommendation, surely, and this man might find it difficult to get one. Well, perhaps we'll have to ship him back to New Orleans after all——"

Suddenly Regret spoke, greatly daring. "I count on the highest of recommendations, Your Excellency——"

"Whose?"

"Yours!"

For a moment Houston stared as if he did not believe his ears. Then he fetched Gatling a great clap on the back and laughed like a hyena.

THREE:

*"Absolute Courage, Absolute
Loyalty . . ."*

1

PAUL REGRET, recruit for the Texas Rangers by grace of the audacity which had tickled Sam Houston's sense of humor, had no chance to dally and sample the somewhat scanty pleasures of Washington-on-the-Brazos.

That afternoon the clouds broke, the rain ceased, and the late sun came through. Accompanied unwillingly by Gatling, who had been ordered by Houston to see him properly outfitted, he set out to equip himself. He would have preferred to leave the man out of it, but Gatling proved valuable after all. The Ranger conducted him to the proper marts, where from his dwindling funds he bought such garments, chiefly of buckskin, as were indicated, a wide hat, boots with huge spurs, a short carbine, and a bowie knife. No Colt revolvers, unfortunately, were available, those weapons being snapped up as soon as they appeared in Texas, at unheard-of prices.

Regret's chief surprise came in the selection of a horse. He considered himself an excellent horseman, thought he knew good horseflesh when he saw it, and he had heard romantic tales of the wild steed of the prairie—the mustang with flowing mane and eye of fire. But at the corral, he saw about fifty poor, lean ponies, of all imaginable colors; each suggesting in its appearance the near approach of death by starvation or old age; all unshod; all branded on hips and shoulders with extraordinary alphabetical vagaries; and all as ignorant of the usages of the currycomb as the average Texan seemed to be of the usages of soap and water.

Gatling, however, seemed to regard these beasts as standard. He shook his head when Regret selected what appeared to be the best, a black somewhat less plebeian than the others.

"Why not?" Regret asked.

"Blind in his off eye."

Regret now perceived this was so.

Three other selections were rejected by the Ranger, who said one was tender-hoofed, the second a "stump sucker," and the third wind-broken, before they finally decided on a creature of drab dun color, frescoed with tufts of last season's hair and chunks of this season's mud. The animal looked unpromising, but it had the spirit to buck when it was saddled and mounted, so that Regret clung to the saddle horn while he wrenched its head up—a practice he was subsequently to learn was not well thought of in Texas —and later proved to be tough and gifted with astonishing powers of endurance.

Next morning the two of them began a three-day ride to the Rio Leon, a remote stream in the northwest wilderness, where a Ranger post was situated as a defense against the Indians.

The country was monotonous, with all habitations soon left behind, and nothing to be seen but rolling plain and thorn brush. Gatling spoke so rarely that Regret had more than sufficient time for his own thoughts, which were bitter.

A remarkable conspiracy of affairs, he reflected, had made him their victim. He thought of New Orleans, of the cafés, the cockpit, the gaming tables, the race track, the Salle St. Philippe, even the dueling Oaks of Allard, with nostalgia. And of the gay companions and charming ladies he had known there. It seemed almost unbelievable that in the period of a few days a connoisseur in elegant society like himself could be converted into a leather-clad nomad of the frontier, forced into a species of involuntary servitude the thought of which he hated.

A duel fought unwillingly—the enmity of an old man—

and the words of a girl. These were what had united to make him an outcast from life as he knew and understood it. And he could not see where he had been gravely at fault in any of it.

Eloise Grailhe—and her beauty, her falseness, and his own bewilderment—kept returning to his mind like some unhappy refrain. Odd, how of all the girls he knew in New Orleans he seemed to remember none but Eloise. He felt he would like to wring her neck . . . a particularly pretty neck it was, he remembered. Damn all women!

Resolutely, he tried to think of something else and Houston's solemn words came to his aid.

Something . . . out there, back of everything . . . as hellishly intelligent as the vampires . . . who live on the blood of human victims . . .

He wondered what that weird menace was, and much as he disliked Gatling, ventured a question about it. The Ranger replied with a grunt. Texans were a taciturn race, treating words with parsimony, but Gatling carried this to an extreme. Decidedly Regret had more than enough of it.

"Monsieur Gatling," he said, "a gentleman would have the politeness to answer me."

"Mister Regret," said Gatling coldly, "in Texas it ain't considered necessary to answer, unless the other party says somethin' important."

"Oh, I know about your Texans, and how they think themselves superior to all other men," Regret retorted bitterly. "But don't forget that I've seen a few of the species in the last day or so, and my opinion is that any of them would be better for a bath!"

Gatling rode his horse over close, and his pale blue eyes were hard.

"Get this," he said. "I'm on duty, and I don't want no trouble with you. But sometime you'll eat that."

Thereafter talk was reduced to the barest minimum between them.

They spent the first night at a stage station, where Gatling was received with respect and Regret was stared at. A bald-headed man cheered them with an account of three men he had found hanging in a tree, and a slatternly female, evidently excited by something said at the table, retired to where a male acquaintance was seated in another part of the room, whispered in his ear, and returned flourishing a villainous-looking knife with a nine-inch blade.

Regret thought he saw a wild glitter in her eye, and watched her, suspecting that she meditated some violence. But it turned out that she had no thought of mayhem, having borrowed the knife only to cut up her tough piece of venison into mouthfuls for mastication.

The second night they arrived at a log cabin owned by a Cherokee Indian named Bacon Rind. Regret had been eager for the sight of an Indian, but this specimen was "civilized" and therefore a disappointment. He was attired in a castoff shirt, a pair of moccasins, a battered hat with a feather thrust in the band, and a breechclout of ancient and most unsavory vintage hanging between his legs, the original color of which was obscured by countless layers of filth. While his plethoric squaw cooked their meal, he sat on his porch gazing at nothing with a countenance of unspeakable stupidity.

Supper consisted of fried meat and corn pone. Regret's appetite was not good, and when he bit into a pone and his teeth encountered a piece of rag with a button on it, he lost all desire to eat. But there was coffee: at least coffee would be boiled. Bacon Rind, having first helped himself, prepared to pour into Regret's cracked crockery cup, when he saw a dead fly in it.

"Wait um minute," he said. He seized the cup in his dirty claw and—oh, horror!—wiped it with the unmentionable breechcloth.

Regret drank no coffee and was heartily glad when their journey was resumed next morning.

The sun was dipping toward the horizon the evening of the third day, when they descended into a valley with a thin straggling of unimposing trees among which a ragged haze crept up from the bottom.

"The Rio Leon," said Gatling. It was almost his first word all day.

Among the trees they saw a weathered gray that was neither mist nor dead timber: the stained canvas of several close-huddled tents. Gatling gave a far-carrying call. At once a loose-jointed frontiersman appeared at the edge of the timber, quite tall, with long, thin arms ending in huge hands that fondled a long-barreled rifle.

"That you, Tom?" he shouted. "Wall, come on in!"

As they rode down to him, Regret saw that he was excessively thin, with a yellow, hollow-cheeked face covered with a coarse stubble of gray-shot beard. One of his eyes turned slightly inward, imparting a jocular expression to his otherwise grimly lined face.

"Mister Regret," Gatling said as they dismounted, "this here's Wyman Cruze."

"Howdy," the man said briefly, favoring the recruit with a squint-eyed appraisal.

"Regret's assigned to this company," Gatling continued.

"Huh!" grunted Cruze.

Was this scarecrow, Regret wondered, also a member of the Texas Rangers? Gatling enlightened him.

"Wyman's our lootenant, second-in-command on the Rio Leon, under Cap'n Blake Henrion."

The recruit was too astonished to speak.

"Speakin' of the cap'n," said Gatling, "where is he?"

"Over yon," Cruze said. He gestured, and Regret saw through the trees a group of men standing together at a distance beyond the camp.

"A barbecue?" he asked.

Wyman Cruze gave him a withering look. "Buryin'," he said.

"Who?" asked Gatling.

The frontiersman's face grew oddly troubled. "Tom——" he began. "It's—well—before God, I hate to be the one to tell ye——"

Sudden terror was in Gatling's face. "It ain't—it couldn't be—Tap Cobb——?"

Cruze nodded.

Incredulity changed to belief and pain in Gatling's face. "Tapworth Cobb?" he half whispered. "I can't believe it—*not Tap*——" He gulped. "Was it—Injuns?"

"Nope. Hoss stepped in a hole. Fell on him an' busted him up inside. He died last night."

Gatling handed his bridle reins to Cruze and almost blindly turned away, walking toward the group that awaited him at the grave.

"He was Tom's pardner," Cruze said, looking after him musingly. "They was like horn an' cantle of the same saddle—never fur apart. Tapworth Cobb was a conspicuous man in his day, Mister Regret. All gall an' stubbornness an' luck. Comanches, range thieves, an' Mexican bandits could never git him, though he had enough scrimmages for a dozen men. An' now—piled up by a stumblin' bronc! We all come to it, I reckon. An' Tap Cobb at last is gittin' a common sidehill buryin' like anybody else." He ruminated a moment. "Wall, Mister Regret, bring yore hoss along, an' come into camp."

3

He led the way. Regret observed that this post of the Texas Rangers, if picturesque, was in no respect military, the tents huddled together without arrangement, the ground strewn with horse furniture and utensils.

The men at the grave began straggling back, looking solemn, two remaining behind to fill it in. From one of the tents three or four of them began silently to carry the personal effects of the dead man—his saddle, blankets, rifle, and other gear—which they heaped near a tree stump. On the stump Wyman Cruze mounted and removed his hat.

"Gents," he said, "we done lost our comrade, Tapworth Cobb, as good a man as ever forked a saddle, an' thar ain't a man of us that ain't sorry. But patrols has to start. Some of us won't be back in camp for days. So it's been decided to sell off Tap Cobb's stuff now. Let's all try an' be gen'rous. Pore Missis Cobb's shorely needin' the money."

Regret could hardly believe it: before the dead man was settled in his grave, these people were preparing to auction off his few possessions. But a moment later he saw this was a kind of charity to the widow.

Cruze was no professional auctioneer, but the sale went rapidly, most of the men bidding right at first what the articles were worth, with as much more as they could afford. At the very last the frontiersman held up a revolver.

"Ye all know how Tap Cobb come by this gun," he said. "It was give to him by Sam Houston hisself, for what he done in the squabble with the Woll outfit on the Salado. If six-guns wasn't so all-fired scarce an' needed so bad, we'd mebbe ought to send it back to Missis Cobb as a keepsake. But Colts ain't to be had easy, an' they're the best answer to a Comanche. Now, gents, what am I offered?"

Regret had been unable to buy a revolver, and he needed one.

He spoke up at once, "One hundred dollars."

A voice behind him said, "A hundred an' twenty-five."

"That's a right fair price, Tom Gatling——" Cruze began.

"One hundred and thirty-five!" Regret interrupted.

Some of the Rangers glanced at him oddly, and he knew that Cruze and the others would like the revolver to go to Gatling.

Gatling said, "A hundred an' fifty."

"One hundred and seventy-five!" It was almost all the money Regret had left, but if they were to be charitable to the widow, he would be as charitable as any. Besides, he did not intend to let Gatling have that gun.

He saw displeasure now on the faces about him, but shrugged. He cared little what opinion of him they, or anyone else, held in this Godforsaken wilderness.

Cruze looked at Gatling, who shook his head. "That outreaches me," he said.

"A hundred an' seventy-five for the gun," said the frontiersman. "I reckon if'n Tap Cobb had his say, it'd go to you, Tom. But it looks like the gent with the do-si-do mustache has done bought it."

The "do-si-do mustache" brought a laugh, and not a friendly one. But as the group about the stump broke up, Regret went forward unruffled to pay for and receive his purchase.

Into Cruze's palm he counted out the money.

"Right," said the frontiersman, surrendering the weapon with its belt and holster, which Regret buckled on. "Tom," Cruze went on, "take this man up to the cap'n. He wants to see ye."

Without wasting words the tall Ranger jerked his head for Regret to follow, and led the way to the upper part of the camp, where a tent a little larger than the rest stood. Within it, at a crude table, sat a short, compact man in his middle thirties, wearing boots that failed to conceal the fact that his legs, from constant riding, were too bowed for elegance.

"Cap'n Henrion," said Gatling briefly, "this here's Regret. The man I was tellin' you about—at the grave."

Captain Blake Henrion had a square, impassive face on which sat a sort of metal dignity. His close-cut brown beard and mustache had patches of gray in them, and his eyes were gray and uncommonly clear, but somehow weary. For a moment he regarded Regret with a quality of resignation, of unhappiness, as if he had just been called upon to shoulder a fresh burden.

"Mr. Regret, why did you join the Rangers?" he asked.

Regret shrugged. "Let us say it was a whim of mine."

The captain's eyes did not change expression. "It takes more than a whim to qualify for this body, sir."

"I believe you have General Houston's endorsement of me, monsieur."

"*Monsieur*. Beginning now, Regret, you will stop addressing me as monsieur. You are in the Texas Rangers now, and you will say *sir* in speaking to your superiors. Is that understood? And while we're on the subject, I understand you're from New Orleans. If you have any other Frenchified ways, get rid of them. I won't have a man who minces and prinks. We take ourselves seriously, sir, and you will school yourself to conform to our standards. Is that clear?"

"It is—sir," said Regret. He was angry, and weary of this toplofty talk about the Texas Rangers. "And if you wish my qualifications for your organization, I'll engage, sir, to shoot with any man you've got—pistol or rifle, offhand, with a rest, at will, or at the word! I'll engage, sir, to ride with any! I'll engage to demonstrate my bravery equal to any man you've got! And I'll engage to show your people a few lessons in politeness that may profit them—*sir!*"

"That's big talk, Regret. You'll get a chance to prove it." The captain was cold and deadly serious. "Since the president has seen fit to recommend you, I'll not inquire into your past history. All we require in this service are absolute courage, absolute loyalty, and absolute integrity. You will be paid forty dollars a month—when you get it. At this post we're now about three months in arrears on our pay."

Henrion paused, and his gray eyes bored into Regret's. "You'll be expected to perform unreasonable duties and make unreasonable sacrifices, without regard to any personal consideration. For this you'll receive little thanks— in fact, very few will ever know of it. If you die, you'll get six feet of Texas soil, with no headstone, and no memorial, except your brief notation in the records of the Texas Rangers. This company's lost five men in a month— two to the Comanches, two to Mexican outlaws, and now

57

Tapworth Cobb. That gives you an idea. And finally, if you find the pace set by the Rangers is too hot, you'll be at liberty to resign—at the end of the year—if you live that long."

Regret stood at attention. He gathered that he had begun his service on the wrong foot. First he had horned in at the auction and outbid Gatling for that revolver, which he wanted for sentimental reasons. The men did not like that. Now he had angered the captain. Unpleasant all around.

But the remark about too hot a pace rankled. He lifted his chin. They would see about the heat of the pace.

Henrion's eyes shifted to Gatling. "You've had bad news, Tom, and nobody's sorrier than I am. But Cobb's death leaves you without a working partner. You will take this man and show him the ropes."

Into Gatling's eyes leaped a surge of protest. But it died instantly, and he nodded, not speaking what was in his mind: that of all men he would have preferred any but this one.

4

The trade of a Texas Ranger was less easy to learn than Paul Regret thought.

One thing was soon admitted: that the new man could shoot with the best. But otherwise life was something less than pleasurable.

For one thing, the conditions of their existence were more abject even than he had feared. The food was crude and coarse, the tents ragged, and of discipline there was none, save for a curious and remarkable personal *élan* in every Ranger. At this post were stationed about fifty men, hard-looking and uncouth, most of them bearded, and lean to the point of the cadaverous. But in them he noticed one thing in common: a certain steadiness of the eye, and a peculiar competence, especially with weapons or when mounted. Also, he discovered as time passed, that they were possessed of a perverse, and to him deplorable, sense of humor.

Little was said of danger: yet danger was their constant companion, and death an accepted probability for every man of them. And riding to the point of exhaustion was a matter of course.

On a patrol Regret one night shared blankets with Gatling under a pouring rain, and became uncomfortably conscious of water running in their bed. His companion slept on undisturbed. At last he roused Gatling.

"For God's sake, can't we find a drier place to sleep?" he asked.

"What for?" the other growled. "We've got this puddle all warmed up now. If we move, we'd only git into another, an' mebbe ketch cold."

Off to sleep he went again, while Regret lay miserably through the night, or rose and shivered over the wet ashes of their fire.

And that was only a sample of the conditions of his life. Sometimes he found himself smiling bitterly over what his friends of the cafés of New Orleans would think now, if they saw him, the connoisseur of fine wines and foods, of sophisticated society, of elegant manners and conversations, with garments soiled and torn, face blackened by sun and storm, as wild and uncouth in appearance as a savage.

In none of this did Regret take pleasure. He learned, but he learned because of a certain exasperated stubbornness and anger. And meantime toward Texans, and all things concerning Texas, he developed a growing contempt and distaste, and particularly for the habit the men had of making the wildest claims for the greatness, beauty, future, richness, and he knew not what else, for their new country. Personally, he thought only of the time when he might escape from Texas.

As for Tom Gatling, the three sentences he spoke on the night of the wet blankets formed almost the longest speech he uttered in their weeks together. Morosely he followed orders, took Regret on his patrols, presided over his blunders, and sometimes saved him from calamity. Again and again he showed his pupil how to find a ford instead of embarking into quicksands that would have dragged him to death. Patiently he gave him little lessons in "reading" the country, following a trail, butchering game, camp cookery, packing a horse, and kindred matters.

But his dislike was so evident and great that they scarcely had a companionship, but rather a coexistence in unsociability. Except when instruction was indicated, Gatling treated Regret with cold though perfectly civil silence. And this was not because he could not talk freely and laugh hilariously, as Regret saw when he was with Cruze or others, in camp. Only with his "partner"—a sorry misnomer, that—did he display his continued icy aloofness.

By chance one day Regret uttered the name of Tapworth Cobb. Instantly Gatling turned on him, his face stiffening.

"What about Tap Cobb?" he said, very low.

"Nothing," said Regret with surprise. "I was only wondering what kind of a man he was."

The other turned this over in his mind, frowning, as if looking for a hidden meaning. Finally, he said, "I'll tell you the kind of a man Tap Cobb was. His name's too good for some folks even to speak."

Oddly, Regret found he did not particularly resent the affront. In a momentary flash he had seen how Gatling still mourned for his friend. And he knew, now, that Tapworth Cobb was riding with them. Every minute they were on the trail together the dead man formed a spectral third. Whatever Regret did, or failed to do, was measured against Tapworth Cobb, and because of his shortcomings he was a constant maddening reminder to Gatling of the friend he had lost.

In June the two of them rode unusually far to the north and made a camp in the forks of a creek where stood a thick little grove of cottonwoods. That night they ate jerked meat for supper, but next morning early Gatling knocked over an antelope with a good shot from his horse's back.

Regret wondered. He understood the truism that a shot in the evening before one camped must be avoided, since it might attract night-prowling foes. But why kill fresh meat now, when they were about to start back to the post on the Rio Leon?

He had a surprise.

"We're goin' over to Cogswell's Corners on the Brazos," Gatling said.

The antelope was to be a gift. Bled and gutted, its carcass was bound behind Gatling's saddle, and that day they forged eastward.

Shortly after noon Gatling grunted and pulled up his horse.

"New place," he said.

It could be seen at a distance of a mile, in a shallow valley, near the straggling line of willows and cottonwoods which were the invariable sign of a small meandering creek. Regret noted its rawness, even as he approached from a distance. The cabin was small, of fresh logs; there was a shed of some kind, possibly for a stable, and a small corral of rails, completed, with another larger one only half finished. A few cattle dotted the vicinity of the small watercourse.

They saw a man, somewhat bowed in the shoulders but tall, standing before the cabin, a rifle suggestively held in the crook of his arm. But as they neared him, he set the gun against the wall.

"Howdy," said Gatling. "We're Texas Rangers."

"Yes, I reckoned ye was," the man said. He was youngish,

in jeans and a hickory shirt, but he looked older than he was because of yellowish whiskers that covered his lower face.

A woman lounged to the door, with an infant about a year old in her arms. She was small, and looked younger than her husband, and she was still nursing the child, for it pawed at her dress front. But she laughed and put its small hand away, and kissed it, and Regret, who had not seen a woman in a month, thought it was a pretty sight to see her and her babe.

"My name's Irvin—Nate Irvin," the man said.

"When did you set stakes here?" Gatling asked.

"Two months ago."

"You done well."

"Some of the folks from Cogswell's come over an' he'ped us raise the cabin an' shack. I built the corrals myself. Me an' Sue Ellen." He was referring to his wife.

She stood with her hip outthrust, holding the child on it, her body soft and rounded in the linsey-woolsey dress which seemed to be its only garment. Her face was small and round, with dark eyes crinkling at the corners. Not pretty, but mighty pleasant-looking to a man starved for feminine company.

"Come in, an' I'll fix you a bite," she said.

Regret hoped Gatling would assent, but the Ranger shook his head.

"Got to go over to Cogswell's by night," he said. He began loosing the thongs that tied the antelope behind his saddle.

"Happened to git in a shot. Could you use this?"

"Why, thankee," said Irvin with pleasure, stepping forward. The dead beast was lifted from the back of the horse, which stepped gingerly away.

Gatling watched him lay the animal on the ground, and said, "Don't you think you're a leetle far out from the settlements, here?"

Irvin stood up from where he was stooping over the antelope.

"Oh, I dunno. We don't see folks very often, but nobody's heard of an Injun around here in months. Seems like they most gen'rally causes their mischief down around the Nueces, or north of here."

"Well," said Gatling. "It's your business. But I'd think a couple of times before riskin' a leetle woman like you got, an' kid, out here at the end of nothin'."

Regret glanced over at Mrs. Irvin. She laughed.

"We ain't scairt," she said. She was young and believed in her husband.

"If any red hides did show up around here," Irvin said, "we got two guns—the rifle an' the shotgun. Sue Ellen kin use the scatter-gun as good as me—an' I reckon we'd discourage 'em plenty."

Gatling gave a little shrug. "Well. Good luck to you," he said.

They rode away, and Mrs. Irvin made the baby wave its tiny hand good-by to them.

Three hours later Cogswell's Corners appeared on the distant plain. Regret counted four cabins, one of them large as log structures went, and some smaller outbuildings and corrals. This was almost a settlement.

A roar greeted them and a huge man came striding toward them, followed by a scurrying of youngsters, all wearing the "toga" of the frontier—a long shirt like a nightgown, the boys' having two slits in the tail to distinguish them from the girls'—and adding their shrill chirps to their grandsire's welcome.

"Tom Gatling! How be ye?"

"Yum Cogswell!" laughed Gatling.

He was a looming giant, white with eighty years, headed and bearded like some Old Testament prophet.

Regret was introduced.

"Light and come in!" the old man said. "Git out from underfoot, ye useless cubs!" He lifted a huge foot, as if to kick, and the children scattered with squeals of mock fear and laughter, clearly in no terror of him. "Hey, boy—you, Chadwick——" He selected the oldest. "Take them hosses to the barn, while I bring these men to the house!" He had a voice like a wave on the shore.

The big cabin was part home, part store, the latter smelling of goods and groceries, as all general stores have always smelled. But they passed through it into the residential part, a big log-walled dwelling room with a huge hearth and rude furniture, a loft, and various smaller rooms adjoining for sleeping, and a kitchen house outside.

"Yettie!" boomed the old man. "Here's two hungerin' friends!"

She came in from the kitchen shack, wiping her hands on her apron, an apple-cheeked woman with black hair shot with gray, her face covered with countless fine lines, and her broad shapeless body quaking with laughter, to shake hands and bid them welcome.

Yum and Yettie. Will-*yum* and Henri-*yettie*, Regret discovered. The Cogswells were landmarks in this part of Texas, patriarchal, with their tribe about them, known to everyone in an area as large as all New England. Their sons, Hogarth, Doughty and Bullard, lived in the cabins near, with their families, and a widowed daughter and her children in the main lodge with her parents. Together they made up a numerous community, ten adults—if a bound girl, Nettie Hare, who worked for Yum and Yettie, be counted as an adult—and eleven children, ranging from fourteen years to babes in arms.

That night the Cogswell tribe gathered at the big house, to feast with the guests on beef and venison and sage hen, and when the meal was over, the youngest son, Bullard, picked out tunes on a banjo, and they sang.

In a great chair sat the patriarch, like a careless work of art, his chiseled face framed in silvered, curling hair. The other younger men yielded him grave respect, but the children clambered over and about him in spite of his mock-ferocious bellowings. The women sewed and chatted, and Yettie, the grandmother, rocked the newest baby to sleep on her pillowed bosom. In and out, timidly like a mouse, stole the girl, Nettie Hare, on the little errands connected with her work as servant. She was a thin little thing, about fifteen, with a face that could have been called pretty, and masses of yellow hair. Regret tried to speak with her, but she ducked her head and hurried away as if alarmed. Yet he knew she was well treated in this house, and only painfully shy.

The talk that night among the men was of cattle, and range gossip, and endless queries about mutual acquaintances. No politics, no knowledge of events beyond their ken, no weariness of existence or wish for anything different. These people, insulated by the distances surrounding them from the yeasty discontents of the world, were perhaps truly happy, Regret considered, and vastly to be envied.

When he and Gatling rode away next morning with hearty urgings to return at an early time, he in his own mind resolved to accept the invitation when he could, for the evening had been a warm and bright event in his Texas experience.

6

Back at camp, and the old routine.

To the Texas Rangers on the Rio Leon, Regret was a constant subject of mirth. His ways were different from theirs, and therefore comical. He persisted, for example, in washing his hands before eating, and this "daintiness" was a subject for laughter. He did not chew tobacco, an evidence to them, perhaps, of effeminacy. When eating he cut his meat into bits, rather than putting a corner of the piece in his mouth and sawing it off with his bowie knife before he masticated it. Though he no longer said "monsieur," he had other tricks of speech, expressions genteel enough but strange, which they repeated with guffaws and nudgings of the elbow. He had a horror of snakes and tarantulas, and the Texans, to whom these creatures were familiar and not fearsome if treated with common sense, found his reflex-shrinking at the sight of a rattlesnake wildly funny.

Always he was the outsider, the ordained butt of practical jokes, some of them maddening, the perpetrators of which he could never discover.

There was the evening when someone slipped a cicada, or summer locust, into his boot, while he was bathing in the river. This is a large but harmless fly-like insect, notable for the loud buzzing sounds it makes in the trees during warm weather by vibrating its wings.

When Regret dressed after coming from the water, he put his boots on last. They were high and tight fitting, so that to get the foot in was a matter of pulling and twisting; to get it out even more difficult.

He had the boot halfway on, when he heard and felt a sudden dreadful whir *in the boot itself*. To him the sound and sensation were unmistakable. How a rattlesnake could have crawled into his boot, he had no time to consider: that it was *there* was the one paramount, pressing thought. He had a frantic desire to remove that boot, and an equally frantic desire to take wings and fly. The difficulty was that he could never stick to either course of action long enough to obtain a finished result.

He turned a backward flip in the air, meanwhile grabbing with frenzy at his boot. His first jump landed him on his shoulders, his feet threshing the atmosphere. His second took the legs out from under Wyman Cruze, who got a knee so badly sprained that he did not ride for a week. His third, an effort that would have done credit to the finest tumbling acrobat in the world, was a three-time pinwheel spin, landing him with a tremendous splash in the river.

There, under water, he finally succeeded in wrenching the boot off. Half drowned, he waded to the bank and from the boot poured—not a rattlesnake, as he supposed, but the insect, sadly soaked, the vibrations of which inside his boot had sounded so like the reptile's murderous whir.

Now he became aware that the whole camp was hilarious, and the enormity of the prank dawned on him. He was furious enough to fight—but on whom to turn his anger? He suspected Gatling. He suspected Cruze. He suspected everyone and anyone. But you cannot bring a man to a serious discussion of fighting you, when everything you say only sends him off in fresh gales of laughter.

At last he stalked away to his tent. Next day he could manage a smile over the incident. A wry smile, but a smile. By this he won approval, though at the time he did not know it.

And a few nights later Regret revenged himself.

A game of poker was organized. At first he was an onlooker only, but after a few deals he was invited to take a hand.

He supposed this was politeness, and was pleased, until he noticed a concealed smile pass among them. Then he knew that these Texans, who esteemed themselves superior to all men in everything they undertook—cards included—regarded him as a fat squab for the plucking.

To not one of them did it occur that in Paul Regret they were inviting an antagonist who was feared in every professional gaming house in New Orleans.

He had no mercy on them.

Unfortunately, there was little money in camp, the paymaster being so long overdue. But what money there was, he got. One by one he "cleaned" their champions. When he rose from the game that night, the men of Henrion's Company, Texas Rangers, were as innocent of cash as Adam, before the Temptation, was innocent of sin.

The poker game won for him a reluctant respect, and by so much bettered his standing. There was this, he gathered, about a Texan: he loathed being bested in anything, but once you did best him, his respect for you was almost devout, since to his eyes the mere fact that you had excelled a Texan lifted you into the category of the remarkable.

He could not say, however, that there was any appreciable increase of affection for him. A Texan might respect the man who mastered him, but he did not necessarily love him.

FOUR:

"Them Moccasins Was Never Comanche!"

1

IN THOSE WEEKS Paul Regret came to feel the nameless dread of the great emptiness to the west, which all Texans knew.

There was nothing to see in that direction except a vast, irregular plain, growing every day more brassy in color with the withering of the buffalo grass. Sometimes a lobo wolf howled in the darkness of night. Once in a while, by day, a few straggling dots of game appeared far out. Occasionally buzzards, those sinister harbingers of death, circled high in the sky. But that was all the landscape afforded to the eye.

Each day the sun swept across the huge archway of heaven, and as the shadows shifted, the Rangers regulated their duties, until at last the red rim slipped over the western horizon and the shimmering afterglow faded into night's darkness.

And each day Regret's strange uneasiness seemed to increase. There—somewhere far beyond—lay the *Back of Everything* of which Houston had spoken, the home of a nameless peril. The mystery of that immeasurable waste was so fathomless, its menace so ever-present, that he caught himself glancing in that direction frequently and apprehensively, as if expecting to surprise some horror in the act of springing out of it upon him.

When the moon approached the full, their patrols became longer and more continuous, their duties more rigorous, for the orb in that stage was known in Texas as *Comanche Moon,* since the full light it offered permitted night movements, and the deadly red raiders invariably came at that time. It was in August, when he had been a Ranger nearly three months, that Regret and Gatling once more rode north on that long patrol from which, two months previously, they had made their visit to the Cogswell settlement. Regret still remembered the night they had spent there with pleasure: the white-bearded patriarch with the bull voice and his lapful of laughing children; his smiling, hospitable wife; their brood of strong, happy descendants; the singing, the merry talk, the hope, the permanence, the content.

More than anything else, the Cogswells had taught him the meaning of human occupation of this land, won him to Texas as a home, justified to him his service as a Texas Ranger. He thought that, when he finished his term of enlistment, he might find a piece of land, perhaps, and settle near just such a bright spot as Cogswell's Corners to begin a life different from any he had known before. It was a half-formed dream merely, not a resolution. But he looked forward with anticipation and pleasure to seeing again those friends he had made.

He could be trusted now to find his way to a given place, so they separated, Gatling to scout a watercourse, he to investigate a range of small hills some miles away, agreeing to meet at the same creek fork where they had previously stayed, for their night camp.

Knowing the moon was near full, Regret should have been more watchful that day. But at first he thought nothing of it when he saw a horse standing not far from a clump of chaparral, its head hanging. Supposing it was a stray, he rode toward it, whereupon it took alarm and turned away—very lame, on three legs. He put spurs to his mount and galloped to head the animal off.

All at once something whipped past his ear with a rustling sound. He mistook it for the passage of one of the large prairie grasshoppers which sometimes made a glinting flight of a hundred feet or more.

A moment later a second object struck the ground right

beside his horse's galloping hoofs. From the tail of his eye he caught a glimpse of it.

An arrow . . .

It dawned on him that in the thicket ahead was hidden a hostile Indian who was trying to kill him.

But they were almost upon the chaparral. Before he could rein up his horse a third arrow struck somewhere with a sharp, rapping sound.

Then from the thicket burst a wild, scarecrow figure, almost naked, leaping away in frantic zigzag hops. A wild Indian! The strange apparition was so grotesque, so almost inhuman in appearance and gait, that it took Regret a second to shake out of his mind the semi-daze it created in him. By then his horse, which had taken it into its equine head that they were playing some sort of game, was almost running the fleeing savage down.

More by instinct than by volition, Regret drew his revolver and fired twice.

The figure pitched forward sprawling, so that his horse had to leap to avoid trampling it, and lay still.

Regret pulled up and glanced about for other foes. But the Indian was alone. His horse must have lamed itself, and he had hidden in the thicket. Regret's gallop to head off the supposed stray, he had mistaken for a charge upon himself; otherwise the Ranger might never have known he was hiding there.

Now Regret dismounted to examine the prostrate savage.

Only the mercy of providence saved him then.

He thought the Indian dead, but as he stooped over him, the creature leaped up at him like a catamount, a knife flashing in his hand. One murderous slash he made, which by a miracle Regret avoided. Before he could close for a second stab, Regret lifted the revolver and blew his head in.

Even after that, with a concentrated rage which was superior to the agony of death, the creature lay horribly kicking and striking, bounding about on the rough ground like a beheaded serpent, until with a mighty shudder he lay still.

Carefully Regret looked his Indian over, to be sure he was now really dead. A more repulsive brute he had never seen. The savage was very swart, his face pitted by small-pox, the forehead low and wrinkled, the cheekbones extremely wide, every feature ugly and vicious, and made more so by the crude red and black paint that smeared it.

A sudden flush of triumph overcame Regret's repulsion. He had met his first hostile Indian and killed him!

So that he would be fully believed, he must take some proof of the encounter with him. For the first time he saw where the third arrow had struck. It was embedded in the fork of his saddle, having missed his thigh by less than an inch. He took care not to disturb it until he had a witness as to where it was planted.

He pondered. Some Rangers, like Wyman Cruze, talked of scalping Indians, and his eye strayed to this fellow's coarse black hair, which fell in two braids, with a feather fastened in the crown. At the sight he shuddered. He was not dainty, whatever the Rangers thought of him, but his gorge rose at the thought of touching that filthy mass all matted with blood and sand.

At last he took the Indian's bow, his quiver of arrows, and the moccasins from his feet, the latter somewhat worn but worked with colored porcupine quills in a barbarically pretty pattern. Lacking tools and time to bury him, Regret left him to the buzzards and rode away to join Gatling.

When he reached the forks of the creek at sunset, Gatling came out from the trees and stared.

"Where'd you get them things?" he burst out.

"From a hostile Indian I killed back in the chaparral," Regret said, his bearing somewhat jaunty. "Look here—this arrow just missed my leg——"

"To hell with that! When did this happen?"

"Four hours ago, or such a matter."

"Four hours! What're you doin' *here?*"

"You said I was to meet you——"

"Meet, hell! You ought to've reported back to camp as fast as that hoss could travel!"

"Report a single Comanche—and he dead?"

"Comanche! So help me God, them moccasins was never Comanche!"

"Then—what are they?"

"Kiowa! The buck that wore them moccasins was a vile, thievin' violater of women an' butcher of children!" Gatling glared at him, and then rushed on in an unwonted burst of loquacity. "The Kiowas is the wust savages on the plains —they don't even have a language any other Injuns understands! The Comanches, who're bad enough, God knows, only tolerates 'em becuz they're devils for bushwhackin' an' scoutin'. Where there's one Kiowa outrider, there's mebbe a hundred Comanche raiders. Do you know what you've done, man? *You've given 'em a four-hour start!*"

Regret was crushed. He thought he had done so well, and had done so ill.

"I'm headin' east," Gatling said. "Mebbe I kin warn them ranches. You git back to camp, *pronto!*"

Long after midnight, when Regret rode into the camp on the Rio Leon and made his report in the darkness, the men tumbled out at Captain Henrion's shout.

2

Now at last it had come, the horror of an Indian raid.

Through the dark they rode, the whole company. Dawn came. Then full day. About noon they saw smoke rising from a shallow valley.

"Irvin's ranch," said Regret, his heart sinking.

"What's left of it," another added.

Crumbled ashes were all that remained of the cabin and outshed. Nate Irvin, the rancher, and the baby, dead, scalped, and hideously mutilated, lay horribly in the front yard. No trace of the wife.

"Took the woman off to amuse theirselves with later," said Wyman Cruze, pale with anger. "She's prob'ly daid now, pore thing."

Regret thought of Sue Ellen Irvin, laughing, with her baby in her arms, saying, "Come in, an' I'll fix you a bite."

He stared at the hacked and butchered bodies of the rancher and the child with the guilt of a Judas. Had he acted promptly, might this family have been saved?

They buried the bodies and rode on, Captain Henrion grimly silent in the lead. Three hours later, the stink of burned timbers again.

"Cogswell's Corners," a Ranger said, and Regret felt sick at the pit of his stomach. He had hoped these, at least, might have escaped. . . .

At this place they found Gatling awaiting them. And surprisingly, with him were Hogarth and Doughty Cogswell, the older sons, and their wives, with the young bound girl, Nettie Hare, and three dirty children, who were picking over the heaps of charred fragments that had been ranch houses. These were the survivors of that thriving little neighborhood, having escaped the first surprise of the Indians and defended themselves in one of the cabins until the raiders withdrew.

Silently they showed the new graves. Twelve of them.

Old Yum and Yettie, the patriarch and matriarch, were gone and dead. And Bullard, the merry banjo player. And the others.

Nettie Hare, the bound girl, gave the most circumstantial account of the raid. The Comanches, she said, came just at nightfall. She was out in the brush, looking for a stray cow, when she heard the shots and savage yelling at the house. She hid in the undergrowth. Though mounted warriors careered all about her, driving off livestock, they did not discover her.

"They must've kilt the whole family right away, except Mr. Cogswell," she said in a light, reedy voice. "They done somethin' awful cruel to him. I could hear Mr. Cogswell hollerin' for hours, it seemed like, afore they finished him an' went away."

Her simple words ran through Regret's mind like a thrill of horror.

"I seen a white man with 'em," she added.

Henrion and Cruze bent their heads suddenly closer. "You sure?"

"He shore wasn't no Injun. Mebbe he was a Mexican—no, he was *white!* He rode clost by where I was hid, an' he wore black clothes, an' had a black mustache. Injuns don't have mustaches, do they?"

"No, child," said Henrion. "Indians don't have mustaches."

The captain's face grew suddenly thoughtful. A white man on an Indian raid. Who was that black rider, and what perversion of his natural instincts carried him on an assault so hellish against his own kind?

3

Midafternoon, two days later, and the sun a flood of infinite fire, saturating earth and sky, sending heat billows almost as palpable as smoke wavering upward from the blinding landscape.

The men rode drooping in their saddles, their horses near the limit of their strength. Regret thought he had known fatigue before, but nothing had ever equaled this. For two days and nights the captain had driven them with scarcely a rest.

There is a weariness of the flesh, and that can be borne. Beyond that is a weariness of the bone, far harder to abide, but possible. But the final weariness, of the nerves and brain, when a man may at any moment pitch unconscious from the saddle, is the worst and most unendurable torment. That stage of weariness the men of Henrion's Rangers were now suffering.

Before them the Comanche trail still danced mockingly.

Never once had they seen an Indian or even been close to one as far as they knew, for the savages followed their usual practice of changing mounts frequently, having a great herd of stolen stock from which to choose. Once the captain had been able to commandeer a remount of horses from one of the large ranches, but even this second relay was ready to drop now, and the men rode drunkenly swaying, clinging to their saddle horns unashamed.

The hope, the hungry hope that by some miracle they might still come up with the red foe, alone kept them going. For they had found the body of poor Sue Ellen Irvin, where she had died an unspeakable death, and other horrors had multiplied in the wake of the savages.

The column halted. Men dismounted and horses slacked off, heads hanging, sweat running down their sides in little rivulets and dripping off into the dust. Up ahead, the captain was talking with a rancher. Yes, the Indians had been this way. They had fired on some cattle herders fifteen miles south, wounding one of them, and had turned west with the stock they picked up.

News, but not good news. Fifteen miles away—six hours before? The Comanches might be thirty miles from this place now, and the horses of the Ranger company were almost done.

Gatling had a dusty mask for a face, and his shirt was drenched with sweat on which the dust had settled and become mud. All of them had dust countenances, with wet scars for mouths, and twin holes in the plastered blankness for eyes.

Up ahead men began mounting again.

"Hossman comin'," came the word down the line.

Regret climbed wearily into his saddle, and it seemed he could hardly get his leg over the cantle.

A dust-stained rider wheeled his horse before Captain Henrion, and raked the column with a hawk-like glare.

"Lookin' for Injuns?" he said.

"That's correct."

"Mebbe ye'll find 'em. My name's Jackson Sime, from

De Long's ranch. Cut the trail of some red hides over that rise, six miles back."

"Can you show it to us?"

"Yep."

Men straightened in their saddles. As the column got into motion snatches of talk came to Regret.

"Comanches must've doubled back. We may be nearer to 'em than we thought."

"What made 'em head back, d'ye think?"

"Rangers south, mebbe."

"A trick, more likely. If that man Sime hadn't cut their trail, we'd be ridin' blind, jest opposite the way they're headin'."

Heads nodded. That was like Comanches.

An hour of riding. The cowman turned his horse with a jerk of his hand at the ground. Sure enough, across the land had passed many hoofs—stolen horses, the loot of this raid.

The Rangers took up the trail, weary animals shuffling; alkaline dust rising from every hoof, filling the eyes, nose, throat, and lungs with torture.

Nightfall. Henrion, his beard salted so thickly with dust that he looked like a hoary patriarch, came down the line, looking at the men, who were sick with fatigue, and their horses, which were even worse.

He lifted his voice. "I want you to listen to me, men! There's just enough in these horses for one more push. *One* more. So we've got just one last chance to catch up with the Comanches." He paused, and looked back and forth along the line. "Jackson Sime says there's a water hole down this dry creek we're on. It's fifteen miles if you follow the meander, but maybe ten if you cut across the country. He'll take us to it. *If* the Indians have camped there, and *if* our horses can reach it, we might make some of those murdering redskins sorry they ever came this way . . ."

The march began again. Ten miles is no great distance when your horses are fresh, but these were stumbling, ready to drop. Sometimes the men dismounted and led them, husbanding with miserly care their strength. In the night sky

76

the moon, almost full, sailed rakishly, its light revealing the country, growing more hilly and broken and covered with scrub oak and cedar, fit for an ambush.

Column leaders halted. Men dismounted and bent over something, then climbed into their saddles again and rode on. The others saw as they passed—a dead man, spread-eagled with arrows, scalped, his upturned face pallid in the moonlight. They had seen many such already.

Another halt. "Dismount . . . dismount," came the whispered order back down the line.

A mile ahead, Jackson Sime was saying to the captain, lay the water hole. They would try a surprise on foot.

Surprise whom? Indians who had the eye of the kite, the ear of the cat, the cunning of the fox, the ferocity and tirelessness of the wolf? It seemed almost foolish to attempt it. Yet the men crept forward through the scrub in a widely scattered skirmish line, trying not to crackle twigs underfoot or rattle branches in their passage.

To his right, Regret saw Tom Gatling. On his left was Jackson Sime, the cowman, going in with them to the kill. For most of the time both of the men were hidden from him in the thick brush through which they were making their way.

Very still the night, with no breeze to cover their faint sounds with rustlings. No clouds in the sky. The broad white moon—"Comanche Moon"—bathed the landscape with pallid, treacherous light.

A horse whinnied. Not very far ahead. Regret caught his breath. Horses . . . Indians . . . just down in that basin.

His palm was sweaty where it grasped the carbine. He tried the hammer, softly raising and lowering it, marking the well-greased smoothness of action. A faint spice of wood smoke prickled his nostrils. In such a moment, a man steps back a thousand generations. He felt a great, gasping excitement, his eyes narrowed, his jaw set, his lips grew thin in the cruel line of the killer.

Shrill as a hawk's scream, an Indian war whoop startlingly split the air.

A great voice shouted, "God damn!"

Another, quickly, "*Open up on them, boys!*"

A carbine cracked. Instantly there was a deafening stutter of reports. The dark basin ahead was marred by little rags of instantaneous flame.

Regret sprang forward. Flattened bullets squealed off in every direction. He threw himself prostrate, and a spray of dirt stung his face.

Somebody, a few feet away, grunted, threshed about under a bush, began coughing with a sudden, momentary pneumonia, and died.

All at once Regret saw Indians for the first time. Flitting, galloping shadows, receding in the moonlight, flogging their horses. Already a long way off.

He fired, and knew he missed.

Suddenly there was Wyman Cruze, his gaunt height against the night sky, with a howl of rage in his throat, shaking his fist at the fleeing foe who had escaped them once more.

4

At dawn the fullness of their failure was evident.

Not an Indian, from any sign which could be found, had been so much as scratched. Nor was this the main war party. Only a handful had camped at this water hole, probably a scouting band.

The raiders were gone, slick and clean, and the Rangers, their horses all but foundered, could not even think of further pursuit.

They found the man who had coughed his life out under the bushes. It was the cowman, poor Jackson Sime, dead with a bullet through his lungs.

Gray with dust and fatigue, Blake Henrion looked down upon him.

"Twenty Texas folks killed—mostly women and little kids," he said, as if he despaired. "Five hundred head of livestock gone. A dozen ranches burned. And nothing to show against those devils. Not one damned thing!"

"One," said Wyman Cruze, slowly.

"What one?"

"The Kiowa that Regret killed."

The captain looked at Regret, his face changing.

"That's right. I had forgot. Regret's Kiowa. Well—they don't go back scot-free." It almost seemed he felt a little better.

After that it was back to the Rio Leon.

The raid left a brand on Paul Regret's soul. At last he knew the full hatred of the wraith-like red enemy, and the thought of that mysterious black rider—the traitor of his own race among them—was the clinching last detail of his bitter anger.

He thought of Nate Irvin and the Irvin baby butchered in their blood . . . and Sue Ellen Irvin, victim of a horror not to be described. And Yum Cogswell, that bull-roaring old grandsire, filled with laughter and fondness for the children that clustered about his feet, lingering out his last hours screaming for an end to his agony.

And he thought of the ruin he had seen. The devastation of the earth by the raiders was not so terrible as the devastation on the faces of the people who survived. The young girl, Nettie Hare, especially remained in his mind. As they rode away that day from burned-out Cogswell's Corners, she gave them a timid smile. It was enough to start the tears in a man's eyes to see it.

The depression of his spirits was not lifted by the fact that he found himself at last accepted by his fellow Rangers.

A place was made for him, now, around the campfire. The hazing ceased. Men listened to him with the same respect that was accorded to others.

Not even his blunder in failing to carry immediate report to camp, after the killing of the Kiowa, was held against him, for Captain Henrion himself stated that it would have made no difference—the Indians had too long a start to have been headed off in any case.

As for the slaying of the Kiowa—it was cherished by all as their only retaliation.

Only Gatling refused to relax his chill reserve and silence.

FIVE:

"By the Same Token, You Stay Out of My Country . . ."

1

REGRET TOOK a purchase on the cinch strap and waited until the horse let go its breath. The animal had the habit of swelling up its barrel while being saddled, and a loose cinch could mean a bad spill. It was a contest of patience. When the horse exhaled, the man smoothly took up the slack, made the under-and-over fastening in the cinch ring, and the saddle was snug.

Ready for another day. On the Rio Leon you started early. Regret glanced toward the east, and the sun was scarcely breaking the horizon. Breakfast had been eaten in the predawn dimness. He and Gatling were going up the river this day, and did not expect to be back in camp before dark.

He checked the carbine in its sling, and the revolver at his hip, to see that both were loaded and capped.

A week had passed since the raid, but there always was an off-chance that a few straggling Indians might be lurking in the country.

Gatling, a few yards away, swung into his saddle.

"Hold up for a minute," someone called.

Regret, his hand on the horn, ready to mount, turned. Stork-legged, squinting and quizzical, with a streak of tobacco juice running down from one corner of his mouth, Wyman Cruze strode toward them.

"Afore ye start out, the Old Man wants to see ye," he said.

"Both of us?" Gatling asked.

"Both."

It was less than a hundred yards to the captain's tent, but Regret had acquired the custom of the habitual horseman, who never walks when he can ride. Together they trotted their mounts over.

Blake Henrion came out, and lit a cheroot, the one luxury he allowed himself.

"I'm ordered to Austin," he said, "to report to President Houston there. Don't know what it's about. Maybe only a little special job on stock thieves. On the other hand, the president doesn't frequent Austin commonly. I'm instructed to bring two men with me. Since you two are up for next patrol, I'm taking you. Get some rations from the cook, and I'll be with you in fifteen minutes."

Going to town. It was the dream of every Ranger at this isolated post, and at another time Regret would have been jubilant over his luck. Austin, he had been told, was larger and more "metropolitan"—whatever the Texas conception of that word was—than Washington-on-the-Brazos. He reasoned that society there might be somewhat elevated, with perhaps charming and cultivated women to illuminate it. Ordinarily, an attractive prospect. But now, because of the ugly feeling caused by the Comanche raid, which had remained with him, the announcement left him almost indifferent.

He did brighten somewhat when, about nightfall of the second day from the Rio Leon, they "raised" the distant buildings of the town in the valley of the Colorado. Half an hour later their horses were trotting into Austin. The "metropolis," it turned out, was no more than another squalid collection of rude huts and cabins, with a few ramshackle stores. Hardly a teeming mart of commerce: a wide, muckish puddle in the middle of the main thoroughfare had been pre-empted by a razorback sow and her litter of gaunt piglets—*actually!*

But as they jingled down the street, Regret saw bright faces and pretty figures. Girls and women. Some of them turned to look after the Rangers, and just seeing them gave a lift to his spirits.

A man hardly realizes how he misses the flutter of petticoats, until he has been deprived of them. Also, it is singular how a chance smile on a woman's face, even when given merely in passing, has the power to cheer a man.

He was feeling better when they dismounted before a shambling, two-story structure, known as Bullock's Inn, and turned their horses over to a black groom. Inside at a counter, beneath a bristling array of horns—deer, antelope, and longhorn steer—a genial, foulmouthed man greeted them. He was Dick Bullock, the tavern keeper, who loved conversation as some men love alcohol.

"Been expectin' you, gents," he said, after they wrote their names on the huge buckram-bound ledger which served as a guest book. "Gen'ral Houston hisself awdered the accommodations, an' I trust you'll find everythin' to your requirements. Supper will be served in the dinin' room, an' if you desire, in the meantime, to cut the dust from your throats, you'll find our line of wines an' lickers to your taste, I'm shore. How are things on the Rio Leon?"

"Active, last week," said Henrion. "Is the general in the tavern now?"

"No, suh. The gen'ral's dinin' with friends in the city," said Bullock expansively. "He info'med me that he intends to look in at the *baile* which is bein' given in his honor at the Hall of Congress, befo' returnin' to this house. I might add that the *baile* is open to the public, an' no doubt you gents will care to attend——" He hesitated, his eye on their soiled and worn garb. "But then, of course, you may have plans of your own——"

Henrion glanced at his men. "Suit yourself, boys."

Gatling stood in leather-faced silence, staring at the antlers above the counter as if he had not heard.

But Regret discovered that the prospect of attending a ball—which he took to be what Bullock referred to as a *baile*—was all at once overwhelmingly attractive.

To move once more among charming ladies, to hear something besides the ordinary gruff converse of men, to press a white hand, to pay a neat compliment, to be rewarded with a sweet smile: to a man who had been accustomed to these things so that he had taken them for granted, they now seemed doubly enchanting because he had been denied them so long.

But, he considered, he *was* shabby. . .

And at that he remembered for the first time that he had in his possession a couple of hundred dollars—his total winnings the night of the poker game at the Ranger camp, just before the Comanche raid. Money meant so little on the Rio Leon that he had almost forgotten how necessary it can be.

He glanced at Bullock. The innkeeper species runs true to form the world over, and Regret knew how to handle it.

"I think I shall attend the dance," he said. "I will need some new apparel—at once."

"Yes, suh," said Bullock. "There's a gent's outfitter's acrost the street."

"Send word to have some suits of clothing brought—to my room—for approval."

"Pleasure, suh. Unhappily, you may find the prices of clothes in this city uncommon steep——"

Regret knew Bullock was thinking of the notorious poverty of the Texas Rangers.

"Expense is of little concern to me, so the garments are passable," he said crisply, and caught in Gatling's eye a gleam of rueful recollection of that poker game.

"In that case, a pleasure, suh," said Bullock, impressed.

"And send a servant to clean my boots."

"Pleasure, suh."

"And a barber to attend upon me."

"Pleasure, suh."

"And prepare a bath."

"Pleasure, suh!" Mine host began to show alacrity. No guest he could remember recently had been so peremptory, or demanded so many things at once, in a manner so superb. To Dick Bullock, these things indicated that the gentleman was Quality. He wondered what he was doing in the Texas Rangers, but forbore asking questions, and began giving rapid orders to his black servants, while he slid the keys across the desk.

To Regret's room came at once a porter for the boots. Two servants carried in a tub of steaming water in which Regret luxuriated. A barber appeared, to whose ministrations he submitted. Lastly, a lantern-jawed individual in a well-brushed black suit arrived with some garments over his arm, and announced that he was Mr. William Jochems, of Jochems & Hess, the haberdashers across the street.

By the time the barber wiped away the last traces of lather, it was dark and the candles had been brought. Gatling, who shared the room with Regret, looked on silently while these matters progressed, save for a low tune he whistled through his teeth. He donned a shirt of dark blue from his saddlebags and shaved himself. Simple as these changes were, he looked not too badly. Now, without a word, he left the room, to have supper with Henrion, no doubt.

Regret did nothing to delay his departure. He preferred the man's room to his company.

With a kind of renewed zest, he turned to a consideration of the clothing brought by Mr. Jochems.

There was a suit of blue broadcloth, with a buff waistcoat, which looked well on him. Also a long-tailed coat of plum color with very tight-fitting fawn trousers. He was tempted for only a minute by them, and discarded them both in favor of a neat suit of doeskins. The blue and the plum colors would do very well in New Orleans, but he discovered that he had curiously lost his taste for finery of this kind.

84

He donned the soft doeskins, which had fringes on the sleeves, across the shoulders, and down the trousers legs. Quite dashing, he thought.

Mr. Jochems stood looking on silently.

"It's remarkable," Regret said, "that all these garments fit me so well. Look at these doeskins—they might have been made for me."

"Yes, suh," said Mr. Jochems. "Dick Bullock said that fo' size an' build you was the spit of Fess McFadden. These was made fo' him."

"Really? Then why didn't he wear them?"

"Fess had an unfortunate likin' fo' livestock, suh—other people's. He was strung up last March by the vig'lance committee down at Goliad, fo' hoss larceny——"

"Thunder and lightning! I am standing in the garments of a dead horse thief?"

"He never had no chance to wear 'em, suh, the vig'lance committee actin' so sudden-like. Pity, too, in a way, fo' he had as purty a taste in apparel as he did in hossflesh—but yo' kin jedge fo' yourself, suh."

Regret gazed into the mirror. After all, clothing was clothing, and the doeskins fit well, almost to a nicety.

"At least," he said, "your Mr. McFadden appears to have had a very fair figure."

"Yes, suh. Neat, I allus called Fess."

Regret made up his mind. "I'll take this suit. After all, when the result's so admirable"—he bowed smilingly to himself in the mirror—"why cavil at the circumstances that make it so?"

He paid Mr. Jochems, and that worthy departed with the two suits which had not been chosen.

Regret returned to the mirror and knotted about his throat a blue silk scarf. Remarkable, he allowed to himself, how clean clothes, a hair trim, and a close shave against the grain could improve a man's appearance.

2

The *baile,* as Dick Bullock called it, was to begin at eight o'clock. It was after seven by his watch when Regret went down to the dining room. Gatling and Henrion evidently had finished their meal and were gone, but this did not concern him. He welcomed a chance to dine alone and at leisure for once.

The meal was such as might be expected at a frontier inn, but still better than the fare at the Ranger camp. And he discovered some excellent brandy. Over this he dawdled, for it was no policy of his to be among the early comers at any social affair.

All at once he lifted his eyes and saw, to his absolute astonishment, at the dining-room entrance a man he knew.

It was Emile Beaubien.

For a moment Emile stood looking about the room. Then he saw Regret. It did not seem to surprise him.

He hesitated briefly, then came directly over. He seemed thin in the face and somewhat pale, although his complexion still was spotted with his chronic and unpleasant acne. But he was dressed handsomely in a fine long-tailed blue cloth coat with brass buttons, pink waistcoat, frilled shirt, white cravat, and yellow nankeen trousers—overdressed, Regret thought. And then realized he had himself affected just such foppish attire no more than a few months ago.

Emile stopped beside Regret's table. For a moment he stood uneasily, while Regret sipped his brandy without speaking. An awkward situation.

"Hello, Paul," he said at last.

"Hello."

"May I sit down?"

"As you wish."

Emile took a chair, and glanced about as if at a loss. He looked immature, almost effeminate, having inherited nothing of his father's vigorous force. Rather he resembled his mother, whom Regret remembered as being given to vapors and snobbery, and whose mind was occupied exclusively by trifles. How Eloise Grailhe could have thought even for one moment of this spoiled and pampered weakling was beyond him.

"I saw your name on the register, Paul," Emile began. "But when I saw you here, I hardly recognized you. So sunburned. And rough-looking—meaning no offense."

Regret took no offense. Observing the other's pallor, he reflected that this was the result of the wound he had given him. Also that the youth had come out of the duel much better than he should have expected.

"I arrived in Austin this afternoon. By stagecoach," Emile resumed. "I have a room at this inn—execrable place, isn't it?"

"What are you doing here?" said Regret.

"That's a strange question, coming from you!"

"It has to do with me?"

"You know well it does," Emile said obstinately.

"It pleases you to deal in ambiguity."

"It pleases you to deal in equivocation."

Regret shrugged, and prepared to rise from the table. He had no wish to quarrel with this fool—again.

"Wait!" said Emile quickly. "I'm sorry. I—I'm not strong yet." His voice had become apologetic, almost pleading. "You put me in bed for a month, you know. My shoulder's still stiff. The ball just missed the lung and an important artery, the doctors said. But by autumn, they tell me, I'll be as good as new."

"I'm pleased to hear it," Regret said.

"You hold no enmity against me, Paul?"

"None."

"Nor I against you. Here's my hand on it."

Regret accepted the proffered palm and was struck by the contrast of its soft whiteness against his own brown and weather-beaten fist.

After a flabby handclasp, Emile played with the spoons,

looking down at the homespun tablecloth. All at once he exclaimed, "Paul—tell me where she is!"

Regret groped for his meaning. "Who?"

"Eloise."

"Eloise Grailhe?"

"Of course. What other Eloise concerns both of us?"

Regret stared. "How should I know where she is? I thought—I supposed—you——"

He had imagined them married by now, but he suddenly found it most difficult to say.

"You mean you haven't seen her?" Emile insisted.

"Of course not."

"Or heard from her? You swear it?"

"I haven't an inkling as to her whereabouts. That I swear."

For a moment Emile looked at him, then he said with a sort of sigh, "So she didn't come out here . . . to you."

"You're telling me that Eloise is *here*—in Austin?"

"To the best of my knowledge," Emile said dully.

Regret's first sensation was a great leap of the heart at the thought that Eloise might be close at hand. His second, like a jet of icy water, was the recollection of how she had publicly announced her love for this puppy Emile, and brought on him the laughter of New Orleans by her preposterous story of whipping him. And his third was the discovery that his resentment against her for these things was gone. Everything was submerged in wonder at what she was doing in Texas, and a longing to see her again.

As calmly as he could, he said, "Why do you think she's here?"

"She left New Orleans, suddenly and without a word of farewell, two weeks ago. Naturally I was—concerned. We checked the outgoing steamboat and stagecoach passenger lists."

Regret nodded. The same obvious process had been employed in his own case.

"I followed her, hoping to talk some sense into her," Emile went on. "If she only knew the discomfort and annoyance I've been to——" His childish petulance effectively quenched any pity for him.

"She knows I'm mad about her—and she uses it to torture me," he continued in his whining voice. "Why, I've begged her to *marry* me. Will you credit that, Paul?"

"It's not too difficult to believe."

"But think—she's an *actress*. Mother had one of her fainting spells when she heard I'd proposed, and father scowled as he does at a prisoner in the dock. Would you think a girl of Eloise's station would refuse such an offer?"

"The honor must have seemed too great for her," said Regret dryly.

"I thought it was because she was in love with you," Emile said, not noticing the irony. "Until you told me you didn't know she was here. I still wonder——" He shot an odd, shifting glance across the table. "Listen, Paul, it might help me get over this—this infatuation—if I knew the truth——"

"Well?" Regret was a little puzzled.

"Tell me—I won't hold it against you, I promise——" Again the twist of the weak face. "You're a man of the world, Paul, and have a devil's own way with women— what about Eloise—did you ever——?"

Regret did not know why the implication shocked him so. Certainly at one time his designs upon the girl had hardly been honorable. Yet a man changes, and he discovered that life in the wilderness had altered his whole viewpoint toward women, and particularly the one they were discussing.

He came to his feet so suddenly that his chair crashed over.

"Eloise Grailhe is as far above reproach," he said, his voice vibrating like a fiddle string, "as you, sir, are beneath contempt!"

He strode furiously from the room.

3

For a moment in his anger Regret could not think clearly. Then his rage against Emile Beaubien faded before a sudden great wish to find Eloise.

The *baile!* Suddenly the public function which was being given in honor of Sam Houston assumed new importance. Wherever Eloise Grailhe was, he told himself, an affair of such significance must be known to her. And her hosts, whoever they were, would hardly fail to be present and bring her with them, if only for the beauty and charm she would add to the occasion.

Memories rushed over him: Eloise on the opera stage, her throat thrilling like a bird's; Eloise across the table from him at Victor's, making magical play with laughing eyes; even Eloise in anger, slapping her dress with his riding whip as she stormed at him to flee from Judge Beaubien.

At the desk he got directions to the Hall of Congress. It was not far, and on the short walk he found himself wondering how she would greet him if he found her there. Suddenly he was very thankful for his new doeskins.

His old assurance seemed to have gone. Like a schoolboy in his first puppy love, he began rehearsing speeches to himself, and casting about for some way of showing to advantage before the girl.

There was General Houston. Perhaps of his acquaintance with the president he might make something. Houston would hardly fail to remember him. If Eloise saw him in conversation with that impressive figure . . .

The Hall of Congress, a drafty, one-story auditorium surrounded by a stockade built as a defense against the Indians, was ablaze with lights, and all of Austin seemed to be present. As he reached the door he heard an expiring blare of music: the grand march had just ended.

90

Regret entered. The place was crowded, and gentlemen already were choosing partners for the first dance.

Across the room he beheld the gigantic figure of the president of the Texas nation. And Houston was leading out on the floor—Eloise Grailhe.

For the moment, as the orchestra began a polka with great enthusiasm but little harmony, the other dancers, out of consideration for His Excellency, left to this couple a cleared space in which they passed through the first steps as if alone.

All things are relative, and especially is this true of the charms of women. Place a beauty in a crowd of other beauties, and she loses value because of the plenitude of graces surrounding her. On the other hand, among ungainly and homely women, one of even moderate enhancements may appear glorious.

Eloise's enhancements had never been moderate: she was born to hold her own in any company. But in this assemblage, to Paul Regret at least, no other member of her sex was worth a snap of the fingers compared to her. Eyes and lips very bright, bare shoulders gleaming, light on her feet as the airy down of the milkweed, she drew the gaze not only of Regret, but of everyone present. He felt a sudden great pride in her, as if he had something to do with the splendor of her beauty.

Then he saw Tom Gatling, standing across the hall with Captain Henrion, gazing at her as if he had never seen a woman before. A sudden throb of jealousy—ridiculous enough—made Regret half angry. What right had Gatling —or any other man—to stare at Eloise like that?

Houston appeared to be enjoying himself; and for a man so huge he danced not badly. Like a tiger upon a gazelle, he grinned down upon her, and she gazed up at him with a smile that fairly provoked Regret with her in his present state of mind. Everyone, he told himself, must behold how silly was her behavior in trying to work her foolish charms on a man like Houston. He resolved to speak to her about it, giving her to understand in a manner kindly yet firm, at the first opportunity, the impropriety of her conduct and the danger of making herself ridiculous before the people of Texas.

The floor now filled with dancers. But still he could follow the movements of the couple in which he was chiefly interested, by the towering height of His Excellency.

When the number ended, the crowd applauded. Houston received the tribute with his rather ferocious smile and an inclination of his massive head; and to Regret's surprise Eloise bowed also.

His annoyance with her increased. Credulous girl! Did she really believe this was anything but a polite acknowledgment to the man with whom, by merest accident, she happened at the moment to be thrown?

And yet, even while he fumed to himself, he heard about him murmuring comments, inquiries as to who she was, and expressions of admiration, until he began to wonder if, after all, the applause was not as much for her as for Houston.

At the same time it came over him that any hope of impressing Eloise with his acquaintance with the president was gone. She was, quite obviously, on a footing of far greater familiarity with Houston than was he. Illogically, this conclusion perhaps served to increase his vexation.

4

A moment later, he noticed Gatling again. As the dancing couples started to leave the floor, the Ranger began elbowing his way unceremoniously through the crowd. Regret did not divine his purpose until he saw Houston catch sight of him and greet him with laughing cordiality.

Decidedly Regret had underestimated the man. He began also to work his way toward where Eloise stood smiling at the two tall Texans, coming up just as Houston, with a bow, presented Gatling to her, and while the Ranger was uttering some chawbacon compliment, which she received with a response so sprightly that Regret could have shaken her.

"Eloise," he said, directly behind her.

She turned, her eyes widening. "Paul!" she cried. "Why, *Paul!* I can't believe it! It's really *you?* Where have you been? When did you arrive here? What are you doing?"

Her questions came tumbling out so fast that they tripped over each other, and before he could answer any of them, she took both his hands and was drawing him toward Houston.

"General!" she said. "An old friend—Paul Regret!"

Her pretty excitement brought a grin to Houston's face. "Mr. Regret and I are acquainted," he said. "I had the honor, personally, of enlisting him in the Texas Rangers."

She released Regret's hands, and looked at him, wondering. "A Ranger? And Mr. Gatling's a Ranger, too? You're probably great friends—and I was just about to introduce you!"

Her laughter rippled, and both men smiled, but wryly, thinking how far she had missed her mark.

For the moment her entire attention turned to Regret. "How you've changed, Paul!"

"For the better, I hope?"

"So brown and fit!" she said. "Yes, it's becoming. It makes you look more handsome, Paul—and I think a little devilish——"

She laughed lightly and teasingly.

"I hope not devilish," he said, his voice lowering.

Her voice dropped also, so that the others were excluded from the conversation. "Perhaps not entirely. I'm sure you're very upright and honorable—except possibly in one respect——"

"What respect?"

"You'd never betray a trust—or anything else more important than a woman."

"I deserve that," he said. "But—it's not true. Not any more it isn't."

"About—the women? You must have strangely changed, sir."

He smiled. "The charming scoundrel—I think you called me that once? The leopard that can't change his spots?" All at once it became to him very important to convince this girl of certain matters which, to be most truthful, he had at that moment just realized in himself. "I suppose," he said, "it would be hard for you to believe that I've scarcely seen a woman in these months?"

"Why not?"

"They don't come where I live—the Ranger post. Once in a long while you see one in an isolated ranch—I knew two families——"

He broke off, his face twisting.

"What about them?" she asked.

"The Indians massacred them."

"Oh," she said with horror.

"Anyway," he went on after a moment, "you miss women. You get to understand what they mean to you, when they aren't there to take for granted. You—you look at things a little differently——"

A shadow seemed to cross her eyes. "If I could only believe that—" Her voice trailed off. It seemed to him that she would have said more, but stopped.

"I don't blame you," he said. "It would be mighty foolish to expect a girl like you to take any stock in that, wouldn't it? Let's talk about you."

"What about me, for instance?"

"Why are you all the way out here in Texas?"

For some reason she became evasive. "For no important reason——" She gave a little laugh.

"Is there some secret about it?"

"None worth discussing."

He said, "Eloise—I've just seen Emile Beaubien."

"Here—in Austin?" she asked quickly.

He nodded. "Just arrived. He told me of your sudden departure from New Orleans."

"He had no right to follow me!"

"Then it *is* something to do with Emile that brings you here! Did you run away from him, Eloise?"

"Emile Beaubien is not of sufficient consequence to run from!"

"He said you refused to marry him. He couldn't understand why."

"Why do *you* suppose?"

"I can't imagine." But his heart was racing.

"The imagination can be cultivated," she said.

"Tell me," he begged.

"It's just that I find Emile Beaubien impossibly selfish and boring!" she said defiantly.

Regret was dashed. "That wasn't what you said to Judge Beaubien!" he said bitterly.

"You heard me? And you hold it against me?" She seemed quite angry. "Tell me how else I could have kept them from searching the premises and surely finding you——"

"In heaven's name, I wasn't blaming you!" he exclaimed, aghast. "As for that fool Emile—you were right—absolutely right——"

Her manner chilled. "It's a pleasure to know you approve of me," she said. "And I'd feel *so* glad to return the compliment." She turned to an elderly female of determined visage who stood near. "Myra, darling, may I present Mr. Paul Regret, lately of New Orleans? Paul, this is my dear friend and hostess, Mrs. Myra Hackett. Now, Mr. Gatling, I believe you asked me to dance?"

5

Never had Paul Regret been more neatly disposed of, and never, he thought, had he appeared to worse advantage. He fumed inwardly, bewildered and indignant at his own stupidities, as Gatling, all long legs and arms, led the girl out on the floor, while he was detained by Mrs. Hackett.

The woman had square steel-rimmed spectacles and a desiccated countenance, and she engaged him in a spate of talk with a voice as sharp as the screech of a slate pencil. In the first sentence she informed him that she was *doyenne* of such society as Austin boasted, that she had the largest house in town, and that she was a widow. Then she sketched brief biographies of herself and her late husband; gave a catalogue of the series of ailments that took the latter off some five years previously; furnished interesting details about her own complicated symptoms; and gave a circumstantial account of her dinner party that evening, in which, it appeared, "dear" General Houston had been the guest of honor, with "darling" Eloise as his dinner partner.

All this Regret took in at one ear, his eyes being occupied with the manner in which Gatling was disporting himself with Eloise.

Disporting, he decided, was the proper word. The dance was a Texas version of the Virginia reel, and it appeared that his colleague of the Rangers imagined that he could make up in violence what he lacked in grace. As the music began, Gatling gave a snort, and with the plunge of a maddened longhorn steer bounded toward Eloise. He seized her and swung her around like a bag of meal. Regret saw her passed, swung, and passed on to the next, until she arrived breathless at her starting point; and his heart would have gone out to the poor creature, had it not been so very obvious that she was thoroughly enjoying this rough experience.

At his elbow the garrulous Mrs. Hackett clacked that Eloise and Gatling made *such* a handsome couple. It was a viewpoint he did not share. Eloise might deserve the description, but about Gatling it was hard for him to concede anything handsome.

The number ended. They came toward Regret, Eloise chatting with her partner in a manner he found disgustingly vivacious. Yet he hoped for the next dance—a waltz, incidentally, in the performance of which New Orleans, at least, had found nothing to criticize in him—and a chance thereby to discover what he had said to annoy her, and why she had treated him so much more mystifyingly than even a woman's ordinary inconsistencies warranted.

Before he could speak to her, however, a sudden stir and tension caused him to turn and witness a strange and surprising moment of drama.

Houston, who had paused for a word with Henrion across the hall, had just departed. The floor for a moment was clear. Suddenly a slim, hawk-like youth appeared at the far entrance and started across, walking with his hand near the holster of his revolver, his eyes fixed on the captain.

At once, with an odd, alert watchfulness in his bearing, Blake Henrion moved forward to meet him. As the two neared each other, Regret saw a most arresting resemblance between them—a mark of breed, of close family blood— though the captain was a good fifteen years the senior of the two, much shorter in stature, and bearded, while the other was clean-shaved.

A stillness fell in the auditorium. The two men halted in the center of the floor, facing one another, the youth seeming to bristle.

"Blake," he said in a flat, menacing drawl, "I heard you got a warrant for me."

"Then you heard wrong, Lanny," the captain replied. "I've got no warrant for you—not yet. But you've been running with some mighty trifling company."

"I choose my own company."

"That's your privilege. But I wish you'd listen to me, boy. Those no-goods will only get you into trouble. Some-day there *might* be a warrant. If it comes, I'd have to serve it on you—like on anybody else."

A smile, cold as sleet, crooked the younger man's lips. "You won't serve no warrant on me, Blake. This is your country. You won't see me in it no more." A dancing devil was in his eye. "By the same token, you stay out of *my* country. If we was ever to meet again—one of us might not walk away."

The captain's face did not change. "If it's good-by, Lanny, I'd like it if you'd shake hands before you go. And take a drink with me."

The other's smile faded. "I'll shake hands," he said after a moment. "But I don't want no drink."

Regret saw their hands meet briefly. Then lightly as he came, the deadly youth walked out of the hall. Blake Henrion stood alone in the middle of the dance floor.

At once, with relief at the passing of the tension, conversation was resumed all over the hall, and the orchestra started to play. Regret glanced at Eloise. On her face was the strangest expression, a look of speculation, or immense interest, or even fear, he did not know which.

"Who was that?" he asked Gatling.

"Lanny Henrion. Blake's brother."

"Strange talk between brothers!"

Gatling gave him a half-exasperated side glance. "He's Blake Henrion's *only* brother. Lanny's a likable kid, game as they come, an' mighty good with hoss or gun. But he's reckless an' wild, an' he's been nothin' but trouble to Blake with the scrapes he's been in. There was talk that he was mixed up with Fess McFadden, who was lynched last spring for stealin' hosses."

Fess McFadden! The dead man who had unwittingly contributed the very doeskins Paul Regret was then standing in.

"But it wasn't proved?" he said.

"Not proved, but thought. A sorrow to Blake, who's more like a father than a brother to Lanny, an' keeps hopin' for the boy, an' fond of him. But the kid's got an anger agin' him for bein' the law. Someday he might be trouble—big trouble——"

He broke off. Across the floor they could see Captain Henrion beckoning to both of them.

Evidently Houston, before he left, had given the captain some instructions. They said their farewells.

For a moment Regret had Eloise alone. "I'd hoped for at least one dance," he said wistfully.

98

"One can always dance," she replied.

"Then may I see you later?"

"It's doubtful. I'm leaving very soon."

"But surely—a few minutes——" He was intensely disappointed.

"They're waiting for you, Paul," she said. Then, all at once, she softened. "Good-by. And if—if we don't see each other again—please try to remember that I am your very dear friend—*always!*"

Her voice, as she said it, had such a quality of unexplained emotion that any petty annoyance was quite wiped out of his mind. As he left the hall with Gatling and Henrion, he still felt on his hand the pressure of her fingertips.

SIX:

"Give Houston Only One Year of Peace on the Border . . ."

1

The captain led them down a hall on the upper floor of Bullock's Inn, opened a door, and they were ushered into the presence of General Sam Houston, the president of the Texas nation.

Again Regret felt the impact of that giant leader of men, with his huge head, his lion-skin waistcoat, and his roan side whiskers. He had been writing and he glanced up as they entered. When his eye fell on Regret, he frowned.

"Is *this* the pair, Blake?" he asked.

Henrion seemed at a loss. "Why yes, sir. They don't come better than Tom Gatling——"

A gesture of impatience. "I know Tom Gatling. Nobody can tell me anything about tall Tom. But *this*——" Regret felt the eyes of all three on him. "I need experienced men —tried Rangers—the best I can get!"

"I had no notion, General, that you wanted picked men," Henrion said.

"Pretty obvious," growled Houston, with a tone of disparagement which Regret would have resented in another. But with this remarkable man resentment somehow seemed futile. It was like being angry at a mountain peak—or a hurricane.

Houston thought for a moment. "Regret," he said presently, "your surmise was correct concerning the nature of the charges against you at New Orleans."

"Yes, Your Excellency?"

"The young man who was—ah—regrettably shot has recovered. I'm happy I didn't send you back, although it's resulted in a mass of acrimonious correspondence with the authorities there." Houston gave his grim half smile. "The exchange of notes in which one nation politely insults another is one of the few diversions of international diplomacy."

"May I ask when you satisfied yourself of these facts?"

"Just a few moments ago, as it happens. The young man himself, Emile Beaubien, left here just before you arrived. I'm surprised you didn't encounter him in the hall —although perhaps he went to his own room, which I understand is on this floor."

"Was his business to inform you of this, Your Excellency?"

"No. He came to present his father's respects—a very correct and polished gentleman, Judge Beaubien, though we do cross each other at times—and to make inquiries about that young lady, Miss Grailhe, with whom I had the pleasure of dining."

Eloise! So they had been discussing her. Very much Regret wondered what had been said. But Houston rumbled on.

"It occurs to me that your enlistment in the Texas Rangers, which came about under somewhat arbitrary conditions, might be reconsidered by you. I'm prepared, under the circumstances, to give executive approval to your resignation, if you should by any chance wish to tender it."

Regret digested that. A month ago he might have eagerly seized upon the offer. But now he said slowly, "By so doing, I suppose I'd be excused, sir, from the particular assignment—whatever it is—that you have in mind here and now?"

Houston nodded his massive head.

Regret found himself suddenly and unaccountably angry. "You expect me to thank you for that?" he burst out. "You have me at a disadvantage, sir, because of your official position, but I'd like to say at least this much: It was your whim to make me a Texas Ranger—and it's my whim to remain so! And whatever you think of me, sir, I'm as good a man as—this fellow Gatling—or anyone else! And furthermore, I know my rights. And one of them is that a Texas Ranger can't be shoved off a job without good and sufficient reasons, until he finishes it. If you have such reasons, sir, I demand to know what they are!"

Houston relaxed back into his chair with his tigerish smile.

"Well, well!" he said. "A fighting cock—with all his hackles up!" For a moment he studied Regret with his flat, opalescent eyes, then nodded. "Blake, I think I've wronged this man. I reckon there's good stuff in him." He continued his odd, perfectly impersonal survey. "Tell me, Tom Gatling, does this man scare?"

"He doesn't scare," said Gatling, as if grudging it.

"He shirks duty?"

"No." It seemed the words came with an effort. "Nobody kin say he shirks duty."

"He must have faults. What are they?"

"By your leave, Gen'ral, it ain't right for you to ask me that."

"Perhaps not. I withdraw the question, Tom." Houston returned his gaze to Regret. "It occurs to me that this man hasn't had the best of times." He pondered. "Sending a man so completely dissimilar from the common ruck of Rangers might be just the proper caper." He nodded again. "We'll forget about the suggestion of a resignation, Regret. You've drawn yourself an assignment."

What a man—what a leader! At his words, Paul Regret forgot to be angry, in a glow of pride.

Houston rose at his desk. For a long moment he said nothing, standing before them as a practiced orator who, in no hurry to begin, awaits the exact moment when the effect on his audience is greatest. Slowly his leonine head turned toward each of them.

"Gentlemen," he began, "you are here to listen to a sheer impossibility. And to tell me if you think it can be accomplished."

2

Nobody ventured to interrupt him. He fell into his curious habit of referring to himself in the third person.

"It has ever been Houston's one plan and hope to bring Texas into the Union of States. Our safety, our interest, our common blood demand it. A great man first saw this vision—a man who is now dying from his sacrifices for his country." He bowed his head. "Andrew Jackson," he said reverently.

"Three times," he resumed, lifting his head, "has Texas offered herself to the United States. Three times has her offer been rejected. It is a humiliation, gentlemen, which is difficult for a proud people to bear. Yet, in this year of 1843, the fourth offer is to be made. It will be the last. Not even Houston could scourge the people of Texas into courting rebuff a fifth time."

He surveyed them gloomily. "Texas is like Issacher, the strong ass, crouching between two burdens. The bill for annexation is fought by the senators of the North, who fear any accession of strength by the South. Yet all their arguments Houston could answer—save one."

His great fist thumped on the desk. "That one is so obvious—and yet so specious! Over and over it's been used by our enemies, until they have begun to lean upon it as their invincible bulwark!"

His craggy features grew cunning, and his voice lowered, almost intimately. "It is to destroy that bulwark that I have called you three gentlemen here."

Now he took a stride or two back and forth. "In simplest terms, this is their argument: The annexation of Texas would bring into the United States two thousand miles of additional wilderness frontier to defend, entailing outlays of money and the stationing of troops beyond any benefits to be expected by the nation."

His eye grew wrathful. "Sophistry! Texas will defend her own frontiers—but how can you tell them that? The value to the United States of her people and her lands is beyond computation—but how can you tell them that? In Washington the timid palterers hesitate, and while they hesitate our cause is lost!"

He resumed his restless pacing. "Houston was the first to see the difficulty of answering this argument—under present conditions. Everyone knows of the incursions of the Comanche Indians upon us." Lightning seemed to glitter under his shaggy brows. "You men have just witnessed a sample of it on the upper Brazos. That's the situation with which we must deal. If we can strike a blow that will quiet the Comanches for a single year, I can get the annexation of Texas through the Congress of the United States!"

Then, very simply, he finished, "I've chosen you three to strike that blow."

They listened, stunned at first; then their amazement and doubt showed. Quiet the Comanches? They were the most powerful tribe of savages on the plains—some said that, in all their bands, they numbered twenty thousand. The task Houston proposed would require an army far

103

greater than any Texas could raise—and he blandly offered it to three men!

For a moment Houston looked at them, appearing to enjoy their amazement. Then he seated himself, took up a dog-eared map and a small sheaf of papers, and gestured them to gather around him.

It was a map of Texas—the coastal plain with most of the settlements, the chief rivers and their affluents, the long range of hills marking the beginnings of the high prairies. His great forefinger strayed to the west, where the map was blank save for a few tentative wavering lines— guesses by the cartographers as to the probable courses of streams never explored.

"There dwell our enemies, the Comanches," said Houston. "Not all together, but in numerous shifting bands. To find them is like seeking fleas in a blanket, for they're never in any one spot for more than a week at a time. Yet they appear to have one chief to whom they give a universal fealty. Have any of you heard of Iron Shirt?"

Both Gatling and Henrion nodded.

"His name is all we know about him," Houston resumed. "No Texan has ever seen him—and lived. But from all accounts, he's a very fierce cut-and-thrust warrior. Iron Shirt might well be called the king of the Comanches. Beware of Iron Shirt!"

His finger shifted northwest on the map. "Here are the Staked Plains. No man knows what lies within them. But I believe that from this unknown land comes most of the sorrow of Texas."

He glanced up at them. "You—who've ridden and fought until you were ready to drop from weariness, yet seen our ranches and settlements in smoldering ruins, the dead scattered over the earth—what if I said to you that it is my conviction the Comanches are not primarily to blame for those raids?"

For a moment he sat savoring their incredulity.

"I don't wonder at your surprise," he said almost complacently. "It took Houston some time to grasp the idea himself. But the Comanches are primitives, without the capacity to maintain the long-continued purpose, or lay the cunning plans which we know to our cost. Minds more sophisticated *must* be behind them."

He gave them time for this to sink in.

"I've questioned every wanderer on the plains who came into my orbit—hunters, traders, friendly Indians, captives ransomed from the savages, outlaws even. Slowly I've become aware of the existence of a people unknown to anybody. A strange, shadowy, cowardly, ruthless people, dwelling like Ishmaels in the wilderness. I've even heard a name for them—*Comancheros*—signifying, 'those having dealings with the Comanches.' The little I know about them is in these reports."

He indicated the papers on the desk. "They appear to be a vicious and debased *mélange* of many nations and races. Whence they came, nobody knows. They have the brains of criminals, without any regard for human life or property. Rather, it is by destroying life and property that they prosper, for they deliberately foster upon Texas the Comanche raids, so that the Indians may bring them plunder—to be exchanged for liquor, arms, and trinkets, to the great profit of the Comancheros." He paused and his eyes glittered around at each of them. "*Theirs* is the superior cunning that developed the Comanche tactics of feinting to draw away the Rangers, then slipping through the gap to kill and burn and loot. All that cruelty and horror for the enrichment of these depraved outlaws! Gentlemen, if history ever recorded the fellow to this hideous plot against a people, I have never encountered it, and my knowledge of history is not scant!"

In dead silence he folded the papers and map and put them in his desk. "Who are the Comancheros? Where is their stronghold? How many do they number? Who is their leader? These are questions that must be answered. Find the nest of the Comancheros, and you find the head of the snake—that we may scotch it!"

"But—only three men, sir?" asked Captain Henrion.

Houston rose and towered. "I would send a company —two companies—three—of Rangers. But such a force would never reach the hidden capital. It would be cut off, or led a futile chase. Yet *three men,* using a plan I have in mind, *might* succeed!"

His voice deepened. "I need not tell you this is a forlorn hope. I order nobody—it's your decision to make. If you undertake it, your chances are less than slim; and if you fail, nobody will ever know what happened to you. Yet to you I say this with all solemnity: *Give Houston only one year of peace on the border, and Texas will be safe in the Union!*"

The man was tidal, irresistible. There and then, standing before him, the three pledged their lives and themselves to the incredible, the insane task he had asked of them.

3

Paul Regret went back to his room alone and sat down to think.

A situation, surely. The full comprehension of what he had committed himself to undertake, now that he was away from the spell of Sam Houston's presence, was enough to make a man grow cold all over.

Whatever was the outcome, he told himself right solemnly, it assuredly illustrated a remarkable change in one Paul Regret—a change he could hardly understand himself, and one scarcely on the side of temperate good judgment.

If anyone had suggested to him, as little as twelve weeks ago, that he would go out of his way—even to the point of losing his temper with the president of the Texas Republic—to demand as his "right" the privilege, most dubious, of going on an errand tantamount to suicide, and, without hope of gain from it in money, reputation, or advancement, he would have regarded that man as a fool or worse. Yet that, exactly, was what he had just done.

An honor, of course, in its way, to be chosen for a mission so desperate and important—if you cared for that kind of honor.

He wondered what New Orleans would say about it, if it knew. There would be laughter, surely. He could imagine the cynicisms of the young elegants who had been his companions. And the ladies gossiping—a shrug of a dainty shoulder, a charming shiver and sigh over poor Paul Regret, who had been so amusing and then lost his sanity.

He thought of Eloise. She was at the Hall of Congress now, probably the center of clamoring gallants begging her for dances, because the ball was still in progress. Would she shrug, and make a *moue* over his foolishness—supposing she knew?

Strange how often that high-headed young creature thrust herself in his mind. He felt again that glow of pride in her in the ballroom; and pleasured in her surprise and joy—he could swear it was that—when first she turned and saw him.

And he remembered how chill and distant she suddenly became. Mere perversity? No, something he had said had changed her, perhaps offended her, and he could not imagine what it was.

All at once he wanted to talk with Eloise. Not about his problem, because that was a state secret. But about herself—and if she did not want to talk about that, she could choose any other topic under the sun. He had a craving, like a thirst almost, just to see her, and hear her voice.

She had, he reflected, given him small cause to think she would welcome him. But he did have an excuse . . . at least the beginnings of an excuse: to ask what he had said and done that was wrong, and make his apologies if they were indicated.

Regret rose and straightened his blue scarf before the mirror.

When he reached the Hall of Congress a few minutes later, the lights and sounds advertised, as he expected, that the revelry still continued. But when he entered the auditorium and looked around, he could see nothing of Eloise. Mrs. Hackett was gone also. They had left the ball before it ended.

Unusual—very unusual—for a girl like Eloise, who customarily delighted in dancing until, toward the very dawn, the last fiddle in the orchestra stilled from sheer exhaustion.

He wondered why, and several speculations, none of them reassuring, came to mind. She was, he remembered, the guest of Mrs. Myra Hackett, and that blizzard-faced female had given him, among much other unasked information, specific directions for reaching her domicile—on the mistaken premise that he might next day ride by and admire its grandeurs. Now this information became suddenly valuable. He decided to go to Mrs. Hackett's, inquire for Eloise, and, if she *would* see him, frankly have several questions out with her. He did not anticipate too much difficulty in rectifying any mistake he might have made with her.

As he stepped out of the Hall of Congress and turned in the direction that had been described to him by Mrs. Hackett, he experienced a rising hope. Perhaps, he told himself, the whole misunderstanding might be fortunate in clearing the air between them. Eloise . . . He suddenly discovered that what she thought of him had become something of high importance, to the extent that he was surprised with himself.

The Hackett house was not hard to find. As he approached it a few minutes later, he admitted to himself that while it hardly came up to the glorification it had received from its mistress, it was quite imposing for Austin. It was of two stories, colonial in style, painted white, with an upper and lower gallery running all across the front. The windows, he observed, were alight.

He halted in the shadow beside the house before knocking at the door, to adjust his scarf and to rehearse in his mind a little opening speech.

In that moment he heard above him an airy little laugh. Among ten thousand he would have known Eloise's voice.

Rooted, he stood in the darkness below and watched her as she stepped through an open door out on the upper gallery, chatting quite gaily.

She was laughing up into the face, her hand tucked most intimately into the arm, of the man Regret had least expected to find with her. Emile Beaubien.

It was a deeper treachery than Paul Regret had imagined. He slipped around the corner of the house, and silently slunk away into the night, thankful that the blackness covered his discomfiture and humiliation.

Back to Bullock's Inn now, stumbling over the uneven shadowed ground in his anger and preoccupation. His conversation with the girl came back to him: Eloise had asked him why he supposed she had refused Emile's proposal of marriage, and when he replied that he could not imagine, said, "The imagination can be cultivated."

His imagination was cultivated in earnest. . . .

It had been a lovers' quarrel, after all, between Eloise and Emile. That had to be it. She had rejected him, presumably, on a woman's whim, expecting him to besiege her with renewed fervor, whereupon later she would surrender on her own terms. Women did insidious things like that, he said to himself savagely. But Judge Beaubien's dilettante son had failed to react according to her expectations. Unlike a hotter-blooded and more impetuous man, he did not pursue his suit. So, as a final resort, she went flying from New Orleans, knowing *that* would bring him after her.

Now things were patched up between them. She would return with Emile, and marry with pomp and ceremony into the Beaubien family and the De Rieux fortune.

All very clear. And very, very bitter to Paul Regret.

His own part in the affair in no wise sweetened the bitterness of it. Without much question he had been used . . .

It would be Eloise who dropped those suspicions about which Emile had questioned Regret—hinted, perhaps broadly, that Regret was the man in whom she was really interested—all to bring Emile to time.

Well, Regret conceded, he got what he deserved. For a man to lose his head over a girl as he had done . . . he was glad things turned out the way they did. Now he could go on with his adventure with a mind free. Scouting out the people whom Sam Houston called Comancheros would be his sole business in life, and the sooner they were at it the better. No backward looks. No regrets.

It was good news when at Bullock's he found Henrion and Gatling ready to leave, horses already saddled. Not even one night was to be spent at Austin. They were starting back to the Rio Leon at once.

Paul Regret did not even glance back as they rode out of the night-shadowed Colorado Valley and left the winking lights of the town behind them.

SEVEN:

"It Must Be Old Iron Shirt Himself!"

1

TOWARD EVENING of that tormenting day, heavy clouds began piling up in the west, promising a break in the superheated drought. It was now the end of August, and they were far out on the inhospitable plains, without exact knowledge of where they were.

To all appearances, they were three broken, lawless men, driving westward a string of "stolen" horses. Captain Henrion's usual dry correctness was submerged now in an ancient buckskin coat and hat with burst crown, shiny and black with campfire grease and smoke. Tom

Gatling looked villainous with unshaved jowl and filthy red shirt. Paul Regret himself was slovenly as any in a Mexican sombrero, ragged short jacket, and "breed" leggings, made by wrapping rawhide strips around the calves as a protection from the thorny brush. Each day they went westward added to the havoc in their appearance.

Three weeks had passed since they left Austin: the intervening time spent in perfecting arrangements for this secret mission, and in traveling thus far out beyond the utmost reaches of settlement.

On this afternoon they suffered from the intense heat and experienced the torment of thirst made more unbearable by their concern over their situation. The horses had not drunk for a day and a night, since in this country no rain had fallen in weeks and the grass powdered under hoof from its dryness. Want of the reviving element was evident in the animals they drove before them. Regret marked their wild and glaring eyes, their broken, nervous and unsteady action, which showed their distress.

Of enormous importance were those horses, for it was a part of Houston's plan that the men should go as horse thieves, the supposedly stolen animals to be their passport into the dark and mysterious land into which they were plunging, since horse theft was second in reprehensibility not even to murder in Texas.

Toward evening they saw in the distance some low blue mounds which seemed to indicate broken country. Hopefully they urged the weary animals forward. Now the terrain began to change, becoming rough and interspersed with cedar and scrub oak. All at once they reached the lip of a high bluff from which they gazed down on a wide valley, very rugged and broken, its bottom covered with dry cedars, evidently killed the previous year by a fire.

"That's the Red River," said Henrion. "Indian country sure. From now on, look for, listen for, smell for, *think* Indians. Every bet's coppered against us, boys."

The horses pricked forward their ears, and smelling

water ahead, at once began to wind and slide down the steep descent to the bottom. They were crazy for water, and at the bottom broke into a brisk trot, the mounted men following. Presently, through the dry cedars, the sound of rushing waters came. A moment later, as Regret rode out in full view of the shallow but broad stream, he saw the nags belly-deep in the river, drinking until they were distended like sausages—an example the men thankfully followed.

Henrion rose from the sandy brink and wrung the water from his beard, glancing at the tumbling masses of clouds which half covered the sky, obscured the sun, and turned blue-black toward their base at the horizon.

"We'll camp here," said the captain. "That storm looks rough, and she's going to hit mighty quick."

They hurried to get their meager supper of jerked meat and hominy, but it was hardly cooked before the wind began to moan through the trees, and the mutter of thunder came with occasional vivid zigzag streaks of lightning. A few minutes spent in gulping the food: and then the tempest struck, with a hurricane wind that bent and twisted the trees, dashed water over the men in bucketfuls, and brought occasional volleys of whipping hailstones. Darkness increased rapidly, and night had fallen before the wild fury of the storm was succeeded by a cold steady drizzle.

No hope of kindling a fire now. Regret wrapped himself in his wet blanket, and cursed all prairie weather, and thought gloomy thoughts. He could not sleep, an icy trickle ran down his neck, and the thoughts of Eloise Grailhe, who had treated him so atrociously, kept coming back, and back, to keep him unhappily awake. Always she seemed to be in his thoughts, and always it was maddening to think of her. Why would not an empty, ended chapter in a man's life slip back into forgetfulness like other unpleasant dreams?

He dozed a little just before morning, which came

112

bright, with a clear sky, and birds singing ecstatically in the dead cedars.

They rose, hanging soaked blankets on the bushes, ate a handful of moist jerky each, and looked around.

As usual, they had the previous evening allowed the horse herd to graze—since the animals were used to them and rarely wandered far—keeping only one picketed at camp to round the others up in the morning. Now, however, they discovered that the animals, driven by the storm, had disappeared somewhere among those hundreds of acres of fire-killed trees; and, what was more serious, the camp horse had somehow managed to pull up his picket pin and had gone off with them.

To recover the horses was the first necessity. It would not have been difficult to follow their trail on the sandy bottom, save for the very circumstance that caused them to wander—the storm, with its wind and rain, which had erased every hoofprint. After consultation, the three men set off on foot, seeking the lost horses in three separate directions.

Regret's route took him toward the valley wall, where for more than an hour he searched fruitlessly among the dead cedars. The sun was well risen now, drying everything, and the day was growing warm. For a better view he clambered to the top of a steep rock outcropping, which stood twenty feet or more above the valley floor, with a flat top a few yards in extent which supported several cedar trees and a thick little jungle of thorny brush which had escaped the fire of the previous year.

From this point he could see nothing of the horses. But it was the one green spot in this part of the valley, the shade was grateful, and he sat down among the bushes to rest. It was pleasant on the tree-crowned little hillock. He had slept little the previous night, and he grew drowsy. He must have dozed off, for he woke all at once with a vague feeling of trouble which he could not at first define.

Before him the wide valley lay, with its forest of dead cedars. A solitary buzzard made wide circles in the blue above. Nothing in any of that to explain his curious feeling of dread. He wondered what had wakened him, and was about to rise to his feet, when something froze him motionless.

He had *felt*, rather than heard, a heavy body moving slightly, within a short distance of him. *He was not alone on that rock.*

What kind of creature was on the other side of the underbrush? He hoped, at first, that it was an animal of some kind, and sat perfectly still, holding his breath. Then he heard a sound, very faint, a tiny tinkling such as might be made by the little tin ornaments which Indians loved to wear on their leggings.

His companion on the rock was *human* . . . almost certainly a hostile Indian.

Some highly interesting speculations raced through Regret's mind. Why was the Indian there? Had he seen the white man's trail and followed it? Perhaps at this very instant the savage was leaning forward, his gun barrel pointing through the bushes, his finger crooked to press the trigger. . . .

Mortal flesh and blood could not resist it. Slowly—as if by some mechanical means outside his control—Regret's head turned, his eyes almost starting, expecting every instant to see the black hole of the rifle muzzle.

There was no gun muzzle. Relief swept over him. Perhaps the unseen foe did not know of his presence.

He tensed again at a shifting of weight beyond the thorn bushes. There was a faint crunch of gravel—in a moment fate would make its decision. Again Regret held his breath.

Luck was with him. He heard the other moving away. Presently a thud came, as the unseen person leaped down from the rock. A horse made a sudden trampling as an animal does when being mounted, there was a deep, harsh command in an unknown tongue. Then hoofbeats receded rapidly.

Minutes later Paul Regret came down from his rock,

blowing the breath out through his lips, and wiping his damp forehead with his fingers. That had been a shave too close for comfort, decidedly.

2

Henrion and Gatling had recovered the horses and were waiting for him at camp when he burst in with his news.

"Did you see him?" the captain asked at once.

"No."

"Indian all right." Henrion thoughtfully tugged at his beard. "A white man would have made a racket when he came and went. Scout, likely, who climbed your rock to look over the valley. Came from the opposite direction, so he didn't see your tracks. Lucky you didn't have a horse below, to give you away. But what kind of an Indian? Comanche? Or Kiowa? A lone hunter? Or a member of a war party? What do you think, Tom?"

"I think we better git out of here."

The captain nodded. "No telling which way the Indian went. But we'll try working up the river, so the trees will screen us."

Hard traveling, compared to the open prairie, but the horses were rested and went willingly, moving up the valley through woods that became green as they left the burned area.

An hour passed, and nothing had happened. Regret relaxed slightly, and indulged a hope that they had escaped that particular danger.

"Bad place," said Henrion suddenly. "We'd better get 'em across in a hurry."

They had reached a bend where the river swung sharply toward the bluffs, and where they must cross a wide sandy stretch devoid of trees, perfectly exposed to the view of anyone who might watch from the cliffs above. Gatling swung a rope, and the others spurred forward as the string of driven horses was put to a trot to pass the open area as quickly as possible.

Right in the middle of it, Gatling grunted and Regret glanced up.

Silhouetted against the sky on top of the bluff was a horseman.

The rider sat leaning over his mount's neck, his face thrust forward, his body bent, peering intently down upon them—a strange, almost deformed figure, short-statured, his head appearing larger than natural, with an unstrung bow jutting out from between his shoulders, and a lance in his hand.

An instant and he was gone, the edge of the bluff empty against the sky.

Regret glanced at his companions. The strange shape of this solitary creature, his dark outline, and his prowling, intent attitude suggested rather a fierce bloodthirsty beast than a human being.

"What was it?" he asked.

"Kiowa," said Gatling, swallowing.

The captain nodded. "Worse luck couldn't happen."

They spurred forward, looking for some place where they might make a fight of it; and the band of horses, sensing their nervousness, moved erratically about.

Suddenly all uncertainty ended in grim certainty. The lip of the cliff above sprouted a frieze of wild riders—thin, wiry horses and swarthy horsemen, sitting forward on the withers, their naked legs hanging stirrupless, their stocky bodies balanced as if they were parts of the beasts they bestrode. Bow and quiver, long lance, and rifle, which each warrior carried, were visible: also numerous fluttering feather headdresses, many of them elaborate.

It was all so picturesque and startling that for a moment Regret simply stared, his nerves numbed, the spectacle seeming almost unreal. Then he came to himself with a start, and hauled the carbine from its scabbard under his leg.

116

Instantly he heard Henrion's quick command, "Don't shoot!"

Wondering, he glanced at the captain. Without a further word, Henrion put spurs to his horse and rode at a gallop toward the foot of the bluff from which the savage horde gazed down.

Regret's knees tightened. But before his horse could move to follow Gatling seized his bridle.

"Stay where you are!" he said.

Bewildered, not understanding, Regret sat still on his horse and watched a series of mystifying actions. He saw Henrion ride to the foot of the bluff and wheel his horse there. Lifting his arm with open palm, the captain shouted something. The leader of the savages above him raised high in air his feathered lance.

Now Henrion began a series of rapid movements with his hands.

Sign talk. Regret had heard of that universaal language of the plains tribes, though he understood nothing of it.

"What's he saying?" he asked, struck by the flowing vividness of the symbols.

"Wrists crossed—prisoner," Gatling translated. "Points to himself. He's offering to surrender."

"Surrender to the Kiowas?" Regret had seen enough in the wake of the Comanche raid to curdle his blood, and he had been told the Kiowas were worse than any Comanches, torture their single art, and one in which they delighted. "He must be insane!"

Gatling glared angrily into his eyes. "Whatever he is— or ain't—you obey orders!" Then he added, "Them ain't Kiowas. They're Comanches. An' there's just one chance in a thousand——"

Regret groped in his mind for an explanation. It appeared that the Kiowa war party, if there was one, had missed them; and the Comanches had come upon them instead. But how could this help them?

Gatling said, "Blake makes the sign for Comanche—the sign for trade—the sign for friend—he's tryin' to say

Comanchero to 'em! Now he makes the sign for hoss—the sign for steal. That's us—hoss thieves. I—I think they believe him. Half believe him, anyhow——"

For the first time Paul Regret saw the magic of the name Comanchero demonstrated, and from it he derived no assurance.

With shrill yelps, the Comanches began sliding their ponies down the bluffs in a cloud of dust, racing toward the white men, swirling about them, snatching away their weapons, gesturing viciously for them to dismount. Hard hands pulled Regret to the ground. He saw Gatling, protesting, hauled off his horse. A moment later Henrion, also dismounted, was thrust into the circle with them.

About the small, disheveled group of prisoners, the Indians crowded, gazing on them with exultant eyes. Most of these savages, Regret observed, were stocky and thickbodied, with legs very bandy from incessant riding, so that they waddled uncouthly when they walked. Their small eyes were deep-sunk in their flat, heavy, hairless faces, which were disfigured by daubs of paint in crude colors. Save for breechclout and moccasins, and occasional blankets held about the hips, most of them were naked, except that all wore fantastic feather adornments in their coarse hair, making more devilish their barbaric ferocity.

The circle suddenly opened, leaving a space through which an extraordinary savage, taller than most of the others and past his prime of life, advanced toward the prisoners.

"God——" Gatling whispered. "I believe—— Good God, it must be old Iron Shirt himself!"

The Indian's face, very wide through the cheekbones, with a conspicuous hooked nose and a mouth thin and hard as the scar of a knife, was framed in a splendid war bonnet of eagle plumes, and did not lack a certain nobility. But it was not at his face that Regret stared.

From his high square shoulders, downward about his body, hung a brownish web. Twice Regret had to look at it before he could convince himself that it was what it was

—a shroud of steel links, covering its wearer from neck to hip.

A shirt of ancient chain mail—there was no doubt of it —such as fighting men wore in the days of the crossbow and the battle-ax. What vicissitudes had brought this armor out on these far Texas plains to cover a savage? Perhaps it had been worn by some *conquistador* of Cortez' time, who fell in battle and lost his linked mail to his barbaric slayers—to be passed on and traded from generation to generation, until three centuries later it appeared here, brown with rust, broken in places, with many links missing, but still usable and recognizable.

Iron Shirt! So they knew at last whence came that name. . . .

A whirl of dust at the top of the bluff, and a new pack of horsemen were looking down upon them. Even to Regret the difference between these and the Comanches was apparent. They were the jackals of the Comanches—the Kiowas—and they had arrived too late for the prey.

For a few minutes they gazed hungrily down, while the Comanches paid not the slightest attention to them. Then they slunk away.

Iron Shirt stood with his fierce eyes going from one to another of the captives. All at once he spoke in a harsh, imperious voice.

The hands of the white men were bound with buckskin thongs; they were forced to mount their horses and submit to the further humiliation of having their hands tied to their saddle horns. A dozen young Indians surrounded them—a guard. These carried the revolver belts and carbines of the prisoners slung on their saddles, but the "stolen" horseherd was left behind.

Guttural cries of farewell filled the air. Leading the horses of the prisoners by the bridle reins, the escort went into motion. Regret glanced back. Iron Shirt stood as they had left him, regarding them with that same grim stare.

Then Regret became too occupied with his riding to look back as the horses began scrambling up the bluff, out of the river valley, and on to the great, terrible plains, which stretched illimitably to horizons where hung a shimmering violet haze.

3

That journey was almost dreamlike in its silence. The young Comanches hardly spoke, and the hoofs of the horses were muffled by the springy sod. In every direction extended the brown, rolling plain, with occasional shallow valleys, so featureless that hardly anything from day to day showed that they had made progress.

Early the first day Henrion remarked that it was lucky they had encountered a Comanche party led by Iron Shirt in person. Only the authority of Iron Shirt could prevent the Kiowas from cutting them off as soon as they were away from the main body.

"What about the hoss herd the Injuns kept?" Gatling asked. "We was to use it to git in good with the Comancheros——"

He was silenced by an Indian who rode up beside him and drove a rifle butt into his ribs. Thereafter the prisoners did no further talking.

But Regret was left with something to think about. Perhaps the Indians were half convinced that the prisoners were of the Comancheros. But what of the Comancheros themselves? Three "outlaws" riding into their country, with "stolen" horses to prove their criminality, might be believed. But three captives unceremoniously thrown among them . . . It led to an unpleasant train of conjecture.

Days passed. One night they camped in the shadow of a mighty wall of cliffs which rose from the prairie and extended north and south beyond the horizons. It was the escarpment of that strange table land called the Staked Plains, which stretches for hundreds of miles, north and south, across the continent.

Next morning they climbed the escarpment and were on the edge of the mysterious blankness which no man knew. Almost impossible to believe was that flat immensity. The prairies they had left at least possessed a rolling quality, but here the earth stretched away perfectly level and featureless. Mirages, dancing on the horizon, only emphasized the deadly emptiness of the desert of withered grass.

Straight across it, however, as if guided by instinct, struck the Indians with their captives. That night they made a dry camp, and once Regret heard the words "Palo Duro" spoken by one of the Comanches. Late the following afternoon they came upon an old Indian trail, marked in the sod by the scars of *travois* poles. Weary though the horses were, the Comanches whipped them forward without slacking speed. Other trails converged into the one they were following, from which Regret reasoned they were approaching some large Indian encampment.

But where was it? By the signs that multiplied almost with every step, they should be seeing hundreds of conical tepees in circles or clusters, in every direction. The plain should be populous with grazing pony herds, while the savages themselves, ahorse and on foot, should be visible in numbers. Yet as far as the eye could see, the Staked Plains stretched bare and level as a floor, without one sign of life in any direction. It was uncanny, spectral.

Then the sun dropped over the horizon, and the swift prairie night cloaked everything.

An hour. Another hour of riding in darkness. Without warning, in the gloom, their horses came to a sudden, snorting halt.

In spite of himself, Paul Regret gasped. Yawning at his feet was that which took his breath away—a colossal crevice which slashed across the plains, hundreds of feet deep and with sheer precipices for sides. In the night, feebly illuminated by a gibbous moon, its profundity and terror were magnified, yet it could not have been seen until they were right upon it.

With awe he gazed down into the inky black depths where the rocky walls dropped straight down below him. His horse swung nervously about, and its hoofs spurned over the edge a rock the size of a man's fist. He heard it strike, bound, strike again, bound once more—and then he heard nothing. So far below was its next landing, that the sound did not come up to him.

That they would attempt to descend into that black underworld by night did not occur to him, until the Indians led the horses off down the canyon rim at a smart trot, snuffing like hounds. Presently they found a trail—if by that name could be dignified what, to Regret's horrified eye, appeared to be a mere crooked, zigzag path down the face of the mighty cliffs, where antelopes, or deer, or perhaps mountain sheep, had found precarious footing to the water below.

The Comanches did not hesitate. One by one they guided the horses over the rim, slipping to the ground and making the descent on foot, although the prisoners, bound to their saddles, were forced to ride. Regret's animal trembled and snorted, but obeyed the jerk on its bridle reins.

Never had Regret liked heights, even by day. Yet in the darkness, down a devil's stairway of uneven boulders, narrow shelves worn into age-old limestone, and occasional shaly slopes which threatened perilously to slide out from under them, along which even the sure-footed Comanches picked their way cautiously, they descended with painful slowness for what seemed hours.

A sense of fathomless space beneath him kept Regret's heart in his throat. Up the canyon shrieked a wind at intervals, seeming to pluck at them against the face of the black cliff.

He clung with his bound hands to the saddle horn, and silently prayed that his horse would keep its footing. He envied the Indians the safety, in comparison, of their foot progress, and alternately cursed them mentally for subjecting him to this added peril, and prayed prayers forgotten since childhood, as they made their way deeper and deeper into that revolting pit of blackness.

Sometimes he closed his eyes in sheer horror, when it seemed that nothing could keep him from toppling into the inky womb of earth. Then, in a flicker of the moonlight, he saw Henrion's face, and later caught a glimpse of Gatling's long countenance. These men were afraid also. The knowledge, for some reason unaccountable, made him feel a little better.

From the depths an orange spurt of flame suddenly leaped upward at them and a ricocheting bullet went screaming across the canyon, while back and forth clattered the echoes of the gunshot. With that a voice below howled out a challenge.

At once the Comanches answered, repeating over and over, "*Camisa de Hierro . . . Camisa de Hierro . . .*"

The Spanish for Iron Shirt. A password evidently. They huddled on a rocky shelf, and Regret could have sworn that the Comanches were as fearful, at the moment, as he.

After ages the voice below shouted, "*Avanza!*"

Downward they moved again. Regret heard the rushing of a stream. Then, devoutly thankful, he found his horse had reached the floor of the horrendous gorge.

About him he was conscious of numbers of armed men, although in the pit-bottom gloom, shadows within shadows—for at this place the moon was cut off from them—it was impossible to see what manner of people they were.

Up ahead, one of the Indians jabbered a mixture of Spanish and Comanche. Presently a figure on foot came down the line of horses. One after another he thrust his face up at the three prisoners, as if studying them in the blackness. Regret had an impression of a lean, dark visage, a black smear of mustache, and eyes that caught a flicker of pallid light from the narrow strip of night sky above— a luminescent gleam, almost, like that in the eyes of a wolf.

The man growled an order and strode away in the darkness. At once the hands of the prisoners were unbound from the saddle horns, though still left tied together; they were pulled from their saddles, and thrust into some sort of small building.

Regret heard the door slammed shut, and a bar fell into sockets on the outside.

In the total darkness, he heard Gatling say, "What happens now?"

"Nothing," Henrion's voice answered, "until daylight."

"And then?"

"And then—there will be daylight."

They stretched themselves on the earth floor, and Regret wished the thongs had been taken from his wrists, which were cut raw.

Within a few minutes, Regret heard both his companions breathing deeply. That they could thus fall off serenely into slumber seemed hard to credit, and for a time he lay awake, filled with ominous speculations. This eerie crevasse was the stronghold of the Comancheros— of that he had no doubt. Those men who had surrounded them in the darkness were not Indians, whatever they were; and their treatment of the captives, throwing them into this prison without even easing their bound wrists, augured very badly for the future.

He became conscious of a drumming, the double beat of Indian tom-toms, so far away that it was like the throb of the pulse in his ears. All at once in the profound and ghostly hush, as from an immense distance, a scream bored through the silence, with an edge of agony to it that made his flesh creep. He sat up.

"What was that?" he said.

"What was what?" Henrion's voice said sleepily.

"I heard a scream——"

He could almost *hear* them listening. Minutes passed. The shriek was not repeated.

"You're liable to hear anything around here," Gatling grumbled.

"Try and get some sleep," the captain said. "We may need it—bad."

Again he heard the deep breathing of his companions.

But he lay awake, his ears straining for that sound. It did not come. Outside in the night, the stream gurgled happily. He heard the call of a distant night bird. Otherwise all was silence.

Then the rush of the river was transformed for him into the long-drawn hum of traffic on the Rue Dauphine in New Orleans, and he was sitting in Victor's with a group of his friends of the old, elegant days, their wineglasses red, their dream conversation as gay and frivolous as of old, and for a time, in slumber, Paul Regret was happy.

EIGHT:

"I Am Musketoon, the Chief of These People . . ."

1

DAWN LIGHT, filtering through cracks and crevices, woke Regret from his uneasy sleep. Outside a man cleared his throat and spat. One of their guards.

Gatling sat up, gaunt and desolate. Captain Henrion was awake also, lying on his back, gazing imperturbably at the roof. By the little light, Regret saw that the building in which they were imprisoned was of adobe, and empty—some kind of storage shed, evidently.

"Well?" said Henrion.

"I was thinking of that scream I heard—I can't get it out of my mind," Regret said.

"Might have been a panther," said Gatling. "They got a scream like a woman's voice——"

"This was a *man*. And by the sound, being hurt."

"I thought I heard Injun drummin' once."

"I did too. Very faint and far."

"Might be a camp of Indians up this canyon," said Henrion.

"Do you think——?" Regret did not finish his question.

But Henrion understood. "Could be. They might have been doing things to some poor devil they'd got their hands on."

"But what about the white people here?"

"They wouldn't do anything to stop it."

That brought silence.

Gatling was the first to speak, and it was as if he tried deliberately to turn the subject.

"I'd give a laig for a drink of water," he said. "How long has it been now? I'm so gander-gutted that my paunch rattles all the time, like somebody snorin' in a hollow log, an' I've got enough wrinkles in the skin of my belly to catch a week's rain."

"Talk just makes you thirstier," said Henrion.

An hour passed. Then another. Growl of conversation came from outside, and an occasional laugh.

Regret suffered, from his bound wrists, from hunger, from thirst, and from apprehension.

Suddenly the door was pushed open, and a one-eyed, lean scoundrel with a gun in his hands thrust his head inside.

"Come out!" he snarled.

Blinking, they emerged into day. Looking up at the sheer seven-hundred-foot walls of the prodigious canyon in which they stood, it seemed to Regret impossible that they could have descended them in the darkness, without disaster. At the bottom of the gorge, through a thicket of cedars, the stream dashed, and at the sight of the water, he moistened his lips with his tongue. Then he saw up the canyon a score of white tepees. Now the mystery of those signs of Indian encampment was explained, and a further sinister corroboration given him, that the shriek of agony he had heard the night before was no product of his imagination. He shivered.

A dozen armed men surrounded the prisoners. It was Regret's first chance to see the breed of Comancheros, and what he saw was not pleasing. Mexican faces, Spanish

126

faces, faces of French *vide poches,* faces of American renegades, half-breed Indian faces—the sweepings and offscourings of a hemisphere were here, without exception depraved, evil, and cruel, and all with the hound look.

"Git goin' down that canyon," said the knave with the single eye.

"Where to?" asked Henrion.

"To the council house."

"At least let us have a drink first, will you? We're near dead of thirst——"

A howl of laughter and someone struck him across the face. Regret winced. The sight of a brave man so mistreated is not easy to watch.

But except for the reddening mark on his cheek, the captain's grave bearded countenance did not alter.

Silently, he set the example for his men, starting down the canyon. They marched along the stream, rounded a sharp bend in the narrow gorge, and Regret saw ahead a thick cluster of adobe huts—wretched flat-roofed affairs, such as Mexican peasants build. There also was a *ramada* of considerable proportions, open at the sides but thatched over with cedar bark; and still farther, high up on the canyon wall, a large white house of Spanish style. Just beyond the white house the canyon narrowed to a kind of gigantic gateway, guarded on either side by a lofty promontory so that the prospect beyond was screened.

Down past the huddling *casas* they walked, and the people came out to watch them: ruffianly men; sullen black-haired women with bare heels in rawhide *zapatas;* and half-naked children, tumbling in the dust, showing that the population of this place was increasing much faster than its honesty.

It developed that the *ramada,* a sort of huge, rustic shed, was the "council house." Regret felt a tightening of his stomach as he noticed a gaunt framework near the entrance—two rough cedar posts about twelve feet high, with a third post joining them as a cross bar on top. A crude gallows. . .

Scurvy-looking Comancheros hung about the *ramada*, eying the captives viciously. As he and his companions were prodded into the building, he saw the place was crowded already. They were pushed toward a rude platform, made of logs faced on top with an adz, on which stood a table and some stools. There they halted, the unsavory mob crowding close about them, with snarling quarrels flaring up here and there over places of vantage from which to watch the fate of the captives.

"Seems to be another prisoner," Henrion said in Regret's ear.

For the first time he saw, to one side, a wretched-looking Mexican, with huge drooping mustaches and spaniel eyes, under guard, his arms lashed to his sides, and a pitiful expression of terror on his face.

Then, almost as if a window had been closed to shut out the noise, all clamor ceased in the place, and stillness fell.

Through an entrance which opened on to the platform from the rear limped one of the most extraordinary figures Regret had ever seen.

He was old and very rotund, with a broad, fat face from either side of which immense gray mustachios thrust like the horns of a bull. All of the features were striking: a hooked beak of a nose, mouth wide and grim, eyes gray and peering from beneath enormous shaggy brows. It was the face of an actor, one might almost have said—rascality evident in it, at this moment ferocious, but perhaps not incapable of geniality or even humor on occasion.

His costume bore out the theatricality of his visage: a sky-blue jacket with gold coins for buttons, a broad silken sash of vivid yellow accentuating his massive girth, a scarlet kerchief bound about his head, over which was pulled a high-crowned sombrero heavy with more gold coins, which were sewed entirely around its yard-wide brim, and enormous baggy white trousers thrust into huge boots.

A step behind him walked another man, dark and tall, about forty years old, with a face still and watchful, a heavy mustache, and a thick, brutal underlip. Regret thought of the shadowy face of the night before and the wolf gleam in the eyes. This was the same man.

Then he noticed something else: the fellow wore a black velvet Mexican *charro* costume, although he was assuredly no Mexican, very close-fitting in thigh and sleeve and waist, and a black low-crowned American hat.

He remembered the words of the young girl, Nettie Hare, telling of the Cogswell massacre: *I seen a white man. . . . He wore black clothes an' had a black mustache. . . .*

This sinister lieutenant, garbed in black—could he be the renegade of the Comanche raid?

One other detail: though the weather was warm, the man wore doeskin gloves, a trick of dandies who wished to protect the fineness of their hands, almost an effeminacy. It gave a final unpleasant quality to him.

The portly personage of the mustachios halted his limping progress at the edge of the platform and glared down at the prisoners.

His voice boomed through the *ramada*, "Who are these, Estevan?"

He of the knavish face and the one eye, who was in command of the guards, replied, "Strangers, who claim to be of us, and are not of us!"

From the crowd rose a deep, threatening growl.

The old man scowled menacingly. "I am Musketoon, the chief of these people," he said. "Take care that you do not lie to me!"

2

Regret caught his breath as the crowd pressed forward with another snarl, then halted tensely, as if only the authority on the platform withheld it from tearing the prisoners to pieces.

"What others are for judgment, Amelung?" old Musketoon asked.

"Miguel Soldano, accused of stealing a poncho from Tafoya," answered the man in black, looking at the bound Mexican.

"We will hear his case first." Old Musketoon seated himself at the table.

The spaniel-eyed Mexican, obviously almost too frightened to stand, was pushed forward. For the first time Regret saw behind him, half cowering, a woman. She was thin to the point of emaciation, with flat breasts and meager shoulders, her face anemic and dull as with weariness. Not once did her eyes leave the prisoner in front of her.

"Witnesses?" the great voice on the platform boomed.

Another Mexican stepped forward. "Sí. Three men have sworn that the poncho was found in Soldano's *casa.*"

"What do you say to this, Soldano?" asked old Musketoon sternly.

The prisoner stood mute and trembling.

Old Musketoon's scowl grew fiercer. "Let him taste the bastinado."

From its sheer unpleasant sound, even though he did not know its nature, Regret felt a qualm at the word "bastinado." As for the prisoner, it restored his speech and his power to act.

With a howl he threw himself on his knees. "Not the bastinado, señor! I will tell! I took the poncho! I sought to borrow only, but—yes, I took!"

Old Musketoon looked at him grimly. "You know the law?"

"The gallows!" yelped the crowd gleefully.

At that the woman flung herself on her knees beside the prisoner.

"Señor! Mercy of God!" she cried. "It was an old poncho, and worthless!"

"It is theft."

"He is my man! He is mine for twenty years—a good man, señor! Let him be flogged—a hundred lashes, if need

130

be! But not death for a ragged poncho worth less than a peso!"

The thin, consumptive-looking creature lifted her face, with a plea in it that was half despair, half demand: as if she offered herself, her life, and yet dared the judge, the entire mob, to inflict the judgment.

Old Musketoon's voice was not unkindly. "I'm sorry for you, Manuelita. But the laws of the Comancheros cannot be changed. Soldano, by his own word, is guilty and must be punished. Stand aside."

To Regret such a penalty for a petty theft seemed ferocious, but the crowd licked its lips with pleasure in anticipation of seeing the man executed.

The guards dragged the prisoner to his feet. Slowly the woman, Manuelita, rose from her knees. Her face seemed even more painfully thin, painfully haggard.

Old Musketoon swung his head and fixed his scowl on the three who stood waiting.

"Who are you?" he boomed.

Regret heard Blake Henrion's cracked voice replying with their agreed story. "We got into trouble in the settlements. Had to shove. The Comanches caught us and brought us here."

Suspicion hardened on the mustachioed face. "What trouble?"

"Well——" Henrion hesitated. "We had a few horses——"

"Stolen?"

"That's what—some folks said——" The captain hesitated, as if unwilling to make the admission.

"The horses," said old Musketoon, "are the lawful prize of the Indians who seized you. Your name?"

Henrion said, "They call me Wood Hite."

"Wanted for?"

"Horse larceny—stage holdup——"

Old Musketoon received this with contempt. "You?" he asked Gatling.

"Canaday is the name. Pete Canaday."

"A horse thief too, I suppose?"

131

Gatling nodded sourly.

"Humph!" said old Musketoon, and from the crowd came a derisive snicker. He turned to Regret with a sneer. "I suppose you're wanted in Texas, too? For chicken stealing, perhaps?"

Regret understood that this terrible old man believed nothing of what his companions had told him. He gazed about at the brutal faces of the crowd, at the fat, sneering brigand on the platform who played with him and his companions as the cat plays with mice. And whence his answer came, he did not know.

"Not in Texas," he said. "Nor for theft. I'm wanted in New Orleans. For murder."

An odd stir of interest came into old Musketoon's face. "New Orleans, you say? You have lived there?"

"All my life."

A crafty look. "The Café des Refugiés, is it still on the Rue Royale?"

"It was never on the Rue Royale. It is where it has always been, on the Rue St. Philippe."

"You are, perhaps, acquainted with some of the prominent men of the city?"

"With most of them."

"A certain Captain Dominique You?"

Regret nodded. This was one of the old Barataria buccaneers of the Jean Lafitte days, who had turned honest and become a picturesque figure in the city.

"His wife and children, how are they?" asked the brigand.

"What is this?" exclaimed Regret impatiently. "Captain Dominique was never married, as anyone should know. He's dead now. I attended his funeral many years ago."

A curious change came into old Musketoon's countenance, and Regret took courage. "Every business house in New Orleans was closed that day," he said. "Dominique You was buried in the cemetery of the Cathedral of St. Louis, with full military honors."

Over the old brigand's remarkable features stole an indescribable combination of pleasure and sorrow. "I had not heard," he murmured. "Many years ago, you say? So are we cut off from the world here! And they gave him military honors—an old pirate like Dominique You?"

"He was beloved by all New Orleans," said Regret. And it was the truth.

For a moment old Musketoon sat twisting his mustaches. All at once, like a lean dark spirit of evil, the man called Amelung leaned over and brooded in a whispered discussion with him. He seemed to be urging something, and the old man was shaking his head. Finally Amelung stepped back, his face deep-bitten with displeasure.

Old Musketoon again turned to Regret. "I have not asked you your name," he said.

Thus far, it seemed, the truth had served well. "Paul Regret," the prisoner answered, instead of giving the fictitious name upon which he had agreed with Henrion and Gatling.

"Regret . . . ?" Contemplatively the old man nodded. "A New Orleans name, certainly——"

"You believe him?" Amelung asked, loud enough to be heard.

"Perhaps."

"By your leave, Musketoon, I don't! Anybody can answer a few questions about New Orleans. And anybody can call himself—whatever he chooses——"

"True," agreed old Musketoon.

"The others are Texans—they admit it!" continued Amelung. "I think this man is, too. Let me have them a few minutes—we'll get the truth out of them!"

From the crowd leaped a great yell, threatening and bloodthirsty. But old Musketoon seemed unmoved. He sat perfectly still for a moment, then held up his hand.

"If this man is lying," his bull voice rose above the clamor, "I will discover it! The bastinado never fails to get the truth!"

The crowd stilled, as if expecting him to pronounce at once the sentence of torment. But he paused grimly, then said to Regret, "There's a chance you're honest with us, monsieur. And it happens that in your case I have a way of learning the truth which is somewhat less painful than the bastinado—and quicker. If, however, you are not what you say you are—may God have pity on you, for I will not!"

From the crowd came a sullen growl of disappointment. Regret's eyes were on Amelung's narrow visage. The man was hard, and bitter, and mean enough to be the renegade the bound girl had described. He was looking the mob over with an odd, speculative glance, almost as if he contemplated an appeal to them—to override old Musketoon, their chief, counting on their lust for torture to uphold him. Then he seemed to decide against it.

In that moment Regret knew that Amelung was a man to fear; that he was cunning, treacherous, and ambitious; and that he was biding his time to work out some plan of his own, of which old Musketoon was not even aware.

3

For a moment, although the three prisoners stood in imminent peril, set down in so desperate a game that they could only hope to win by continual luck and unflagging effrontery, they had a respite.

Surrounded by their guards, they passed out of the *ramada*. The crowd already was gathering around the crude gallows. With some horror Regret realized that they were about to witness the hanging of the wretch who had admitted to the theft of the poncho.

Over the cross pole a rawhide rope was flung, one end a noose, the other held by half a dozen ruffians, who, by the look in their faces, relished the part they were to play. Soldano, blindfolded, his lips pattering prayers, was led tottering beneath the gallows, and Estevan, the one-eyed guard, began to adjust the noose about his neck.

It was too much for the woman who had pleaded for him.

"No! No!"she screamed. "It was a loan! He borrowed, only—you heard him—all of you——"

She looked about her, appealing to them, but not one Comanchero face showed a softening line of mercy.

She turned to the condemned man.

"Miguel!" she wailed, and flung her arms about him, wildly trying to drag him away. Then she sank to her knees in the dust, sobbing, her poor scrawny arms clutched about his legs, her head hidden.

Soldano, unable to see her, unable to touch her because his arms were tied behind him, half stooped, pulling the noose up over one side of his face as he leaned over her, saying something to her in a low voice inaudible to anyone else.

"Take her away!" snapped Amelung, and two of the guards dragged the woman back.

"Musketoon! Señor Musketoon!" she shrieked desperately. "Stop them! You can stop them! For the sake of the Holy Virgin, order them to stop!"

A guard muffled her harrowing cries with a corner of his *serape*.

Impatiently, Amelung jerked Soldano back under the gallows, and began readjusting the noose. The rawhide rope was stiff and his gloves hampered him. Holding the prisoner by an ear, he pulled off his right glove with his teeth, drew the noose about the neck, and fixed it to his satisfaction.

Not a dozen feet away stood Regret, and in the moment before Amelung drew on the glove again, he saw something: a curiously formed scar on the ball of the man's thumb.

Amelung gave an order.

The ruffians pulled on the rope; their victim was drawn upward, struggling, until his grotesquely twisted head was less than two feet beneath the cross bar. Then the end of the rope was brought about and fastened to one of the side posts.

Regret had been told that hanging was a merciful death; that the pressure of the noose on two arteries brought quick unconsciousness. He had, however, never known anyone who came back from the experience to affirm that theory. But at least there was this to say for hanging, which was not always the case with shooting—you knew when the victim was really dead.

For minutes that seemed hours the poor wretch spun, knees up, elbows out as far as the bindings permitted, tongue protruding horribly. Then, all at once, the knees sagged, the body hung limp, and Regret, at least, sighed with relief that the suffering was ended.

Manuelita, Soldano's woman, had watched silently. Now she turned on old Musketoon with an almost maniacal stream of curses, as if she held him solely to blame for what had happened.

Without moving a muscle of his face, old Musketoon listened to her, until from lack of breath she stopped, and commenced sobbing again. Then he gave a gruff order, "Bring these men and follow me."

Without another glance at her, he limped away. The guards signed to the prisoners to follow. As he turned his back on the symbol of Comanchero brutality dangling on the gibbet, Regret saw the woman seat herself in the dust beneath the gallows, pulling her black *reboso* over her head, a picture of crushing despair and woe.

4

On the plains above it was now full day, but heavy shadows still so shrouded many parts of the canyon that the unnatural adumbration emphasized its peculiar advantages as a stronghold. Old Musketoon led the way, limping, up a rather steep path or narrow road, which led along the canyon wall, climbing ever higher, toward the white Spanish house Regret had noticed before on the cliffs, some distance down the gorge.

With him walked the lean black figure of Amelung.

Once they heard the old man curse. "A thousand maledictions on this foot!" he grumbled.

Halfway to the white house, they came to a halt before a small adobe hut, built in a niche on the cliff.

"Remove their bonds," the old brigand ordered. "Put the two in here and watch them. Four of you bring this man to the Casa Blanca."

The one-eyed scoundrel took charge of the guard at the hut, and Gatling and Henrion, who were to remain, glanced at Regret, who was to go on. At another time he might have found their expressions almost amusing. For once they were mere followers of his, their fate depending on his wits, and there was nothing they could do about it.

Chafing his sore wrists, and keeping his face carefully expressionless, Regret followed old Musketoon and Amelung up the hill, in turn followed by his four guards.

The Casa Blanca was a structure quite pretentious for so wild a setting. Built on a wide shelf against the cliff, it contained several rooms. They mounted hewn cedar steps, and a Mexican *mozo* in white cotton shirt and drawers admitted them to what Regret took to be the main *sala,* which was not without richness of furnishings. At once the guards took up positions at the doors; the lean-jawed Amelung chose a stool, and old Musketoon sank with a vast sigh into a wide-armed chair of rawhide and wood, reclining back like a wicked old Falstaff of the wilderness, his legs outsprawled, his great belly heaving.

"Would you believe it," he said to Regret, "once I was able to bound up that path like an antelope?"

His tone was half apologetic and almost friendly, but Regret noticed that the guards had placed themselves so there was no possibility of his escape.

To the *mozo* the old man said, "Convey my compliments

to my daughter. Request her to favor us with her presence here, if it is convenient."

The servant bowed, was gone.

A daughter? There was a time when Regret might have considered that a bit of luck, even if she were perhaps somewhat advanced in years and less than beautiful. But the days when he was a New Orleans exquisite, with a sublime belief that he understood the sex, seemed now a part of another man's life.

And to meet any woman as he was at that moment—dirty, unshaved, and ragged—was an ordeal he did not welcome. No way, however, to avoid it. He waited, and tried to assume a bearing that might impress a country female, even though his plight was so sorry.

Old Musketoon and Amelung helped themselves from a decanter. His thirst caused him to try to moisten his lips with his dry tongue at the sight of the liquid trickling into the glasses. But they offered no glass to him.

It was taking some time for the daughter to appear, and from this Regret decided she must have the natural vanities of her sex, which he had always held to be one of the less objectionable weaknesses of women—if it be a weakness at all—since it encouraged them to enhance their charms in all possible ways. Since a vain woman is the easier to flatter, he argued from this some slight encouragement for himself, and tried to rehearse in his mind the little compliments which once had come so glibly to his tongue.

At last they heard a whisper of silk, and a step.

He turned. To his dying day he would never experience a more stunning surprise.

Standing in the door was Eloise Grailhe.

5

At first it was impossible for Regret to understand that she—the girl in the doorway—was the daughter to whom old Musketoon had referred. But the musta-chioed brigand clambered to his feet, and Amelung rose also, with the first smile Regret had seen on his face—a smile rather odious than pleasant.

"Forgive me, *ma chérie,* for disturbing you," said old Musketoon, in a tone which showed deep fondness.

"It was nothing, Father." Eloise's voice, so warm and familiar, cleared Regret's head.

"The Palo Duro seems to agree with you, Miss Eloise," said Amelung with his grin. "I declare, you look more fetching every time I see you."

She acknowledged the compliment, and glanced at Regret. Then her eyes returned to Amelung's, involuntarily, as if fascinated, and fell at once, but not swiftly enough to veil the disturbance in them.

Regret gazed at the two: the man, lean, hard, and brutal; the girl, delicate and beautiful and feminine. And in Amelung's eyes he saw the cause of her agitation. The Comanchero's look was direct, possessive, with a gleam no woman—Eloise Grailhe least of all—could fail to comprehend.

She was in terror of him. All at once Paul Regret knew that. And in that moment her fear became his fear also—a wild, helpless fear—for now he knew at last that in ways he could not even express to himself she was above all other things dear to him. Dear to him. And lost to him. And beyond his power to help.

Old Musketoon, as if unconscious of this byplay, sipped from his brandy glass and spoke to Eloise.

"I wished to ask you a question, Daughter," he said. "This man asserts he has lived in New Orleans. Have you ever seen him?"

Regret had a new sensation. A numbed wonder at what she would say. She knew him for a Texas Ranger, and must understand why he was here. If she was the daughter of the old brigand, who obviously doted on her, what could he expect from her?

She hesitated, and his heart sank. Then she said, "But

certainly, Father. Everyone in New Orleans knows Monsieur Paul Regret."

Regret found time to thank his lucky star for that inspiration which had made him give his right name. Old Musketoon relaxed slightly; but Amelung cast a sudden hard, suspicious glance.

"Perhaps," said the old man, "you know the circumstances under which he left the city?"

She glanced from her father's face to Regret's, as if debating what to say, and the prisoner waited with his breath in his teeth.

"Why, yes, Father," she said. "He shot a man in a duel."

Old Musketoon's eyebrows flew up. "And this is your *murder*, Monsieur Regret? Since when did a duel become of such moment in New Orleans?"

"The man he shot," said Eloise, "was Emile, the only son of Judge Beaubien." She stopped, her eyes on her father's face, as if to keep them from straying to Amelung's insistent gaze.

"Judge Beaubien! That explains many things," said old Musketoon. "I knew him in the old days. Ah, yes. Judge Beaubien *would* erect a murder charge out of such a duel." He grinned. "Monsieur Regret, your flight to avoid the hemp is most understandable. Pray take a chair! I'm truly sorry for the inconvenience to which you have been put. Will you have a little of this brandy?—I can recommend it highly."

"Water—with your indulgence, I would prefer water. I —I have not drunk in two days——"

"Of course! *Mozo!*" The brigand clapped his hands, and the servant appeared. "A pitcher of water, *pronto!*"

When Regret had most gratefully satisfied his burning thirst, the old man looked at Amelung. "You can forget your concern over these people, Jack. Dismiss the guard, both here and at the hill house. Order water taken to them there—immediately. Also victuals. And restore their arms——"

"Their *arms?* You can't mean that!" Amelung burst out.

"Why not?"

"It's enough to trust them without a guard—but to give them weapons——"

"My dear Jack," said old Musketoon, as if reasoning with his subordinate, "there is no danger. What could these people do, supposing they were enemies, even with arms? Three against so many—it is ridiculous. But they have come to join with us, and I for one believe they will be a good addition. It is the legal right of every Comanchero to carry whatever weapons he desires——"

"*They* came to join *us!* We do not seek recruits. Not men we do not know, and who have not been proved——"

"We both remember *one* recruit, who came unasked and unknown to us. Where would Jack Amelung be now, if I had enforced such a policy?" Amelung for a moment seemed unable to reply. Old Musketoon went on, "This gentleman has proved that he speaks the truth. From my own knowledge I know it. If he vouches for his friends, I am prepared to accept them."

"I'm not!" growled Amelung. "I smell bad off them like smoke in a house!"

"That is discourteous," said old Musketoon, growing for the first time stern. "Be so good as to obey my orders!"

For an instant Regret saw anger, or rebellion, leap into Amelung's bitter eyes. Then the look masked itself. He jerked his head at the guards and led them out of the house.

NINE:

"It Adds Up to Worse Than I Thought . . ."

1

AMELUNG and the guards were gone. Old Musketoon smiled at Regret benignly.

"You must forgive him, if he is perhaps oversuspicious," he said. "Jack Amelung is a bitter man. He came to us as a fugitive, you know. You have heard of the Murrel clan of the '30's?"

Regret nodded. "There was considerable talk about it—when I was a very young man."

"Yes," nodded the brigand. "About ten years ago, if memory serves. Amelung told me the story. I will refresh your memory. It may help you to understand him, because I hope you and he will get along well together. That man is very important to our organization here."

Old Musketoon took up a wooden box, beautifully inlaid, opened it, offered from it an excellent cigar to Regret, then took one himself. They lit the tobacco and puffed for a moment. Eloise sat silently on a sort of lounge, and Regret, stealing a glance at her, thought she was the handsomest female creature he had ever laid his eyes on. But she took no part in the conversation.

"John Murrel—the great land pirate, they called him," the brigand said. "I doubt there ever was a more daring and desperate conspiracy than his. It involved the entire southern United States, a plot to destroy great cities, cause the bloody deaths of thousands, and create an anarchy which would have had to be stamped out by nothing less than military forces—all for the enrichment of Murrel and his men. And it came perilously close to succeeding."

"How did that plan go——?" Regret asked.

"In its simplest terms, there was to be a general revolt of all the Negro slaves in the South. It would have created a holocaust, naturally. In that moment of terror and destruction, Murrel and his well-organized clansmen were to strike."

Regret remembered some of these details, but they were confused in his mind. He asked another question. "On what basis did they think they could get the Negroes to revolt?"

"Extravagant promises were made to them. Help in the form of armed legions of sympathetic whites would march to their assistance, they were told. Arms would be furnished to them. The example of Haiti, where the servile rebellion of 1804 resulted in a black empire and the massacre of every white person on the island, was cited to them."

"But such a revolt could not hope to succeed in the United States!"

"To be sure. But the Negroes were ignorant and unable to discern the difference between an island uprising and one on a continent where well-drilled troops and the resources of a great nation would be employed to restore order. Murrel and his men, of course, were completely cynical in the matter. They intended to leave the slaves to their doom after seizing the riches of the destroyed cities. As I say, it was a tremendous conception—think of it! New Orleans, Natchez, Vicksburg, a score of other cities in flames! White planters by the hundreds with their throats cut, their wives and daughters raped and murdered! And Murrel's close-knit gangs of looters moving through the smoke, all equipped with the sign and password to insure their own safety in the rioting, reaping the unprotected wealth of banks, stores, and plantations, and carrying it away in a fleet of ships already anchored off New Orleans for their getaway to some South American or Pacific island rendezvous! It was almost epic in its scope!"

"Why did it fail?"

"Because of a chance conversation overheard between a house servant and a field hand. It came that close to succeeding. The planters were alerted, the conspirators were rounded up, scores of them were hanged, Murrel himself was sent to the penitentiary, where he lost his mind and died an imbecile."

Regret glanced over at Eloise. Her face was perfectly expressionless. She was looking off into space as if she hardly heard this recital.

"What if I told you," old Musketoon went on, "that our friend Jack Amelung was the brains behind the whole conspiracy?"

"I could hardly believe it!"

"Nevertheless, it is true. Amelung was the shrewd planner whose imagination and ruthlessness were behind John Murrel, his chief in name only. You can see how fortunate we are to have such a strategist for our own operation here."

"How did he escape when Murrel's men were captured?"

"He did not escape entirely. When the conspiracy was revealed, Amelung was arrested—in a Texas town, as it happened. News traveled slowly and the full implications of the conspiracy were not at first understood by his judges, fortunately for him. Otherwise he might have been taken out and hanged at once. Instead he was convicted of horse theft—he had taken an animal out of necessity· in getting away from Arkansas when the disaster took place. For this he was sentenced to the penitentiary, but escaped. Not, however, before they branded him. That branding was as much a scar on his pride as on his flesh. It is the one thing even I dare not mention to him."

Regret had once witnessed the branding of a criminal in Louisiana. A sickeningly barbaric penalty that set his teeth on edge even now.

He remembered how the convicted man was brought into the crowded courtroom before the judge, and his hand bound to the rail before the bench. The sheriff took from a tinner's stove, brought by a slave, the branding iron, glanced at it, found it red-hot, and put it on the ball of the prisoner's thumb. The skin fried like meat and the smoke rose two feet in the air, while the victim bared his teeth, writhed, and turned pale with agony. When the iron was removed, the sheriff examined the burn, and in the obligatory phrase said to the judge, "A good mark, your honor." Then the prisoner, with the letters *H.T.*—for "horse thief"—burned into his thumb for life, was led back to jail to begin his sentence.

That was what Amelung concealed with the doeskin gloves . . . a mark of shame to him, and a cause of his hate and bitterness against all law and society . . .

"Jack Amelung is a remarkable man," old Musketoon continued. "He has a certain polish and some education, yet in some ways I never knew anyone so savage. The failure of his conspiracy with Murrel was a stunning disappointment, and it left him with a rage against everything, but more particularly against Texas, where he was branded. To us he is invaluable, because he knows better than anyone else how to deal with the Indians. It is he who lays the plans for their forays. Sometimes he even rides with them."

The rider in black . . . It confirmed everything Regret had suspected.

"Yet he is not really a gentleman," said old Musketoon. "He began as a slave overseer on a plantation in Tennessee. He could hardly be expected to understand gentlemen—such as you and I are, Monsieur Regret." He smiled politely.

"In my own case, a gentleman much the worse for wear. I beg both of you to excuse me, at least until I can make myself presentable——" Regret was frantic with anxiety and the desire to inform his comrades of the strange turn of affairs.

The old man merely smiled under his wide mustaches. "Pouf! My daughter forgives your appearance, monsieur.

145

I'm sure she's as eager as I to compare notes with you."

But the girl said nothing.

2

Old Musketoon rose to draw the decanter close. As he shifted his weight to seat himself again, he winced.

"*Sacr-r-re!* This accursed foot! Do you believe, monsieur, in the efficacy of vulture grease for the relief of gout? I have my people bring in every one of the birds they can shoot."

"I have never heard of it," said Regret, "but garlic is sometimes mentioned in that connection."

Old Musketoon's face lit up. "Garlic! Now, I'm glad to hear this from you! I am bothered by the disease and shall take to consuming the vegetable—which I favor anyway— to remedy it."

He called the *mozo*, and with some rapid-fire instructions sent him hurrying down to the village.

Then as if this simple suggestion had cleared every lingering suspicion from his mind, old Musketoon for a time asked eager questions about New Orleans, listening as rapt as a child to Regret's replies. Over and over, he said, "Ah, monsieur, you know not how welcome it is to these old ears to hear the gossip of the city I love!"

But in spite of this apparent good will, Regret was figuratively sweating. His suggestion of garlic had been casual, an idle remark to fill in the talk, not intended to be taken seriously. Actually, he had never heard of garlic as a remedy for gout, and had no belief in the world that it would be efficacious. That old Musketoon should immediately accept it and pin upon it his expectations of relief surprised and concerned him. What would happen when the garlic was tried and found to have no effect whatever? Very much he was wishing he could recall that statement, as he sat trying to reply to the questions the old man showered upon him.

146

In all this time Eloise, strangely, had not spoken a single word. Regret, who at first had been afraid she would say too much, now understood that she had purposely said just enough to save him. He was wild to talk with her alone, and he wondered at her silence, so that it was most difficult to sit conversing with the mustachioed savage who was her father.

Her father . . . Comparing the two of them, Regret could see a faint family resemblance between the girl and the old furioso before him. Yet Musketoon must be past seventy, while Eloise was just twenty. It was evident that she was the fruit of a very late fatherhood—and, as a late fruit often is, the more perfect because of it.

"You wonder how I know so much of New Orleans?" old Musketoon was saying. "I will tell you. I, whom they call Musketoon, was born Armand Sazerac de Grailhe, of the best New Orleans descent. This beautiful young woman, who stirs my heart with pride each time I gaze upon her, is my legitimate daughter by a wife I married somewhat late in life. Eloise was born after I was forced to leave New Orleans—things, you must understand, went badly for me. Her mother died in her childhood. Until recently these eyes had never beheld my child."

He bestowed a grin upon her. "As for myself, monsieur, like many adventurous young men, I was a friend of Jean Lafitte, whom some call a pirate. Yes, I was one of Lafitte's captains, along with Dominique You, René Baluche, and the rest, and from him I learned my lessons. After his fall, I wandered to many far places, including the Greek islands off the Turkish coast, where opportunity for privateering is constant, and where I learned some strange customs and practices. At last, by circumstances too lengthy to recite, I arrived here, among these traders."

"Only traders?" Regret could not help it.

"Traders only. As peaceful as lambs, monsieur. The Indians bring us livestock and other merchandise to sell, which they acquire—who knows?—by warfare, perhaps. It is not our business to inquire. We trade. We buy."

147

The old man considered the end of his cigar, as if in admiration either of the long ash on it or his own casuistry. He went on.

"It is I who organized the Comancheros and established our capital here in the Palo Duro canyon. This place is a natural fortification, monsieur. Not only does it have the peerless advantages of concealment and inaccessibility, but it is as if it were designed expressly for defense. A body of resolute men, I am well persuaded, could hold off an army equipped with artillery if it approached from the lower valley. As for the upper gorge, it would be almost impossible for a force to get at us because of the sheer canyon walls."

Regret had a vivid recollection of those walls and an immediate personal agreement with the conclusion.

"We do not anticipate such an attack," said old Musketoon. "The Texan government would give much to know just where we are located—but it is impossible for it to find out. Between us and the frontiers is a constant cloud of Comanche warriors, through which it would be very difficult to penetrate."

"To that I can testify," Regret said sincerely.

"When I came here, the Comancheros were scattered, wandering, disorganized," continued the brigand. "They loaded their *carretas* with trade goods, came out on the Staked Plains in hope of encountering the Comanches, traded on the best terms they could, and made a quick return to the Mexican settlements in Nuevo Méjico beyond the Pecos River, never quite sure whether or not the Indians might turn on them and kill them all before they got back."

He blew out his mustaches and chuckled at the amusing thought of the traders scuttling off for safety because of fear that the Comanches might repent of their bargains.

"I changed all that. First, I recognized the need of a stronghold the Indians would respect, and which would at the same time be a rendezvous for friendly Indian trade. This canyon was the answer. Next, I reached an understanding with the Comanches, and also the Kiowas.

148

Finally, I arranged for markets—we carry on a continuous thriving business with the Mexican cities beyond the Pecos, such as Santa Fé, Albuquerque, and Mesilla. Each month our *conductas* set forth, and you can find roads deep-bitten by the wheels of our loaded *carretas* and the hoofs of our livestock from here to those settlements."

It was at this moment that the servant returned from the errand on which old Musketoon had dispatched him. He glided into the room with several small dried pods on a plate.

"The garlic!" exclaimed the old man. "How much does one take at a time, Monsieur Regret?"

"I—I really don't know."

"One clove, I suppose?"

"I should think that would be sufficient."

Old Musketoon selected one of the sections, placed it in his mouth dry as it was, and commenced to chew. Regret, to whom even the smallest suggestion of garlic in food was sufficient, wondered how the other could stand the strong and pungent taste of the quantity he was consuming. But the brigand chief champed away with a look of immense pleasure.

"Where was I?" he said. "Oh, yes. My organization of the Comancheros. It was I also, monsieur, who gave these people their laws. Amelung deals with the Indians. But I am the father of the Comancheros, and their judge. Although we are peaceful traders, our laws are based on the best of all codes—the code of the sea rovers."

"I have heard of such a code," Regret murmured.

"It was developed by centuries of practice and is fair to everyone. Having lived under it so many years, I was familiar with its smallest details. Simplicity is its keynote—for example, we have a system of shares. At first everyone chaffered for himself, providing his own articles for trade, and trying to strike his own bargains with the Indians. Now everything is put in together, and we trade as a unit. The advantages are obvious.

"We vote on all important matters, have elective leaders,

149

and laws governing conduct. As an instance, a personal difference may be settled with weapons, but the fight must be fair. Unfair attack is murder, and a murderer dies. No Comanchero steals from another on pain of death. You witnessed the fate of poor Miguel Soldano. I could do nothing for him, since the law is specific and necessary."

Old Musketoon paused, chewing his garlic, and the taint of his breath came to Regret's nostrils unpleasantly.

"Treachery has a terrible punishment," he went on solemnly. "We turn the culprit over to the Indians. I myself abhor cruelty, but these people require strong controls, monsieur, else we should have chaos here. The fear of this fate keeps them from contemplating disloyalty. The Kiowa Indians, in particular, are said to be ingenious in the ways of torturing and in keeping a victim alive under torment to exact the fullest anguish from him. This is another of the duties—an unpleasant one—which falls to Jack Amelung when it needs to be done."

Regret glanced at Eloise. For the first time her eyes showed expression—a look of horror.

Old Musketoon rambled on. "You are fortunate, monsieur, that my daughter was able to identify you and corroborate your story. Otherwise you would have experienced the bastinado, which is a punishment I myself introduced here, having learned it in the Greek isles when I was privateering there against the Turks. It is superior to the whip or the hot iron in gaining a confession. One does not die from it, but one wishes to. I know—for the Turks once captured me and gave me a course of it. It consists of blows on the bare soles of the feet, where are concentrated some of the most sensitive nerves in the body. After the tenth blow—*Mon Dieu!*—I would have confessed anything!"

Under the vast mustache he gave a reminiscent grimace. "As it happened, I could speak no Turkish; there were none of the Turks who understood English, French, or Spanish; and my Greek was so wretched and stumbling that a rescue party of my friends fortunately arrived before I could get

150

out a confession that would have revealed all our plans to our enemies. For weeks after that, you may believe, I did not run—although eventually I recovered fully. There is this about the bastinado, monsieur, it does not cripple permanently. But—*mort de ma vie!*—my feet tingle now at the thought of it!"

He looked at Regret very straight. "I have never seen the bastinado fail to get a confession—even when the culprit knew it would deliver him to the hands of the Kiowa torturers."

At that he broke off, and smiled. "Well, well! I have been greatly refreshed, monsieur, by this conversation. Which reminds me that you must need refreshment also. You may return to your quarters now. You will find food there. I hope you enjoy our hospitality."

Regret was dismissed.

He rose, and glanced again at Eloise. Once more she was expressionless. She did not meet his eyes. Throughout old Musketoon's long discourse she had been silent, and this seemed strange. There was no secret about her acquaintance with Regret. He could only conclude that, having saved his life, she wished no further speech with him.

He bowed slightly to them. "Thank you, Monsieur Musketoon. Good-by, mademoiselle."

Without a smile she inclined her head.

"You and your friends will be assigned to your duties here later," said old Musketoon in parting. "In the meantime you are at liberty to go anywhere in the village. I advise you, however, to be careful in how you conduct yourselves for the present. Some of my people do not yet fully believe in you. And do not attempt to leave this part of the canyon. You will be observed constantly, and such a move might arouse unpleasant suspicions from the consequences of which not even I could save you."

3

More haggard, more tired than they could remember being, Blake Henrion and Tom Gatling half sat, half sprawled on the dirt floor of the hut by the pathway high on the canyon wall.

They spoke little, because of their croaking thirst, but even more because the door was open, and just without lounged their guards, leaning on their rifles, under the watchful single eye of Estevan, who understood and spoke English only too well.

Each of the Rangers was wondering what was taking place up at the Casa Blanca, to which Regret had been taken. And each, in his own way, had little hope that it would turn out well.

Henrion doubted Regret's ability—or the ability of anyone—to withstand long-continued cross-questioning, for the simple reason that there was such a tangled skein of subterfuge that remarkable adroitness would be required to do so convincingly.

Gatling's pessimism was based on disbelief. For months Regret had been his undesired riding partner, and in those months they had exchanged not one friendly word. His prejudice, based on the clash of their personalities, made it difficult for Gatling to admit even to himself that Regret could do anything well and he strained his ears, expecting every moment to hear the executioners coming for them.

After a time they did hear the trampling of several men walking down the hill. Estevan called out something in a voice slightly raised, as if speaking at a distance.

"Take the men and go on down," said Amelung's voice.

"All of them?" Estevan asked.

"Yes."

"But—what about——?"

"Musketoon's order."

152

Henrion and Gatling exchanged stares almost incredulous.

For a moment the men outside hesitated, then their boots made a confused, unrhythmic trampling on down the hill, and their voices receded, low, wondering, questioning.

All at once Amelung was framed in the doorway.

"You gentlemen are at liberty," he said, his face impersonal. "I am ordering food and water brought to you. I suggest that you remain here, in these quarters, until you get further word."

They nodded, aching with questions, but not daring to ask them.

Amelung departed down the path after his men.

For a moment neither of the men in the hut spoke. Then they rose simultaneously and went to the door. They saw the receding group of guards headed for the village, with Amelung, looking very lean in the tight-fitting black *charro* costume, striding grimly behind them. Not a face was turned to look back.

Above, the path climbed a hundred yards to the Casa Blanca. In that direction nobody was visible.

"What happened?" Gatling burst out.

"I don't know," said Henrion. "But it had to be something Regret did——"

"What could he do?"

"It could be that we haven't been figuring that man high enough," said the captain soberly. "The way he sprung that New Orleans business at the council house—how could he know that old Musketoon was acquainted with the place?"

"Hunch. That's all. Blind hunch." Gatling's tired face was grudging.

"Maybe. But a gold-plated hunch if it was."

They went back into the hut and sat down to wait. For a long time neither of them spoke, the effort being too great.

A step came, and a shadow at the door.

153

"*Agua*," said a woman. Her face was a brown mask like wrinkled leather, with black nails hammered into it for eyes. On her head was an earthenware *olla*.

The men leaped for the jar she set down, and took their turns satisfying their thirst in great gulps.

"Good—wonderful good," Gatling said, wiping the moisture which had run down his chin, and smiling for the first time in days.

"Makes a man feel mighty different," the captain agreed.

The woman stood aside and a girl, brown and shy, her face almost covered by her *reboso*, set upon the floor a wide traylike pottery dish covered by a cloth.

"*Guisado*," she murmured. Both women disappeared.

And while Henrion and Gatling were eating of the stew, three men pushed their way into the hut, loaded with saddles, blanket rolls, and weapons. A miracle, of some kind . . .

4

When Regret appeared some minutes later, they first began to ask him questions, then, knowing his hunger, desisted and sat to watch him wolf his food until the first edge of his appetite was gone.

Regret did not eat with his fingers as they had done. Instead he broke off a piece of tortilla and converted it into a makeshift spoon. This was a fastidiousness which Henrion knew probably would remain with him always. But the captain was willing to accept it, as also a number of other little idiosyncrasies, in view of the way he had developed.

His eye surveyed the outline of Regret's lean, hard body under the ragged garments, and Regret's lean, hard face covered with the unkempt stubble of beard, with the highest kind of approval. This man was a long way from the New Orleans popinjay whom Henrion first had seen. A metamorphosis hard to believe, but one of the satisfactions of being a captain in the Rangers. It either killed men or made them—serving as a Texas Ranger. Blake Henrion thought to himself that he would about as soon have Regret next to him if it came to a tight spot as anybody in his company—even Gatling, who was as good a man as ever stood in boot leather.

Regret leaned back, wiped his mouth with a torn bit of scarf, and looked at them.

Henrion said, "We never expected to see you again. I don't know what you did, but it was something mighty good and splendid. What did old Musketoon have to say to you?"

"He gave me a briefing on Comanchero laws, and in return I gave him some gossip about New Orleans."

"As simple as that? He didn't cross-question you?"

"He didn't have to. He has a daughter."

They stared at this apparent *non sequitur*. It was Gatling who asked, after a moment, dryly, "Well? Is she purty, or plain?"

"I leave that to you," Regret said. "You know her."

"I—what do you mean?"

"She is Eloise Grailhe."

For a long moment they simply gaped at him. Then, incredulously, Henrion said, "That girl at Austin, who was with Sam Houston?"

"The same."

"How in the name of God did she get out here?"

"I didn't have a chance to find out. But it appears the Comancheros have longer tentacles than anyone supposed."

"What did *she* say when she saw you?" Gatling demanded.

"She greeted me as an old acquaintance."

"And that satisfied the old man?"

"He believes in me fully. Unfortunately, his lieutenant, Jack Amelung, does not."

They digested this.

Regret glanced over at the blanket rolls, saddles, and

weapons. "I see they brought up our stuff," he said, in a manner unsurprised.

He went to his blanket roll and took out his shaving things. Using cold water, he began to lather his face.

"Still the ladies' man," sneered Gatling.

"Sometimes it appears to pay off." Regret carefully began shaving.

"I reckon he's got you there, Tom," said Henrion with his infrequent smile.

"I reckon he has," said Gatling. Slowly he rose, got his own shaving things, and began lathering his face also. Henrion remained seated on his blanket roll, combing his fingers through his short beard.

"Hard to believe that girl is old Musketoon's daughter," he said. "And still harder to figure how she made it out here—when we had the kind of trouble we did reaching it."

Regret scraped carefully at the stubble on an angle of his jaw, without replying.

"We're sitting on a powder keg for sure," the captain continued thoughtfully. "With that girl knowing all about us——"

"I don't believe she'll expose us," said Regret.

"Why?"

"Old Musketoon told me what happens to those guilty of 'treachery.' They get the bastinado—he gave some unpleasant details—and then they're turned over to the Kiowas for torture. That's a Kiowa village up the gorge. I could see that Eloise was horrified. She'll think some time before devoting us to a fate like that."

"Women are mighty chancy." The captain said doubtfully, studying Regret, "You going to see her again?"

"I don't know."

"The girl's the key," said Henrion slowly. "She could tell us some things we need to know mighty bad. You say she's a friend of yours? Try to play up to her—why don't you?"

"I said she *greeted* me as a friend," said Regret. He

thought of Eloise's silence. He had, furthermore, received no invitation to return to the Casa Blanca.

"If you're handin' out petticoat detail, what about me, Blake?" Gatling grinned maliciously. "I'm a friend of the lady's, too, only I ain't scairt to admit it."

Regret, tired and overwrought, felt his temper snap. "Damn your impudence!" he cried.

Gatling's big fists closed. "I've took jest about all I kin from this rooster," he said in a low, tense voice.

Regret became cold and sneering. "Perhaps it would amuse you to try to clip this rooster's comb?"

White-faced with fury, Henrion leaped between them and pushed them apart. They stood back, relapsing into gloomy silence, and the captain glared at his angry, over-strained men.

"Listen to me—both of you!" he said bitterly. "I've looked at some witless performances in my time, but never has it been my misfortune to see anything as imbecile as this before! We're looking into the muzzle end of loaded death—all of us—and you two get into a jangle that would shame a couple of school kids!"

They looked at the ground, and Regret tugged his mustache viciously.

"I call it your fault, Gatling," the captain continued. "Riding a man's all right in camp, where everything's relaxed. But not out on this kind of an assignment when a mistake means death!"

"Yes, sir," said the Ranger in a subdued voice, his eyes still on the ground.

"As for you, Regret, you had no call to flare up like that. A man's got to control his feelings when he's in a tight spot. Grow up!"

Under the reprimand, Regret shifted his feet. His head was clearing. The captain had brought him to his senses, although he still smoldered at Gatling.

"You two shake hands," Henrion ordered.

And they did it, though without enthusiasm.

"Now," the captain said, "concerning what we've been

157

discussing, the only tap line we could have to the girl is Regret. As for you, Tom, just you pray that she acts as if she never saw you before—or me, either. Do you see that?"

Gatling nodded.

"What have you to say, Regret?"

"If I get a chance—I'll do the best I can to talk with her, sir," Regret said. "But—I think we ought to get out of here. Why not tonight? Our job's done, isn't it? We know where their town is."

Henrion shook his head. "We couldn't. No horses."

It was manifestly true. Without horses, Indian trailers would hunt them down in twenty miles.

5

Time dragged. Under Henrion's close questioning, Regret made a full report. In particular the captain was interested in the details of the Comanchero trade relations with the Mexican province to the west, in the laws governing them, and in the criminal records of old Musketoon and Jack Amelung.

At the end he said, "It adds up to worse than I thought —worse than Sam Houston ever imagined."

The others nodded gloomily, oppressed by a heavy weight of danger, almost doom.

Toward evening sitting in the mud hut had become unbearable in their nervous tension.

"Did you say old Musketoon gave permission to go down into the village?" the captain asked at last.

"Yes," Regret said.

"Let's go then. We can stretch our legs. Leave your weapons here. Keep together. Don't act surprised at anything you see. But take everything in."

Together they walked down the long path toward the settlement.

Between the towering walls of the canyon Comanchero Town squatted on both sides of the small river, evil, filthy, and ill-smelling—surely the most squalid capital of a people ever seen. Its mud houses were straggling hovels, probably crawling with vermin. From refuse and offal cast in the crooked alley that formed the only street, flies rose in disgusting swarms.

Above the town a sharp angle in the gorge hid the Indian village from sight. In the canyon below the settlement, under the cliffs from which the Casa Blanca looked down, there were no houses. Instead, the space was interlaced by the fences of rude corrals, with a narrow alley through them toward the exit, facilities capable of holding hundreds of stolen cattle and horses. Beyond these, screening the view of the further valley, narrowed the great natural "gate" with its lofty buttresses. All about, their vision was confined by those sheer cliffs of rock.

They walked past the *ramada*, empty now, with the gaunt gallows standing before it, and the dead Mexican, his body sickeningly elongated, still dangling from it. Beneath the swaying corpse still sat the woman, as she had been sitting all day, her black *reboso* pulled over her head, a patient pyramid of sorrow.

"You say these people go on shares?" said Henrion, speaking low. "There's one less share of loot to split up."

"We ain't exactly welcome, neither," Gatling said. "Three more to share with, they think."

The scowling looks they received from the Comancheros they saw seemed to justify the conclusion.

"No love wasted on us here," Regret said. "Look at that devil with the red sash. He'd as soon slip a knife into your ribs as not."

"He'd stab you in the back, maybe," the captain said. "But there aren't two real face-to-face fighting men in this whole canyon."

Gatling nodded. "A company of Rangers could clean it out in an afternoon—supposin' there wasn't no fightin' Injuns around—an' have time for a barbecue after."

It was an opinion they all shared. Depravity, degeneracy, a slinking pot-hound manner, and cruelty, without honest manhood, were written on the Comanchero visages. Sodden drinking was evident—here and there sprawled figures snoring off a debauch in the open air, with nobody to pay attention to them. Groups sat or squatted with dice or greasy cards, for gambling appeared to be the universal vice and almost the sole occupation of this foul settlement. The women, old or young, turned sullenly away from the strangers.

Sounds were harsh—a shouting quarrel, a sudden distant snarl of laughter, a woman shrieking at the blows of her man. Odors were unpleasant, the smell of decay, of unwashed bodies. And the sight was offended by the shiftless disarray.

"There's mebbe two hundred here—men, women, an' kids—not countin' the Injuns up the gorge," Gatling estimated.

"And buildings for twice that many," the captain added. "Those extra dobies must be storage sheds. Gives you a notion of the quantity of loot they get in here. Look at those *carretas!*"

An open space was completely filled with a parking of the crude Mexican vehicles. The enormous wheels were made from huge logs, sawn across to make flat disks, clumsily framed together, and revolving on loose axles which from experience the men knew were innocent of any grease from the time they were put into use, so that they screamed as if in torture with each revolution. The bodies of the carts resembled giant baskets consisting of frames of slats bound to the side posts with rawhide and covered over with frayed canvas or skins. Not one piece of iron was used in an entire vehicle, yet these *carretas,* slowly lumbering over the prairie, drawn by half-starved oxen, were remarkably serviceable, and could transport immense quantities of goods.

Henrion halted and the others with him. The sun dropped behind the canyon wall, and almost instantly the gorge was shrouded in the shadows of dusk.

"Growing late," the captain said. "I don't want to get caught down here in the dark. Better get back."

They retraced their steps through the straggling town, heading for the foot of their path which led to the cliff-side quarters.

From the upper gorge, where the Indian encampment stood, two horsemen trotted, overtaking and passing them. One was Jack Amelung, riding a beautiful thoroughbred gelding, with the brand of the Texas ranch from which it had been stolen visible on its shoulder. His saddle was equal to his mount—hand-tooled, and glittering with silver ornaments. A rifle stock thrust up from the boot under the saddle leathers, and the man was double-gunned with revolvers. He gave them a single glance as he jingled by, but did not speak.

His companion, far less handsomely mounted and equipped, was the knave of the single eye with whom they were already too well acquainted.

"Fixin' some deviltry with the Kiowas," muttered Gatling.

Henrion nodded. "That Estevan fellow seems to be Amelung's personal *segundo*."

Lights began to spring out in the *casas* as darkness descended swiftly in the canyon. Unconsciously, they hurried their pace.

There was the *ramada* again. With a certain relief they passed it, for the foot of the pathway up the canyon wall was just beyond.

In the gloom the dead man still swayed on the gallows; and the woman still crouched beneath the swinging feet, not weeping, hardly breathing, it seemed.

TEN:

"Without Regard to Any Personal Consideration . . ."

1

TOWARD EVENING it grew cooler, and Eloise sat for a time with her window open, feeling for the breeze. Later she would close it, not only because the canyon grew uncomfortably chill at night, but because it gave her a slight feeling of security.

The Casa Blanca, alone of all the houses in the Palo Duro, boasted glazed windows. In this she found an illogical comfort: illogical because she knew it was unwarranted. Glass is easily shattered—really no protection at all—but all women come to think of glass as a barrier and a safeguard, because in a civilized world glass is respected as such.

It was, Eloise considered, like the law. One comes to depend on the law with the same illogic that one depends on window glass, for the law is as flimsy as glass, and as easily shattered.

How she had come to experience the terrifying and confusing changes that she had undergone still seemed incredible. It was, of course, her own fault. Her impetuosity, and inexperience, working together against her. If only she had gone to someone for advice . . . but the whole matter seemed so mysterious and entrancing. How could she possibly have envisaged a plunge into a life so utterly foreign to anything she had known that she could not even have imagined it before she actually became a part of it?

Only two weeks . . . and she had gone through a whole disintegration of her beliefs. Until *this,* she had thought always of the world as a sort of enlarged New Orleans, with a comfortably universal set of customs and disciplines and well-laid-out modes of conduct on which one could count. Most people, she had been assured, were good—in the larger meaning, of course—observing the laws, carrying on their own businesses or conducting their households. A very few people were bad, and broke the laws. But the police caught them and put them in jail for it, and they hardly created a ripple in the peaceful orderliness of life.

Now she had discovered a community where the exact opposite was terrifyingly true. All the Comancheros were bad, despising and breaking the law . . . outlaws, all outlaws, even her father to whom she had come in that breathless journey across the plains, and to seeing whom she had looked forward with such extravagant expectations.

Old Musketoon was like a child in his affection for her. He would roar at others, but to her he spoke with an awkward tenderness, as if he hoped wistfully and almost fearfully that she could find it in her heart to return the love he had for her.

He was wicked. Her father was wicked—she knew that fully now, although sometimes she could hardly make herself believe it. She remembered her first shock at seeing him—the gross, corpulent, savage figure, outlandishly dressed, who advanced to embrace her. She shrank, and he stood back. Then she went to him. She had seen the look on his face, the hurt, and even in that moment of her first realization and fear of what she had come into, her heart went out to him. Even now she could not help feeling the pathos of his age, and his yearning, and a protective instinct for him.

That man Amelung . . . Something within her cringed at the thought of him. He was worse than her father, far worse, and in her mind she was sure that old Musketoon was driven to some of the things he did by Amelung.

A devil of a man. He could not be called ugly, she conceded, except that about him was something hateful as a toad. He repelled her and terrified her at the same time.

That afternoon . . . when Paul Regret was brought to the Casa Blanca.

As soon as she saw him, she knew that he was on some dreadful trial through her. She did not know what to say, but she had to say something. So she said the truth.

An immense relief when the truth served: and when she knew that Paul also had told the truth, whatever his reason for being in this canyon of malevolence.

There had been a time when Eloise regarded Regret as wicked. Not, however, in the same sense that she regarded Amelung and the Comancheros as wicked. Paul's offense was not so much that he violated written law, as that he did things contrary to unwritten social custom. A world of difference in those two things, she had discovered.

Paul Regret was one of many young men whose iniquities had to do with the whole secret, exciting game of sex. A woman has a female body, and it is a source of pride and power to her. Because of it, she is cared for and provided for, surrounded by adulation, a creature most precious and treasured. Because of it also, she becomes aware very early of the game of pursuit and escape, especially if she is pretty.

Men forever are wickedly seeking an opportunity to seduce a girl: she had been told that continuously all her life, beginning in the convent. But though she knew it, there was about it an overwhelming magnetism, an excitement, a gaiety, a little thrill of danger, and the constant stimulation of admiration in male eyes and longing in male voices that made it almost impossible for her to refrain from playing the treacherous game of coquetry, even though it was close to the verge, and one might easily slip over into disaster.

Paul Regret now . . . How wholesome he had looked, dirty and unshaved as he was, that morning, compared to . . . to Amelung. He was honest, at least after his own code, and did not despise a woman. To have lost her head

with him would have been easy, at one time. But she had
kept her head. And there was the important point in the
matter: a girl did not need to be seduced, unless she
wished to be. Not in New Orleans. Because her refusal was
the final answer to even the most fervent young man.

How different here . . . in this place . . .

No woman had any standing. Anything as respectable
as marriage simply did not exist. There was no protection
. . . not even for Eloise Grailhe.

From the very first time she saw Amelung, he had looked
at her as if he knew too much about her. He grinned at her:
narrow dark face, black brush of mustache, prominent
sharp dog teeth. A grin evilly intimate.

And his eyes . . . appraising, demanding, assured . . .
making to her continual indecent suggestions, as plainly
as if he spoke them to her. His eyes said to her insolently
that to him she was just another woman, with no more
rights or privileges than the women down in that stinking
village; but that he desired her for the fact that she was
shaped to his particular fancy.

Shaped, to his fancy . . . as if it were an honor to her.
A woman cannot help how she is shaped. She cannot help
it if the accident of her body's architecture arouses in men
lusts and passions. Especially in the wrong men.

For the first time in her life Eloise Grailhe wished that
she were not a woman. A woman is wonderfully and
beautifully made for the things for which she is intended,
but in other things, the girl told herself, she is a physical
incompetent. She has no strength, nor agility, nor skill to
do for herself. In all the world there is no despairing help-
lessness equal to hers, if she is in peril with nobody to aid
her.

Eloise knew she was in peril. The most dreadful peril.
And she had nobody. She was alone. Alone.

She rose and closed the window, fastening the wooden
latch securely. Then she lit a candle and pulled together
the hangings. It gave her privacy in her room, at least.

165

She wished she could see Paul again. And at once she hoped she would never see him.

Above everything, she must remember never to let him know that he was of the slightest interest to her. She must keep him away, out of her orbit, for his own sake.

If Amelung knew even what she was thinking . . . She shuddered. In all her life she had never even imagined the terror that she felt when she thought of Amelung. . . .

2

Waiting, without knowing what you are waiting for, is the hardest of tasks, as Regret was learning.

Full night had descended into the abyss of the Palo Duro. They sat outside their hut, on the lip of the cliff, and gazed down at the pin points of light from Comanchero Town in the darkness. Long since they had eaten their evening meal of *enchiladas* and water, brought up by the silent women.

After a time Gatling said, "Hoss comin' up the path."

The dim mounted figure rode easily, breasting the hill. As it neared the three sitting at the edge of the cliff, the horse slowed and then came to a full stop. The rider was Amelung.

"Evening, gents." He greeted them with surprising courtesy.

They returned his salutation.

"Saw you down in the town," he said.

"Yes," Regret answered.

"What do you think of it?"

Regret shrugged. "Good as any."

Amelung smiled thinly in the night. He leaned forward in his saddle, his crossed arms on the saddle horn. "Good as New Orleans?"

Regret allowed himself to smile also. "For me—better."

Amelung nodded. "Skipping out from the rope put you a long way from home, mister."

"Farther than I ever expected to be."

"Counting on going back?"

"No. I'm here—for good, I hope."

To that Amelung did not directly reply. Instead he said slowly, "I knew New Orleans once. Natchez, and Vicksburg, and Nashville, too. Knew 'em well—where to have the best times—to find the prettiest girls. I knew some of the best people, too—at least some that were considered the very best——"

He broke off. They waited, but he did not elaborate. And this was as near as he ever came to mentioning his previous life or his experience with the Murrel clan, which included in its shadowy membership "some of the best people" of the South.

Presently he said, "Tell me something, Regret. How long have you known Miss Eloise?"

"Why?"

"Just curious." But Amelung was insistent.

"Oh—I don't know," said Regret. "She was *chanteuse légère* at the French Opera. A year or so, I suppose. Slightly, of course."

"Why *of course?*"

"Well, I don't know why I said that, particularly. She belonged to the music, and art, and fancy-ball crowd."

"And you?"

"I belonged to the tavern crowd, you might say."

Amelung studied him, exactly as if his eyes could see better than most men's in the darkness.

"It was God-awful lucky for you that she knew you," he said.

"So I reckon."

Again a pause, and Amelung said, as if all the preceding were a preliminary, "One thing hasn't been cleared up. How did you men know there was a settlement out here, and that we are called Comancheros?"

The question caught them unprepared. For a moment they sat uneasily, then Henrion attempted an answer.

"We were on the run, you see—thought we might reach

the Mexican settlements west. The Comanches caught us—
and brought us here."

"That was all there was to it?"

"All I know."

"Curious," said Amelung. "Because I talked with the
Indians—*and they informed me you made sign talk for
Comanchero when you surrendered.* That's why they
brought you instead of killing you on the spot."

A bad error by Henrion. They should have remembered
that colloquy with the Comanches on the bluff.

Unexpectedly, Gatling's dry voice said, "That was a
desperation bet, Amelung."

"Explain yourself." The Comanchero's voice was cold
and deadly with suspicion.

"You kin blame me for comin' up with that hunch," Gatling drawled slowly. "Somebody mentioned the name
Comanchero to me once—months ago, it was. When I saw
them Injuns, it come back to me. I thought mebbe it was
our one chance to keep from bein' scuppered. So I told
him——"

"Who mentioned that name to you?"

"Fellow name of Fess McFadden."

An utter shot in the dark. The name was that of the
elegant horse thief who had been lynched the previous
spring, and whose admirably fitting doeskin suit Regret
had worn to the ball at Austin. Almost without breathing,
they awaited Amelung's reply.

"You knew Fess McFadden?"

"Done some speculations with him," lied Gatling.

"Where?"

"Around Goliad." It was where McFadden was hung by
the vigilance committee.

Another long silence. Then Amelung said, "It could be
the truth. In a couple of days *we'll know.*"

It startled them.

"It can do no harm to tell you that McFadden worked
for us—him and his people," Amelung went on. "Our look-

168

outs. Kept tab, for one thing, on movements of the Ranger companies."

Spies in Texas . . . white criminals acting as an intelligence force for these supercriminals, the Comancheros, and their beastly red raiders! Into Regret's mind leaped a vision of Sam Houston's face, when he told of Comanche raids following close upon the shifting of the frontier guard, and his words, *You think that's a coincidence? By the Eternal, it was no coincidence!*

Amelung went on, "A couple of days ago we could have settled the whole business about you at once. We had one of McFadden's men in camp."

Henrion asked, "He left?"

"You might call it that. Fellow named Bernard Hare. Happen to know him?"

"Why, yes," said Henrion surprised. "Redheaded? Crooked finger on his gun hand? I *do* know him."

"*Did* know him, you mean." Odd, the way Amelung said it.

"What happened to him?"

"You might as well know. We believed he was reliable. But it seems he had a sister in one of the settlements against which we'd projected a Comanche raid early in August. He'd have carried warning. Luckily he was intercepted and brought back. We kept him until he confessed everything."

"And when he confessed?"

"The Kiowas up the canyon aren't hard to keep happy. A victim, once in a while, to whet up their ingenuity on. They'll search out a prisoner's nerves, I promise you, and trace them right to the roots of his quivering soul."

Regret felt his body grow cold. "Was that—I believe I heard—some kind of outcry——"

"Last night? After they brought you down into the canyon?"

"Yes. . ."

Amelung nodded. "That would be Hare. They finished him then. Kept him alive a very long time—thirty-six hours

169

it was, and after he'd almost ceased to resemble a human being. I went over twice to see it. Not that I particularly care for that sort of thing, but out of curiosity that the spark of life could stay in a body under that kind of endless torment."

He let that sink in.

"Thought you'd be interested. It gives you an idea of what happens to folks who turn traitor on us here."

He touched his horse with a spur, nodded coldly in the darkness, and rode on up the path toward the lighted windows of the Casa Blanca higher along the cliff.

"Hare . . . who had a sister?" Regret almost whispered. "That would be Nettie Hare—you remember the bound girl, of Cogswell's Corners?"

"That's so," said Henrion slowly. "I never put her and Bernard Hare together. But I told the truth when I said I knew him. Had an arrest order on him. Cattle thief. Killed a Mexican over in Brazoria. No damned good. But nobody's bad enough to deserve—what happened to him!"

"That Amelung—he dazzles me," Gatling said. "Goes over twice, he says, *out'n curiosity*—to see them torture Hare. 'Not that I partic'larly care for that sort of thing,' says he. Like a man would say he didn't care for sugar in his coffee, but could take it if it was offered!"

Regret thought about Nettie Hare, the thin girl with the honey hair, telling how that magnificent old patriarch, Yum Cogswell, was put to death. What would she think if she knew her own brother had died even more horribly— and because of his loyalty to her?

"Boys," said Henrion, "it's Amelung—and us. He's the big devil in this hell."

"What about old Musketoon?" Gatling asked.

"Musketoon's chief, but I'm thinking it's in name and no more," the captain said. "Who was with the Murrel gang, the worst in all America? Amelung. Who gives the orders like the one to hang that poor Soldano? Amelung. Old Musketoon bumbles and pulls his mustaches, but he's losing his grip. One of these days Amelung will get rid of him and be the boss, officially. Amelung's the power. Amelung's the menace. He's cunning as a wolf and twice as mean. Amelung's the man we've got to watch—as sure as he's watching us every minute, waiting for us to make one wrong move. . . ."

3

An hour passed. Amelung did not return down the path. Henrion and Gatling pitched the stubs of their cornhusk *cigarrillos* over the cliff, and watched the little winking red coals drop until they dashed themselves out against the rocky wall in showers of sparks. Then they entered the adobe hut and spread their blankets to sleep.

But Regret could not sleep. Outside, alone in the night, he continued to sit. He kept wondering what was going on up at the Casa Blanca. And he kept telling himself that Amelung, probably, was there for no other reason than a conference with old Musketoon. They must have a lot of business, those two, running a thieves' joint as big as this. There were records, likely, and so on, to be gone over.

It was no affair of his, anyway. He ought to turn in with the others and get some sleep.

But it was no use. He could not. In spite of himself, he kept thinking of Amelung when he gazed on Eloise, and Eloise's frightened, fascinated look in return. The snake and the bird . . .

Then a phrase poked itself into his thoughts: *Without regard to any personal consideration . . .*

The iron code of duty of the Texas Rangers, as laid down by Blake Henrion. A Ranger was not a human being, he was a machine to carry out his responsibilities. Regret was a Ranger, and a Ranger on the most perilous assignment ever. An assignment so weighted with importance that his fate, or the fate of his companions, or the fate of anybody else could not be considered in comparison with it. You cannot trifle with history, when a nation's fate is

171

being decided. It was up to him to keep on the top of his mind that fact, and be as inconspicuous as possible, arouse no suspicion of any kind, and stay out of everything not in the strictest line of business.

As for that girl, he reflected, he had no call to involve himself in her affairs. Evidently she had come out here of her own accord and quite willingly. But how . . . ?

Well, maybe that mystery would be explained someday, and maybe not. She had, he conceded, saved his life. But she'd likely have saved the life of a yellow pup, in the same way. Otherwise, she had made it mighty plain she wanted to have nothing more to do with him. He remembered, bitterly, Emile Beaubien walking out on the gallery with her back in Austin. . . .

Very well, he would attend to his own business. And with that a thought came suddenly: Strange she hadn't spoken a single word—not in an hour's time while he conversed with her father. Not natural, for a woman to keep so silent. *Was there a reason for it . . . ?*

Another hour passed, and a mounting anxiety, a nervousness, took possession of him. After a time he could stand it no longer.

He listened, to make certain that the others were asleep. Then he rose silently in the darkness. If it cost him his life, he had to know what was going on at the Casa Blanca.

Square oblongs of saffron light up the path were the windows of the chief's house. Regret stole toward them along the face of the cliff with the shameless purpose of window peeping and eavesdropping. No very dignified occupation, but the only way he could think to settle that nagging worry in his mind.

He halted, just before he reached the wide shelf which had been carved out by man or nature for the house, and pressed his body against the rock, his hands flattened on it like a lizard's. The moonlight was too bright here, highlighting his body and setting it off with a contrasting shadow black as ink.

In there—close beside the house—he saw what appeared to be a deeper niche, black with shadow.

Across the open moonlit space he slipped, and slid into the blackness. Just about big enough to hold him, almost cavelike, where some big boulder had been pried out of the wall and rolled over the cliff. He felt better in this concealment, and it gave him what he wanted—a direct view through the uncurtained window into the main *sala*.

His immediate sensation was relief. Nothing very bad was going on in there. Nothing very important, even.

He saw the three of them—old Musketoon, Jack Amelung, and Eloise.

Musketoon was sitting back in his huge chair, talking with Amelung. At their elbows was the brandy decanter, and to it they were paying due attention, particularly the old man.

Eloise appeared out of it. She sat on the lounge across the room, her eyes lowered, her hands idle in her lap. To Regret she seemed subdued and depressed, and he observed she took no part in the talk. It was as if she were there unwillingly, sitting with them because she could not well refuse to do so, but disliking it.

Regret now bethought himself of the fact that he was playing the fool to an extent that it would be hard for him ever to explain, supposing his action was known.

He had better get back before Henrion or Gatling awoke and began wondering where he was. And before somebody happened to discover him lurking around outside the chief's house. *That* could be pretty fatal. . . .

He hesitated. The windows of the house were closed, and it kept him from hearing what was being said within. Now and then the two men laughed, and he heard the sound of their laughter, but the words of their conversation did not reach him.

Old Musketoon appeared to be drunk, grimacing, and now and again closing one eye ludicrously, as if better to focus his vision. Amelung seemed unaffected by the brandy, but Regret judged that his drinking would likely make him more dangerous. Now and again the man glanced over at the girl, but he did not speak to her.

Without regard to any personal consideration . . . Whew! Regret had certainly done sufficient violence to that rule.

He moved, to slip across the narrow moonlit space and reach the path which would take him down to the hut.

Then he stopped. Old Musketoon was lurching to his feet. He stood swaying, with a drunk man's foolish giggle, and then staggered from the room.

Back into his black niche crouched Regret. A changed situation, in an instant of time. Amelung was alone with Eloise now. . . .

It was as if what followed was a dream, a bad dream, in which Regret could not lift a hand, could only watch.

He saw Amelung speak to the girl directly for the first time, now that her father was gone. She replied, a monosyllable, not lifting her eyes.

Amelung grinned and put down the cigar he had been smoking. With complete leisure, as if he had all the time he could want, he lifted his gaunt black figure out of the chair in which he had been sitting, and walked over to her. For a moment he stood looking down at her bent head almost derisively. A maddening sight to the watcher outside.

She seemed to shrink. The man's grin widened and he leaned over, half whispering something in her ear. She shook her head violently, and drew her shoulders to one side, away from him. It seemed to amuse him.

Would old Musketoon never return? Regret, crouching angry and helpless in his cavernlike niche, prayed that Eloise's father would come back and relieve her from the humiliating embarrassment she seemed to be undergoing.

Amelung said something more. She did not reply. As if he had reached the end of his patience with her, but still with his odious grin, he abruptly stooped and seized one of her hands, as if he owned it.

She struggled to free herself, pulling and twisting her

wrist weakly as women do, her head averted. A pleading, hopeless look had come on her face. Holding himself in check while he watched that was the hardest thing Paul Regret had ever done.

It came over him suddenly that old Musketoon was not coming back at all. . . .

Still with his hateful grin, Amelung pulled Eloise roughly to her feet, wound his arms about her, and jerked her body against his.

Personal consideration . . . Hell! A man cannot be expected forever to watch a woman he loves being manhandled!

Almost without realizing what he did, Regret leaped forward, forgetting that he would destroy himself, his companions, the whole plan for which they had undergone such infinite risks, and on which Houston counted so heavily.

He was at the window, ready to shout.

Amelung bent Eloise's struggling body backward. No grin on his face now. His mouth came down toward hers.

Like an angry little cat, the girl unexpectedly twisted about, avoiding his lips, and sank her teeth in Amelung's forearm.

In sudden pain and surprise, the man released her with an oath.

For a moment she stood looking at him, wiping her lips as if they had touched something loathsome, with such an expression of hate that even he seemed set back by it.

Then, with some bitter word, she was gone.

Regret realized how exposed he was, and stepped back into his niche, thankful that he had not uttered that shout, still panting from his excitement and fury.

Alone in the room, rubbing his bitten wrist and looking at the door through which Eloise had gone, stood Amelung. His back was to Regret, who could not see his expression. It could not have been pleasant. Yet the man was good at dissembling. A moment later old Musketoon

175

did return, after all—with some papers—and Regret saw Amelung's face, and it was cleared of any emotion.

As if nothing had happened, he bent his head beside the old man's over what appeared to be records of some kind. A few minutes later he left the house, mounted his horse, which was tethered in front, and rode back down the path. When he passed the niche in the canyon wall, Regret could almost have reached out from the shadows in which he crouched, and touched his spurred boot.

Old Musketoon swallowed another dram of brandy, and retired, blowing out the candles and plunging the room into blackness.

No more to see here. Regret began to steal toward the path, to get back to his quarters.

He heard a door open. From the darkened house a figure came, and stood silently at the top of the steps.

Regret stepped out into the moonlight.

"Eloise," he said.

4

With a violent start the girl turned and saw him. Instantly she held out her hand in a hushing gesture.

"Paul!" she whispered. "Go away—at once—please! You're in danger here!"

Instead he walked forward; and she came down the steps to him in a manner so fearful that it went to his heart.

"This moonlight," she half whimpered, "it's like day!"

"Come here—just around the corner——"

She hesitated. Then as if the decision was made for her, she allowed him to draw her into the black niche in the canyon wall.

"Some things I've got to know," he whispered. "First—how did you get here?"

She clung to his hand, and answered quickly, as if she had little time.

"It's not difficult to explain. You know I'd thought my father dead. Then—just before you left New Orleans, it was—I received a communication from him, describing himself as a trader on the plains, and sending some articles that had belonged to my dead mother——"

"I remember. You spoke of problems you had—that day in my rooms——"

She nodded. "I replied. Another letter came, begging me to come to him. I resolved to go——"

"Giving up your career in the Opera?"

She drew a deep breath. "Can you possibly understand what it is for a girl, who has believed herself an orphan, to learn that she has a living father who loves her and wants her to come to him?"

"Of course."

"When I saw you, in Austin, I was on my way—to him. That's why I couldn't explain my errand. . . ."

"I thought," he said slowly, "it was Emile Beaubien."

"Poor Emile! Poor silly, weak Emile!"

"Eloise, I've a confession. I came to see you that night. Before I could knock on the door, I saw you step out with him on the gallery above. You seemed so lighthearted—so gay——"

She gave a little weary smile. "What should a girl do when she's just told a man there's no hope for him? Make faces at him?"

"No," he said. "I suppose not."

She hurried on, "The very next day—after you went away—envoys of my father took charge of me and spirited me across the plains by easy stages to this place. I rode a horse all the way, but it didn't weary me. Every care was taken for my comfort, and every respect shown to me." Then she added casually, "That young man—Lanny Henrion—was in charge of my escort."

It was no casual piece of information to Regret. Lanny Henrion . . . the hawk-like youth who had walked out on the dance floor and challenged the captain! So *this* was what he meant by "his country." And he had brought

Eloise, in perfect safety, through the lands of the most dangerous savages in the world, under the overshadowing arm of the Comancheros!

"Is he here now—Lanny Henrion, I mean?" he asked quickly.

"No. He's away, I believe. Something to do with the Indians."

Regret breathed easier. "I must tell you something, Eloise. Lanny's brother—the Ranger captain—is here with me. And Tom Gatling, also."

"Mr. Gatling! The tall man who danced with me?"

"The same. If you see either of them you must act as if you never saw him before."

She unclasped her hand which had clung to his, and for a moment she thought.

"I don't know what to do," she said. "You ask me to be disloyal . . . to my own father——"

"If that's your feeling, why didn't you denounce me this morning?"

"I—I couldn't! It happened so suddenly—I needed time to think——"

"And now that you've thought?"

"Everything's so different from what I supposed—my father, in this nest of ruffians—and I know he's been wicked all his life, Paul—but he loves me—and he's old——"

"What about Amelung?"

She shivered. "I loathe that man!"

He leaned forward. "Eloise, I'd kill him gladly—*gladly*—for annoying you——"

"Oh, no!" she gasped. "You must never show any resentment toward him. Never! Or any especial friendship for me—that's why I wouldn't talk to you this morning—I was afraid of what you might say——"

"Is he in love with you?"

"Not in love. He doesn't know what love is. But he's mad for me. He would—would do anything to get me——"
She hesitated, as if it were an indelicacy she found it diffi-

cult to express. "This very night he asked me—if I would——"

"Marry him?"

She gave a bitter little laugh. "Nothing so honorable!"

It shocked and angered him. "What about your father?"

"He wouldn't—he couldn't—do anything. He's old, and under Amelung's power. I wouldn't even dare to tell him, for fear that something terrible might happen. Oh, Paul—I've gotten myself into the most horrible mess—and there's—there's no way out for me! I'm afraid, Paul—so afraid——"

He took both her hands. "Eloise, darling—it breaks my heart—finding you here—like this——" he began brokenly.

She cried out sharply, "Paul! Watch out! He's upon you!"

He had just time to throw himself aside as the knife snicked past his ear. He rolled over on the ground, and saw the dark figure turn to pounce on him with the naked blade.

His outstretched hand clutched a jagged piece of rock the size of his two fists. With all his strength he dashed it into his assailant's face.

The man went down without a sound.

Regret came to his feet, breathing hard. For an instant he bent over his attacker. In the moonlight that hard-lined, one-eyed visage was unmistakable. Estevan. Amelung's man. Probably placed to spy on just such a meeting as he had seen.

The man stirred. He was only stunned.

Back into the shadows Eloise shrank, and Regret glanced about. A dozen feet away the edge of the cliff was sharp and clear under the moon's brightness, where it pitched off from this shelf two hundred feet into the canyon below.

With the strength of a maniac, Regret seized Estevan's feet and dragged him to the verge. He gave a groan. Consciousness was beginning to return.

Regret heaved him off into space.

For a moment he stood listening, and heard the dreadful crash far below. Estevan, the one-eyed, probably never knew what happened to him.

From the shadows Eloise darted, and suddenly she was in Regret's arms.

"Paul—oh, Paul!" she sobbed.

"I had to do it. He was Amelung's spy."

"I know. But what will happen to us now? They'll find him—they'll know——"

He swore that he would get her away from that place, not knowing how.

All at once her lips were on his. For a moment she clung to him as if she would not let him go. And fled back into the house.

ELEVEN:

"I Think They're the Bravest Men I Ever Knew!"

1

"Suspicion will naturally turn on us," was the first thing Blake Henrion said when Regret woke them and related what had happened.

"How can they prove it?" asked Regret.

Gatling gave a short laugh. "There's always the bastinado."

It was a chilling thought. Together they stepped out into the moonlight and strained their eyes into the chasm below, fruitlessly trying to see the body of the fallen man. That part of the canyon was occupied by empty corrals. Nobody in the village, evidently, had heard the crash of Estevan's fall.

After a moment, Regret said, "Lanny Henrion brought Eloise to the Palo Duro."

"Lanny? Explain that!" the captain demanded harshly.

180

"That was what he was doing in Austin."

"She told you that?"

"Yes."

"*Where's he now?*"

"Gone—for the present. Out on the plains somewhere with the Comanches."

In the moonlight a powerful emotion of some sort twisted the captain's bearded face. "Lanny—so the boy's mixed up in—*this*," he said, in a sort of whisper to himself.

As if he were suddenly very tired, he led the way back into the dark hut.

Gatling and Regret lit *cigarrillos*. Henrion stretched himself on his blankets. A long silence. After a time the captain gave a little exclamation, almost a groan.

"I half knew it—when Amelung mentioned Bernard Hare," he said aloud. "Hare was with Fess McFadden—and—some said Lanny was, too."

"Nobody never proved it," said Gatling loyally.

"*This* proves it! A thief—a murderer—anything but a—a *Commanchero!* My brother—my kid brother—God!"

They could not say anything to comfort him.

"I blame myself. Only myself," they heard him say presently. "He was a good boy, Lanny was. A fine boy. I handled him wrong."

"You done everything a man kin do—you was like a father to him," said Gatling.

"I tried to be—and I shouldn't have. I was his brother. He didn't want me to be a father—tell him what was right and wrong, what he should and shouldn't do——"

"Somebody had to."

"It's been on my mind—ever since I saw him in Austin. I knew then he was gone—something God-awful had ahold of him. It's bothered me, night and day. But I didn't dream of anything as bad as *this!*"

Regret remembered Blake Henrion's long, abstracted silences on their journey across the plains. This good man, this brave and honorable man, had been suffering, alone and secretly. . . .

"Some colts have spirit, some don't," the captain went on drearily. "Some you can just hitch up, or saddle and break. But some must be taught differently, to get the best out of them—a good thoroughbred's like that. If you try to handle him like some range plug, you'll break his spirit, or he'll break you. But if you show him the way easy, he'll learn better, and do more for you than any other kind of animal."

He seemed to ruminate. "Trouble was, I didn't treat Lanny like . . . a thoroughbred." He paused. "I'm just a kind of work horse myself, I reckon, and I couldn't understand he was a finer strain. You know him, Tom."

"I shorely do."

"He's got everything, hasn't he? Does everything well. And he's afraid of nothing, and mighty pleasing to be around, and not a sneaking thing about him——"

"That's right, Blake."

"And I ruined him." A groan, with agony behind it, was almost ripped out of him. "Oh, God, *Lanny!*"

In this bitter grief words were useless. Gatling and Regret sat and smoked in silence.

Blake Henrion rolled over on his side. He spoke no more, but Regret, in all his life, had never felt more mortally sorry for a man.

All at once Henrion sat up. "*Two days . . .*"

In the darkness they stared at him, not understanding.

"That's what Amelung said," the captain continued. "In a couple of days—he'd *know*. About us. *That has to be Lanny!*"

"You mean he'll be back in the Palo Duro in that time?" Regret asked.

"That's it! A Fess McFadden man—and he'd tell them whether Tom was lying or not. It means our time's already too short——"

"To do what?"

"Get out of here. I was figuring that, give us just a little time, we'd have these people used to us. Then we could slip out some night, lift three horses, and get a long head start by morning. Riding for hell and liberty that way, and scattering, one of us had a chance to get through with the word for Sam Houston."

He stopped. "But now—well, there's just one hope for us. Just pray that Lanny doesn't come."

There was no sleep for them that night. Every hour of the darkness Regret counted over in his mind. He saw the first false light before dawn. He saw the slow coming of day. He thought of Eloise and of his companions, and his despair deepened and darkened with the new and added complications of danger that seemed to draw their deadly network closer and closer.

About nine o'clock in the morning a great shout came from below, followed by the calling of many voices. It was almost a relief.

"They've found your friend," said Gatling.

Regret could not stand it. In a moment he was out on the edge of the cliff. Two hundred feet below the lip of the precipice on which the Casa Blanca stood, a growing crowd milled around the broken body of the man he had killed.

Henrion and Gatling joined him. They saw Jack Amelung stride into the mob, and quickly examine the dead man. He glanced up at the cliff above him, and must have seen them peering down.

Presently, with many following, Amelung came up the path.

To them, as he passed, he did not speak. They followed the jostling crowd along the pathway toward the Casa Blanca.

There Amelung spent a few minutes in a swift survey of the ground. Regret was sure he noticed the jagged stone. Something else the man picked up, and put it into his jacket—the knife that Estevan had dropped when the rock struck him.

Blear-eyed and gray, old Musketoon came to the door.

"What happened?" he rumbled.

"A man has been found dead," said Amelung.

"Where?"

"Just below here—at the foot of these cliffs."

"How did it occur?"

"Don't know," said Amelung slowly. "Perhaps he lost his footing in the dark and fell."

But in that moment Regret encountered his eye, and in it was full understanding, or at least a guess so close that it amounted to the same thing. And it flashed over Regret that not yet was Jack Amelung ready to let Musketoon know that a spy had been placed to watch his house. On this slender circumstance hung their safety for the moment.

Knuckling his eyes, the old man went back inside. Amelung wordlessly led the Comancheros down the path back to their village. With a sense of suspended doom, Regret returned with Henrion and Gatling to their hut.

No use even to discuss what would happen now. The next move would come from Amelung, and they could only wait. They spent the time cleaning their revolvers.

2

About ten o'clock a Mexican went up the pathway past their hut at a run. In a few minutes he came back on his way to the town, and half an hour later they heard old Musketoon puffing down in the same direction. He stopped, as he saw them at their door.

"A good morning to you, messieurs!" he exclaimed. Evidently he was in the most jovial good spirits, and upon Regret he bestowed a grin of vast approval. "Observe me, Monsieur Regret—I do not limp? A miracle, for which I have you to thank!"

"I'm glad to hear this," Regret said.

"Yesterday, after you spoke to me about it, you remember that I dispatched my *mozo* down to the village for garlic. It is a comestible not commonly carried by us, but he succeeded in discovering a small bag of it. I consumed a clove of it at once, you observed, and felt immediate relief of the gout. Later I ate more. Last night I drank—between ourselves—more than was good for me. That would, ordinarily, cause an aggravation of my disability. But, *voilà!* I skip like a fawn!" He attempted a skip, a clumsy fat man's effort, and chortled. "Well, perhaps not exactly like a fawn. But at least without wincing. And though from the garlic I have a breath like a destroying angel, I am a happy man—and a man most deeply in your debt, Monsieur Regret!"

He expelled through his mustachios a breath so rank that it was all Regret could do to avoid stepping back from it.

Old Musketoon's gratitude was received by Regret with complete astonishment. His suggestion of garlic appeared to have been a most fortunate inspiration. He was quite certain it had nothing to do with benefiting the gout—but the Comanchero chief had experienced one of those unexpected periods of relief that sometimes come naturally, and now gave full credit to the garlic and Regret. For the moment—until the pain returned to his foot—they were in high favor.

"You behold me going down to the council house," old Musketoon continued. "A messenger has just brought word that a party of Comanche warriors, under the chief Iron Shirt, is coming in from a raid. I am on my way to receive Iron Shirt, who is a most important personage, if he *is* a savage."

"Iron Shirt?" said Regret, surprised. "We encountered him on the way here—in the Red River Valley."

"Yes, it was he who sent your party here, wasn't it?"

"But—it's hard to believe. That was five hundred miles from the settlements. After we left him he must have ridden all that way, and then come back to here—say another thousand miles—how is it possible in so few days?"

"Did you observe a peculiarity concerning Iron Shirt?"

"He was wearing a shirt of iron links."

"Genuine chain mail! And very old. Because of that the

Comanches believe him invulnerable and invincible, even gifted with supernatural powers. He is the head and heart of the Comanche nation. As long as he leads them they cannot be defeated, for to him they owe both their remarkable *élan* in battle, and their organization which has never been achieved by them before."

"But—even so——"

"Iron Shirt rarely makes a raid in person," went on old Musketoon. "Rather he directs them, as a general, sending this party out on a feint, another on the true thrust home. These are the tactics that our friend Amelung taught him. When you encountered Iron Shirt he had two parties out, and was awaiting their return with his own strong following of warriors—ready to go to either of his advanced groups if they were threatened."

The fat old rascal plumed his mustachios and grinned. "Most ingenious, don't you agree? I await eagerly the day when some rash company of the Texas Rangers, unacquainted with this stratagem, follows too far into the Comanche country, and is destroyed."

Again he chortled. "Now, I must make my apologies. If you care to walk along the path past the Casa Blanca, it will bring you out on a promontory overlooking the lower valley. From it you will see the war party arriving —a sight you may find worth the effort."

A wave of his hand, and he was gone down the path without a limp, and whistling as lightheartedly as if he were a child on some innocent errand for its mother, instead of the bloodiest of businesses.

Henrion stared after him. All at once he exclaimed, "Lanny! *He must be with those Indians!* Didn't the girl say he was with the Comanches?"

Silence fell. Regret saw Gatling moisten his lips with his tongue. If Lanny Henrion was with these Comanches, he was ahead of his schedule in returning to the Palo Duro. This would be the final capstone on misfortune.

3

"Get your guns," said Henrion. "We've got to watch those Indians come in."

He went to the hut and began buckling on his revolver belt. They followed.

"Please God Lanny isn't with the Comanches," the captain said. "But we've got to know!"

Regret picked up his belt with the hanging holster. His eye fell on the handle of the revolver.

That was Tapworth Cobb's gun. He had almost forgotten its former ownership.

Slowly he buckled the belt about his middle, feeling the familiar heavy weight of the weapon on his hip.

All at once he said, "Gatling."

When the other turned, he drew the revolver and held it out.

"Trade guns?" he asked.

"What for?" said Gatling.

"It belonged to Tap Cobb. I thought maybe——"

An odd pulse of feeling came momentarily into Gatling's face. But it was instantly gone, and he coldly shook his head.

"I'm used to the one I've got," he said.

Regret slid the revolver back into its holster.

Wordlessly, he followed the others up the path past the Casa Blanca. The door of the house was closed. No sign of Eloise.

Beyond, perhaps a hundred yards, they came to the natural gateway where the canyon narrowed to the two lofty buttresses. Old Musketoon's *mozo* was there, standing on a flat space perhaps twenty feet across, which topped the promontory on their side of the gorge. The rest of the Comancheros, however, had remained in the village.

As he neared the lookout point, Regret glanced back.

A crowd already had gathered about the council house. He noticed once more the crude gallows. During the night, the body of Miguel Soldano had been removed.

Then he stepped up on the natural platform of rock and saw the lower valley. From the gate of the gorge it widened to about half a mile, its floor fairly level except for occasional rock outcroppings, including one large upthrust of boulders forming a sort of island in the middle, near the river, which was marked by the line of cedars and willows that bordered its course.

But this he hardly saw. At their feet the Indian war party was already entering the canyon gate—a spectacle unforgettable, magnificently barbaric.

In isolated grandeur at the head, rode the kingly Iron Shirt, in his chain mail and his noble plumed war bonnet. Next came a group of subchiefs, feathered, with lances and round bull-hide shields. Then the whole brilliant cavalcade of warriors cascaded past, a blaze of gaudy paint, flashing steel, and fluttering feathers—five hundred, at the very least, of deadly, murderous Comanches.

A mile to the rear rose a huge cloud of dust where was driven the herd of stolen cattle and horses. In the parade itself trotted pack ponies laden with boxes and bales, silver candlesticks and other ornaments, cloth, utensils, and all the heterogeneous loot taken from Texas homes laid waste.

Regret saw one painted brave with a fluttering streamer on his lance shaft. Hair—soft brown hair—the long hair of a white woman. An uncured scalp. Then he noticed here and there other scalps, on lances and shield rims, all still to be smoked and hooped, and more than one of them torn from the heads of women. Enough to sicken a man.

But nowhere down the long line was there a white rider —only painted faces, brown bodies, and savage decorations. Lanny Henrion was not with these Comanches.

The Indian cavalcade passed through the canyon gate and on up into Comanchero Town.

The *mozo* hurried back to his duties at the Casa Blanca.

188

Henrion looked at his men. "I reckon we're in luck— this time."

As they started back, he seemed to walk with a freer stride, as if a weight had been lifted from him.

"The Indians might give us our big chance," he said. "Lots of horses here. Most likely a big drunk tonight. We'll watch for an opening—take three good horses—and have a thirty-mile lead on 'em before morning——"

His feeling of hope communicated itself to the others.

Yet that was the very moment of the black disaster.

The path made a curve about their hut. They turned the corner . . . and almost collided with the very man for whom they had been watching.

Later, Regret concluded that it had been Lanny who brought to the village the first message announcing the arrival of the Comanches, which was why he was not in the procession. But at this moment his sudden appearance stunned them.

Lanny seemed equally surprised. For a moment the brothers—the graceful youth and the quiet bearded man —stared at each other.

Then Lanny said, in his menacing drawl, "You broke our agreement, Blake."

The captain's face grew taut. "I made no agreement, Lanny."

The youth laughed unpleasantly. "I set out the terms. You was to stay out of my country, if I stayed out of yours——"

"I'm not here because I want to be, Lanny. And it isn't anything to do with you. I'm on duty——"

"Always pratin' about your duty," Lanny sneered. "Well, I got a duty, too! A passel of Rangers amongst us? I'm damned well goin' to give the alarm——"

"Lanny!" said Gatling. "I might not mean nothin' to you —or Regret—but Blake's your *brother*——"

"Brother, hell! You're spies!"

What followed was almost too quick for the eye.

Regret saw both brothers draw. Their shots thudded out almost together.

But Blake Henrion's flew wild. Already, as he pulled his trigger, he was spinning backward, struck through the body by Lanny's quicker bullet.

He hit the ground, writhed, then twisted his legs together.

Lanny swung his smoking muzzle on the others.

"Drop your belts," he ordered.

Neither Gatling nor Regret had stirred. They complied, unbuckling their revolver belts and letting them fall to the ground.

"Stand back," was the next order.

Lanny stepped forward, took their weapons, and gave a glance at his brother. Regret could have sworn there was a sudden horror and sorrow in his face.

He shifted his gaze back to the two Rangers. "Get into that doby," he commanded.

They began a backward retreat, hands over their heads, toward the door of the hut a few feet behind them.

Blake Henrion, lying on the ground behind Lanny, was finished, his eyes already glazing. But now Paul Regret, looking past the youth who was menacing them into the hut to lock them in, saw something he never expected to see—the triumph of an inexorable will over death itself.

He saw Blake Henrion stir, feebly prop his numbing arm on its elbow, and cock his revolver. As if hypnotized, he watched the dying captain's almost sightless eye live again in one last momentary blaze of concentration as he aimed, and pulled his trigger.

It was as if he willed the bullet to strike its mark in the back of his brother's head. In mid-step Lanny toppled forward, dead instantly.

So, on the cliffside path, high above Comanchero Town, the brothers Henrion, as brave men as ever walked, and under their feud loving each other, slew one another.

4

Regret and Gatling pounced on their own weapons, dropped from Lanny's dead hand, and buckled on the belts.

"Do we make a fight from the doby?" Regret said.

"Stay where you are," said Gatling. "Lanny can't say nothin' now."

Regret knew what he meant. They must see if the sacrifice Blake Henrion had made—his life, and the life of his brother—would justify itself.

Already, to the sound of the shots, a scurrying crowd was coming up the hill. Among the first was Amelung.

A few minutes later old Musketoon came puffing up the path. Then Regret saw a flitting figure. Eloise had run down from the Casa Blanca, and was clutching her father's arm, looking at the dead men with horror.

"What happened here?" demanded Amelung.

"They shot it out. Killed each other," said Gatling.

"For what reason?"

"Argument. Row of some kind——"

Amelung looked at him, then he studied the two faces. With a clutch at his heart Regret again saw how strikingly the Henrions resembled one another.

"They sure look alike, don't they?" said Amelung. "Enough to be brothers," he added, then broke off short, as if something had occurred to him. "Lanny told me once he had a brother who was a Texas Ranger! Seize those men!"

No use to resist. Regret and Gatling were disarmed and held.

"What's this for, Jack?" old Musketoon demanded.

"These are Texas Rangers!"

Never, until he heard that sudden roar of amazement, followed by the screaming snarl of rage, had Regret fully known the fear and hate in which the Comancheros held the Rangers.

But the old man seemed bewildered rather than convinced. "You're mistaken, Jack," he said. "You must be. Monsieur Regret—my daughter knows him well——"

Amelung spoke with deadly meaning. *"Then she also knows what he is!"*

"That's a lie!" roared old Musketoon.

"Ask her!"

Old Musketoon's lips flapped, but no sound came from them. For the first time he appeared to believe. And also to understand the pit that had been digged for him, and that this was his finish. Suddenly he seemed stricken with age.

From the mob a throaty, menacing growl rose.

As if to shield her, old Musketoon put an arm around Eloise, patting her shoulder. Then he gathered himself.

"My daughter knows nothing of this!" he trumpeted.

There was a silence like the lull in a hurricane, as they waited for what he would now say.

The next moment old Musketoon stumbled forward, fell on his hands and knees, and began coughing blood on the trampled gravel of the pathway.

So strange, so unexpected was it, that it took Paul Regret a moment to understand what had happened.

He saw the blood, staining and spreading on the shirt on the old man's back. Then he saw the woman behind him, the knife in her hand.

It was Manuelita, whose man Musketoon had sent to the gallows.

She leaned over him, her meager bosom heaving, her eyes opened widely and filled with sharp, peering intensity, as if to see whether a second blow was needed. Before, when Regret had seen her, she was pathetic in her sorrow. Now she was horribly fierce and alert.

No second blow was necessary. Old Musketoon collapsed, the dreadful coughing ceased.

Eloise flung herself down beside her father, and her wail

came only faintly in the sudden outcry of amazement from the crowd.

Whether Jack Amelung was pleased or disappointed, Regret did not know. But the man took instant command, as if for many months he had been ready for it. And his authority was as instantly recognized and obeyed.

"Disarm that woman and hold her!" he shouted.

Manuelita was seized, her knife wrested away. But Regret did not believe any very terrible thing was likely to happen to her.

"Take this girl back to the Casa Blanca," was Amelung's next order. Weeping and struggling, Eloise was dragged up the path.

"Now," said Amelung, "you two——"

He was silent for a long moment, while he looked Regret and Gatling over, minutely, as if memorizing their appearance, or striving to understand what brought men on an errand as certain of failure as theirs.

"We appear," he said presently, "to be highly honored by the Texas Rangers. It remains to learn why."

"The Kiowas!" a man yelled. "Give them to the Kiowas, and we will watch!"

It was taken up with a roar by the mob.

Amelung leaned forward, a terrible threat in his eyes. "You are spies," he said to the prisoners. "As spies, you will die. I can't give you life, but I will give you a choice of deaths. One quick and easy? Or the Kiowa stake?"

"For what?" asked Gatling.

"Truthfully answering my questions."

The Ranger shook his head.

Amelung's eyes turned on Regret. He felt himself sweating, his tongue gone dry. To die—that was one thing. But to die endlessly, in insane prolonged agony—as Cogswell had died, or Bernard Hare had died—it was too much to ask of a mortal body.

His eyes met Gatling's. Gatling doubted his courage.

Regret also shook his head.

It was the end of hope.

In a cul-de-sac formed by the canyon walls, at the foot of the very promontory from which that morning they had watched the Indians come up the valley, they stood lashed to posts of cedar. Except for one open side, they were in a sort of large roofless room, the rocky walls of which reflected upon them the sun in a baking heat. Three armed guards watched over them.

Regret suffered already. He tried not to think of what would happen when the Indians began their fiendish work. But he had too good an imagination, and in spite of himself it continually pictured to him horrors committed upon his own body, which brought the chill sweat out upon him. He wondered how long he would last . . . and how he would behave while his quivering flesh was being maimed and seared.

But this suffering was increased by another kind of anguish. That of the mind. He was in agony of concern and fear as to what had happened to Eloise. The terror of his love for her sometimes made his fear for himself seem a little thing. Not a sign had he seen of her, nor heard a word concerning her. Ah, God, he could have died almost gladly in the fire, he thought to himself, if she were safe. . . .

Gatling looked over. "Scairt, Paul?" he asked.

It was the first time he had ever used Regret's given name.

Regret gazed about. It was a beautiful world to be leaving. He saw the golden haze above, where the sun shone on the tops of the towering walls of the Palo Duro. He listened to the gurgling of the stream nearby, already a sound of torment because they could not reach the water, and their thirst was growing. He watched a white cloud like a swan's wing floating in the sky above. Very beautiful the world was, and very sad to leave.

But he shook his head. "No, I'm not afraid."

Gatling grinned, and the grin was strangely friendly. "We'll have somethin' to scare us before the night's over, I'm thinkin'," he said.

The grin faded. They both went silent again. Enduring.

The long afternoon dragged through its interminable hours. Lashed to their posts, standing in the insufferable heat, their tongues began to swell with thirst made the worse by the sweet sound of water only a few feet away. Between them and the village were the corrals, and these were full now of the sound of the bellowing of cattle and the stamping of horses, the stolen livestock which the Indians had brought.

Over this noise of animals, distant shouts and laughter came occasionally from Comanchero Town itself. There, in front of the council house, loot was piled in heaps. Bargaining must be concluded with the Indians, before any other business. Meantime the two prisoners in the rocky cul-de-sac could wait—and learn to know agony in anticipation.

Again and again the guards were changed. Sometimes curious onlookers, Comanchero men and their slatternly women, even children, wandered down from the town to look at the two Rangers.

Once, toward nightfall, a group of Indians came, and Regret found himself under the gaze of Iron Shirt. He viewed the face, the projecting, predatory chin, the deep chasm of broad-set eyes, the monumental calm of the great savage. Iron Shirt did not speak. After a brief survey, he turned indifferently back toward the village.

Evening descended. Still Regret and Gatling stood, the tight thongs cutting into their upstretched arms and wrists, their legs aching now. From the town new sounds came—throbbing of drums, distant barbaric singing.

Gatling interpreted. "Feast for the Comanches," he said. "We'll be next on the program of entertainment."

195

But the singing and drumming continued. All that night it continued. And still the torturers did not come for them.

By morning Paul Regret was sagging, in such anguish and weariness he hardly knew where he was or what he was doing; sometimes bracing himself on his trembling legs to ease the thongs which cut deeper and deeper into the wrists stretched above his head; sometimes, because of the weariness of his legs, hanging his weight on those bonds in spite of the torment, and in spite of the blood that ran down his arms.

Hours had passed since he and Gatling had exchanged a word. The sounds of revelry in the town had stilled. Comancheros and Comanches alike slept.

With a shrill crowing of gamecocks in the village, dawn came, and in the chill of the early breeze he aroused himself somewhat.

He heard Gatling croak, "Water! For God's sake, water!"

For answer, a guard spat spitefully.

Infinitely slow, the sun lifted itself into the heavens until the shadows of the canyon were banished, and Regret estimated it must be midday.

Then Gatling lifted his haggard face. They both heard it: the Comancheros were coming for them at last.

Vivid colors—sombreros, sashes, and *serapes*. Avid faces for the spectacle. The crowd jostled around them.

Indians also. Imperturbable Comanches with eyes like pieces of flint. Uncouth Kiowas with visages of bottomless cruelty.

Regret's eyes were too dulled by misery to take much note until he heard a horse's hoofs, and a voice. Amelung, lean-jawed, black in his *charro* costume, sat his fine horse, looking down at the prisoners.

"You wouldn't talk yesterday," he said. "Perhaps we can persuade you to talk today."

Regret's glance met Gatling's. When Amelung was through with them, the Kiowas would get them. How much of Houston's plan and the fate of Texas was safe from the mortal weakness they might in the end display?

"Bring up the girl," said Amelung.

It was Eloise. Two guards pulled her forward. She was disheveled, her eyes hollow from lack of sleep, her dress all but torn off one shoulder, but still defiant.

"Look at them," Amelung said to her. "What do you think of your friends now?"

"I think they're the bravest men I ever knew!" she flared.

He smiled. "You may change your opinion. Watch."

The realization that this monster intended to force Eloise to witness what was going to be done to them was to Regret the final touch of horror.

A man, however brave, becomes a thing of raw nerves under torture, so that he may lose all control of himself, and screech and gibber, or throw himself about, and pray and entreat for mercy, in a manner inhuman and crazed.

Regret had no experience with great anguish. He feared his own power to endure it without making a sorry spectacle. Tom Gatling, lashed to his post yonder, had spent his life on the frontier under hardships and exposure. He was all lean sinews and bones, probably with nerves as tough as his body.

But Paul Regret, who lived his life in gay places and among dainty pleasures, had nerves attuned to delicate perceptions, as do all of artistic temperament, whether creators or connoisseurs. What Gatling's nerves could withstand, he was afraid his own nerves could not withstand.

Death did not terrify him. He would have welcomed it at this minute.

But torture—to have his manhood broken down, to become an abject thing of sobbings and moanings—before the eyes of Eloise . . .

The shame of that was the final refinement of all cruelties.

He forgot his pride enough to beg. Not for himself, but for the girl.

197

"Amelung!" he croaked. "If you have one spark of mercy —send her away! Don't keep her here——"

"Why not?" the man on the horse said. "She is guilty of treachery, too. But a woman's penalties are different from a man's. And our little Eloise is too pretty a piece of flesh to maim or torture—don't you agree, Regret? She has another purpose to serve. Meantime, it's good for her to watch—and learn the value of obedience."

A sickness of heart, a despair exceeding all other hopelessness, swept over Regret. In that moment he knew they were dealing with a madman, a beast whose insane brain, brutalized and twisted by crime and hate, no human consideration could penetrate.

He had no time to dwell on it. Amelung gave an order. Immediately the prisoners were loosed from their posts and flung face downward on the ground.

Men leaped and pounced upon them. Regret did not resist. He felt his wrists tied to stakes. His boots, even the socks, were drawn from his feet; his knees were bent backward and lashed to other stakes, so that the naked, tender soles turned helplessly upward. In this position he was fixed, virtually unable to move.

On either side of him a ruffian stood, and two more beside Gatling who was similarly trussed, in their hands tough, thick rods cut from the willows by the river.

"The bastinado," said Amelung, "isn't pleasant. You'll cry out—that I promise you. From time to time you'll be given a rest, and a chance to answer my questions. If you refuse, the punishment will continue."

Regret closed his eyes tightly.

"You, with the sticks—begin!" came Amelung's voice.

Regret felt a shock of pain on his right foot, anguish so exquisite and dizzying that it sickened him. He thought the blow had fallen on the sensitive bottom arch; but he could not be sure, because the anguish was so all-pervasive.

A second blow. On the other foot. It brought a pain different and more frightful than the first. After that each blow was a fresh, blinding agony. . . .

He thought the bones of his poor feet were being shattered and crushed; his spine and brain were jolted by the violent shocks of anguish that racked through them; he felt searing sensations, as if red-hot irons were being run up and down his body; his bowels were gripped by a vertigo; he could feel a scream of agony welling up in his throat, ready to burst out of his mouth.

He threw his head about. All at once he saw Tom Gatling's eyes upon him. Gatling, too, was prostrate, bound and tortured. In his eyes was a question. . . .

Regret did not utter his cry.

The blows ceased momentarily. They heard Amelung's question, "Tell me how much Sam Houston knows about the Comancheros?"

They set their teeth and did not reply.

"More," ordered Amelung.

Regret heard Eloise cry out piteously. "No! Please no! Do anything you want with me—*anything*—only let them go——"

Amelung answered her roughly. "Shut up! You've had your chance. I'd have been good to you. But you were high and mighty, weren't you? Well, your time for bargaining's over now!"

She tried to shrink away, but the guards held her where she was, where she could not hide her face.

The blows began to fall again. Voices were blotted out in an eternity of red martyrdom which submerged, suffocated Paul Regret. He writhed and bit his lips until they bled.

But he did not cry out. Nor did Gatling.

The blows continued to fall. . . .

TWELVE:

"Tapworth Cobb Wasn't No Better ..."

1

He had lost consciousness. With a sense of shuddering pain and to the sound of sobbing, he returned to it.

He tried to move, but could not. He was staked out still, face down, the soles of his feet two horrid, bloody pulps.

Somebody was fumbling and working with the knots of his bonds. The sobbing continued.

Eloise . . .

Now he knew it was Eloise, on her knees beside him, struggling with her delicate fingers to untie him. Beyond lay Gatling, still bound also, his face turned weakly toward them, haggard beyond description, all color drained from his features.

Regret became conscious of voices in the distance. One mighty voice was shouting out something in the Comanche tongue.

Eloise finished untying him, and ran to loose Gatling.

Sick and weak, they dragged themselves to the little river to drink. Blessed water!

When he quenched his thirst, Regret turned on his back to breathe the painless air, and then . . . ah, God, the girl covered his bloody face with kisses. . . .

"Oh, my darling," she breathed. "My poor, suffering darling! Believe this—please believe it, Paul—I love you! I've loved you always and always! In New Orleans—in Austin—wherever you were—and never more than now——"

From the sweetness of her lips he seemed to draw life again.

They heard Gatling's voice.

"Hate to interrupt." The Ranger was grinning at them, still lying by the stream. "Fine thing to watch, you two—wonderful gal kissin' a shore-enough man. But—what's happened to everybody?"

It brought Eloise to herself, flushing and embarrassed. But she said, "It was like a miracle. There was a great alarm—they left us here—all of them, Comancheros and Indians too—and rushed back to the town. Even the guards. It was a panic."

"What would cause a stampede like that?"

"They said the Rangers are coming."

"Rangers?" In his surprise, Gatling propped himself up on an elbow. "But—but that would be impossible——"

"Where's Amelung?" Regret suddenly demanded.

"I saw him riding up the path that leads past the Casa Blanca," she said. "He must be on the lookout point. That's just above here, isn't it?"

The men glanced upward. They lay at the foot of the gigantic rocky buttress from which they had the day before watched the Indian procession, and from which the whole wide lower valley could be seen to greatest advantage. Rough, rocky and very steep, the canyon wall seemed almost to overhang them. From where they were it was impossible to see anything on top.

But it was as if the same thought came simultaneously to both their minds.

They did not speak. They could not walk. They could only crawl. But together they began the climb . . . a silent, painful, creeping, inexorable progress up the face of the cliff.

It was impossible to do it, crippled as they were, weak, their feet useless. Yet up the almost perpendicular rocky wall they struggled foot by foot, using their knees, their fingernails, their teeth almost.

Moments passed like ages. A narrow shelf along which they inched on their bellies, with a drop-off, which would mean instant death, threatening every second, let them creep around a complete overhang. Another dreadful climb, straight up, hanging at times by their hands alone, like bats to the roughness of the cliff, while their lungs fought for air. Yet always grimly struggling upward again.

A last sheer wall of rock to surmount, almost smooth, with a fall of three hundred plunging feet if they slipped. . . .

They did not slip. Their knees were as bloody as their feet before they reached the top. But they accomplished the impossibility.

And there they saw Amelung. Alone.

A few yards down the path toward the Casa Blanca was his horse, trained in the western manner to stand when its reins hung to the ground. The animal pricked forward its ears at them. But so intent was Amelung, watching something through an old ship's telescope which must have been Musketoon's, that he did not at first hear them.

When he turned, suddenly, they were almost on him. His face went white with the chill of fear at their haggard, maddened faces.

They were unarmed, injured, almost crazed with suffering. And he was heavily accoutered with weapons. Yet, crouching and bounding on hands and knees like animals, their teeth bared in hate and fury, they leaped on him before he could draw, and bore him down, throttling, biting, striking—anything to destroy.

With their bare hands, on that rock pinnacle, they killed Jack Amelung, breaking his neck, smashing his skull with stones, pulling his throat out. . . .

While they still crouched over him, bloody and gleeful, Eloise reached them.

2

That the girl had made that climb alone was perhaps more wonderful than that Regret and Gatling had made it. Her dress was torn and soiled, but somehow she had followed them up the cliff. She hardly glanced at what was left of Amelung, as they took his two revolvers and rolled him off over the precipice.

Instead she stood looking off down the valley.

"There they are!" she cried.

The men, who had been too intent on their killing to look anywhere, now saw also a distant column of horsemen, just passing the island of upthrusting boulders which Regret had noticed from the pinnacle the day before.

"It *is* Rangers!" Gatling exclaimed. "Our company! There's that fog hoss Wyman Cruze rides!"

"What are they doing here?" asked Regret. "Nothing of this was in the plan when we left the Rio Leon. And how did they find this place, when it was so much trouble for us to find it?"

"I dunno," said Gatling. "But I do know them boys out there is ridin' into a trap. They've got no notion of it. An' they'll never git out of it——"

Regret glanced around, up the canyon behind them.

Because of the isolated character of this buttress of the great gate, helped by a curve in the cliff, the little drama they had just enacted seemed to have been unnoticed. Up the gorge a quarter of a mile the Indians were too busy laying out their battle lines to pay any attention to them. As for the Comancheros, they were streaming in a wild flight, with whatever possessions they could carry, through the canyon beyond.

Regret could make out Iron Shirt directing his riflemen as they swarmed up the rocky walls to line the cliffs with concealed death. It was the chief's voice, calling out orders, that he heard when he first came to consciousness below.

Iron Shirt's plan was evident. At the entrance of the gorge the cliffs were too steep and bare to afford cover. The Rangers, therefore, were to be permitted to ride through the great natural gateway, with no hint of the danger that awaited them, and up the canyon into the deserted village, where they would suddenly be overwhelmed by the ambuscade from above.

"Can't we signal them?" Regret said, looking toward the distant Rangers.

"How?" Gatling said. "We couldn't make 'em understand."

"There's Amelung's horse——" said Eloise.

Gatling studied the far column. "If someone could only reach 'em—they could git back in them big rocks," he mused.

He glanced back at the horse standing down the path. Regret knew they both had the same thought. One rider, with great luck, might get down to the canyon floor and out through the gate. Possibly even two. But the horse would not carry three.

"Paul," Gatling said, "you take her—an' go."

Regret shook his head. "You'd be more likely to make it."

"I got seniority on you. I order you!"

"No!"

Gatling considered. "We could leave it to Miss Eloise—let her say which——"

"Oh, no!" came her horrified cry. "I couldn't—don't ask me!"

"I reckon it *would* be kind of cruel," said Gatling. He gave Regret a glance. "We could gamble for it, if there was a way. Got a coin on you?"

They searched their pockets. Not even a copper had been left them by the Comancheros.

"If we hadn't been in such a hurry to roll Amelung over the edge—I'll bet *he* had money on him," said Regret bitterly.

Gatling thought for a moment. "Tell you what. We'll play 'Hand' for it."

"Hand?" said Regret. "I never heard of it."

The other looked about him and picked up a small round pebble about the size of a hazel nut.

"White folks doesn't play it," he said. "It ain't complicated enough. But Injuns plays it. I've seen 'em bet anythin'—saddles, guns, hosses, squaws—on it. I even heard of two bucks that bet their scalps—an' the loser had his top-knot collected. Are you game?"

"How is it played?"

"Simplest thing. I put my two hands back of me, an' swap the leetle pebble back an' forth between 'em any way I want. When you say 'Hand,' I bring both closed fists out in front. You point to the one you think the stone's in. If you guess right, you win. Winner stays here. Loser takes the hoss an' Miss Eloise, an' makes a try to reach the boys out yonder. O.K.?"

It was no more than the guessing hazard schoolboys play with each other the world over. To Paul Regret, who knew every intricate form of gambling that the ingenuity of men had invented, it seemed almost ludicrous that they were to settle a matter of such importance with a child's game.

Yet whatever they did must be done quickly. Eloise's fate was at stake on this, too.

He nodded. "All right."

"Sudden death—or best two out of three?" Gatling asked.

All a matter of luck anyway, and time pressed. "Sudden death," said Regret.

Gatling placed his hands behind his back.

A strange moment of drama, there on the flat top of the rock pinnacle, with men riding toward their death up the wide valley, and savage warriors laying their ambuscade in the gorge.

The girl looked at Regret and Gatling, and the tears sprang to her eyes. So gallant, so fine, she thought. This gamble was to decide something utterly unreasonable by any ordinary rule—not which of these men should escape death, but which of them should have the privilege of laying down his life for the other. And for her. She felt a sob, and choked it back; fought away the tears, and held her breath.

Neither of the men could stand, so they sat, crouching toward each other, Gatling's hands behind him, for all their pain tense antagonists in this contest of furious elemental meaning.

Regret spoke a single word. "Hand!"

The other presented his two big fists.

Swiftly Regret looked them over. Strange how important was the momentary instinct of competition in him, even in this contest of reversed interests.

He glanced at Gatling's face. The long, tanned countenance was expressionless. He compared the brown, corded backs of the fists.

The left seemed to him a little more tightly clasped than the other, the center knuckle perhaps a hair's breadth advanced. Could that be caused by a grip on the small stone in the palm?

He reasoned. Gatling would try a trick. No, that hand was too palpably intended to deceive him.

He pointed to the right fist.

Eloise seemed to give a little gasp.

A flash of triumph in Tom Gatling's face. He opened his palm. It was empty.

"Tried to outguess me, didn't you?" he said, and grinned. "Figgered I'd make one hand look as if it had a pebble in it, to fool you? But I went further. I figgered *you'd* figger that out. So I let you outsmart yourself! Oh, Paul, Paul! You've beat me in shootin'—an' in poker—but I won at last!"

He was actually happy in this victory, by which he had at that moment condemned himself to die!

Regret gulped.

"Git goin'," said Gatling.

"Tom—I can't do it——" Regret began.

Gatling's voice was gruff in his ear. "We settled it fair, didn't we? It ain't you or me we got to think about—it's *her*. An' there's no time to lose."

Regret nodded dumbly. They wrung hands.

Gatling said, "Sometimes I had my doubts about you, Paul, but I was dead wrong. I never thought I'd feel toward you as I do, an' that's the truth. But you're a man all through. Tapworth Cobb wasn't no better. I can't say more than that!"

Coming from him, it was the greatest compliment Paul Regret had ever received in his life.

He could not answer. But Eloise took the Ranger's gaunt face between her hands and kissed him full on the lips.

3

The ride out of that canyon was such a piece of audacity that Regret wondered how it could possibly succeed.

Amelung's thoroughbred was well trained and gentle. He hitched himself toward it, and with the girl's help somehow got into the saddle in spite of his beaten and bleeding feet. He held the reins and checked the horse as she, using his stirrup, climbed up behind. The gelding shifted his hoofs about, but he would carry double.

Gatling had Amelung's two revolvers, busily examining them. He pulled himself to the edge of the cliff, where he could look up the gorge toward the Indian ambush, and gave them a grin and a wave of the hand in salute and farewell.

The thoroughbred took the downward path. First they must travel along the cliffside for hundreds of yards, straight toward their enemies who lay back up the gorge. Sure-footed as a goat, the horse trotted past the Casa Blanca, past the adobe hut where the two Henrions and old Musketoon had died, and down to the canyon floor.

No notice of them yet.

Comanchero Town stood deserted, with the stark gallows empty before the council house.

They turned. Eloise's arms tightened about Regret as the thoroughbred suddenly broke into a full run, down the lane through the teeming corrals, toward the canyon gate above which Gatling lay.

Still not a shot was fired. Regret could not understand it.

Then he decided that the Comanches did not know who they were, or what their purpose was.

They had ridden down from above, whereas they had been left at the foot of the cliff. That climb they had made, and the killing of Amelung, had occurred in such a manner that they were not observed. The Indians must at first have supposed they were two of the Comancheros, perhaps Amelung himself with someone behind him, until they suddenly whirled away down the canyon in a burst of speed.

Suddenly a rifle report echoed in the gorge. Another. Regret heard the spiteful whine of lead.

Then no more shots.

Iron Shirt was waving his blanket for his warriors to hold their triggers. A full volley would give away his trap. Instead, the chief signaled to a dozen young braves, on superbly fast horses, to overtake the fugitives.

Sound reasoning by the great Comanche. The sight of a few Indians pursuing two riders on a single horse out of the mouth of the gorge would not stop the Rangers from advancing. More likely, it would hurry them to the rescue. And the pursuers should overtake the double-burdened mount long before the man and girl could reach help.

What Iron Shirt did not count on was that a rear guard had been left behind. Lying above the canyon gate with Amelung's revolvers, was Tom Gatling.

Regret and Eloise heard, rather than saw, the sharply explosive little battle he fought, after they were well out of the jaws of the gorge. He must, at first, have driven the Indians back. But he had only the twelve shots in his revolvers—the rest of Amelung's ammunition was at the bottom of the cliff with his shattered body. So Gatling's diversion lasted no more than a few minutes, and he gave his life in the end, with his own last shot probably, to avoid being captured for torture. But the delay was enough.

By the time the first of the Comanches issued from the throat of the gorge, there was no chance to overtake the quarry. One look they gave, then with a flourish of their lances disappeared.

Out in the wide lower valley the Ranger company had halted at the flurry of shooting up in the canyon. Two or three threw themselves from their saddles and knelt on the ground as if to fire at the oncoming pair. But their leader raised his arm, and the rifle barrels were lifted.

"Back! Get back!" Regret shouted at them, as soon as he was near enough to be understood.

Then they were among the Rangers. The gelding's ribs were heaving from the hard run, and Eloise's arms tightened about Regret again as the animal sidled about, still excited and ready for another effort.

About him, Regret saw the faces of men he knew—homely, quizzical, taciturn, daring, stubborn faces. Some exclaimed at the sight of his bloody, swelling bare feet. Others did not hide their stares at the girl who clung to him.

"Regret!" said Wyman Cruze, reining his gray horse over to them. "What are ye doin' hyar? What in the hell happened to them feet of yourn? Whar's Henrion an' Gatling? An' who's this young lady?"

Almost incoherently Regret answered the questions.

He heard the Rangers' comments around him.

"Bastinado? What's that?"

"Both daid—the cap'n an' Tom?"

"The murderin', tormentin' bastards——"

At the end Wyman Cruze swore. "Ye mean to say the Comanchero roost's jest beyond them narrers?"

Regret nodded.

"Je-humpin' Jehoshaphat! We'd no notion we was near sech a place!"

"Then—what brought you here?"

"Trailin' Injuns," said the frontiersman. "There's been a God-awful raid, the wust yet. The count of the daid wasn't near complete when we left. But the stock herd the Comanches took—the biggest ever—left a trail it seemed criminal to miss. We follered it. Now it looks like mebbe we've caught the infernal red hides at last!"

"Do you have any notion how many Comanches you've *caught*—as you put it?" Regret asked.

"Nope. Enough to make it wuth while, I'm hopin'."

"I think you'll find it so," said Regret grimly. "Up that gorge are not fewer than five hundred of the picked warriors of the Comanche nation. And Iron Shirt himself is at their head!"

Cruze gave a low whistle. "We're in a showdown for the jack pot, shore. Injuns, Comancheros, Iron Shirt—all in one deal!"

"You'd better fall back to those rocks behind you. It's your only chance!" Regret pointed to the outcropping.

Cruze gave it a squint-eyed glance. "Makes sense."

He raised his voice. "Boys, we got hot work comin' up! Skedaddle back thar, all of ye, an' take yore places whar ye'll do the most good!"

A highly informal command, but like the rush of a whirlwind it was executed. Helter-skelter, men and horses tore for the solitary position capable of being defended in that broad valley floor, and Regret and the girl went with them.

The "island" of limestone rocks, very rough, heaped boulder on boulder, covered perhaps an acre of ground, with the stream running near it, and a small grove of stunted cedars behind. Among these little trees the men tethered their mounts, then melted into every sheltered place among the rocks.

Eloise slipped to the ground. Two tall Rangers helped Regret down. He noticed Jack Amelung's rifle, still in its scabbard under the stirrup leather, and drew it out. The thoroughbred was fastened in the trees, and with Eloise going ahead, Regret was almost carried up the rocks, for he could not bear his weight on his tortured feet.

They found a depression, deep among the boulders and protected all around, and there Eloise promised Wyman Cruze she would remain.

Regret wriggled forward to where he could see. For the

first time he examined his feet. They were swollen badly, lacerated, aching and sore, but he did not believe the bones were broken in them, actually. Hopefully, he remembered old Musketoon's saying that the bastinado did not cripple permanently. . . .

About him men began exclaiming. He looked over the boulder in front of him, and for the moment forgot about his feet entirely.

Out of the gates of the gorge was winding a long string of horsemen. Iron Shirt, that savage tactician, having been disappointed of springing his trap, was preparing to close with the Texas Rangers in the open.

He would destroy them, every man of them. To him and his people it was vital that not one white person should return to Texas to carry word as to where lay Comanchero Town.

THIRTEEN:

"Invulnerable and Invincible . . ."

1

FROM THEIR leisurely movements it was evident that the Comanches were perfectly sure there was no possible escape for the Texans. Slowly their panorama of battle unfolded, until the whole upper valley, half a mile away, seemed filled with dancing horses, tossing plumes, and sparkling steel.

All at once a rifle's sharp, peremptory report echoed across the canyon. Immediately the echo was drowned in the long, spattering roll of an irregular volley.

One of the Rangers near Regret swore and wrung his right hand, from the fingertips of which came a little spray of blood. Beyond him another man, who had been peering over a rock, sat down abruptly and leaned forward, his head resting on his arms, which were folded on his knees. So natural were the movement and attitude, that it was hard to realize that he was dead—shot through the head.

The others flattened behind their boulders to escape the screaming, ricocheting bullets, refusing to reply to the Indian fire at this range. Back through the rocks crept the wounded man, and once, above the noise, Regret heard Eloise speaking to him. The girl was giving him aid of some kind.

Some of the distant Comanches were shooting from their horses' backs. Others had sprung to the ground, and Regret could see their crouched forms as they knelt to get a steadier aim. But after a time the rolling roar of rifle fire degenerated to quick, sharp throbs in twos or threes or ones, then ceased altogether.

The Indians who were on foot began mounting again. Regret could hear the Rangers talking to each other.

"Hank, yo' got any spare bullet patches?"

"This here riflin's leadin' up on me, drat it!"

"How's that wrist, Dode?"

"Aw, jest creased me. The leetle lady fixed me up—look at that thar bandage!"

"Pore ole Buck! Right atwixt the eyes, they got him."

Wyman Cruze's voice said, "Better keep yore purty haid down, miss. Comanche bullets ain't no respecters of ladies."

"Where's Paul?" Eloise said.

"Over thar. Safe as a church."

A moment later Regret saw her eager young face above the boulders between them.

"How are you, darling?" she said. "Your poor feet! This is a *battle*, isn't it? Really, truly? Oh, when I tell my friends about this!"

Her eyes were brilliant with her excitement. He realized, with pride in her, that the thrill of being involved in an event so unusual for a woman as a full-scale battle obscured any fear in her of the danger she was in.

212

"You must get back," he said anxiously. "The Indians may open fire again, any minute."

Wyman Cruze's worried visage appeared above the rocks near the girl. "I got to order ye back whar ye was, miss," he said. "The Comanches is about to strike up the grand march."

"I'm sorry." She was quickly contrite. "It's a bother—having a woman here—isn't it? I'll be good—I won't make any more trouble—I promise."

She gave the frontiersman a smile and disappeared.

Cruze was right. Up the valley the Comanches appeared to be forming for their charge.

Regret examined Amelung's rifle in his hands, and recognized it as a masterpiece of the gunsmith's craft—single shot, bullets twenty to the pound, the barrel octagonal and true, the metal on the stock chased silver, the stock itself hand-carved of curly maple and specially built so that when he put it to his shoulder it seemed a part of him. Assuredly Jack Amelung had treated himself to the best. This was a weapon about which a man could wrap his heart.

He glanced out toward the Indians. Now he saw Iron Shirt himself, riding back and forth before his array, making his dispositions.

The eagerness of the young, less disciplined braves, hot for renown, was shown by the way individuals frequently broke from the main body, "letting out" their ponies in bursts of speed toward the Ranger position, then suddenly curving back, throwing themselves over on the opposite sides of their steeds, and flourishing their lances as if challenging the white men to fire at them.

All at once the wild eagerness burst its bounds. With a sudden distant drumming of hoofs, and that peculiar bloodcurdling scream of the Comanche war yell—once heard, never forgotten—a full half of the Indian array broke away from the rest, and launched itself against the Rangers in their rocks.

Like lizards, the Texans flattened themselves among

their boulders, clenching their teeth as they gazed down rifle barrels, but not a shot was fired, for Wyman Cruze had passed the word that he would give the signal.

Moment after moment, in sheer fascination, Regret watched the hurtling horde bear down upon them, fierce young warriors whipping their ponies, as they vied with each other to be the first to strike their enemy. Five times the number of the defenders in the outcropping rode in that juggernaut. He wondered how anything could stop it.

Half the distance to their goal the savages had come. Still Cruze held his order for fire. The shriek of Comanche war cries and the nearing thunder of galloping hoofs grew in volume. They were a furlong away, a hundred yards . . .

"*Now!*" came Cruze's sudden shout.

Regret hardly had time to catch the sights of his rifle, but the gun handled so beautifully that it seemed to aim itself. He swung it on a scampering redskin devil, and the bullet drove center with a smack. The Comanche bounced a couple of feet from the back of his galloping horse, and hit the ground with his legs jerking, dead before he struck.

At the same instant, with a single clap like an explosion, the volley of the Texas Rangers burst out. Back over the rocks drifted a choking cloud of white powder smoke, and now Regret heard the spitting, snarling chorus of the six-shooters, taking up where the rifles left off.

Smoke cleared. He almost gasped. It was hard to believe the execution they had done. One hundred paces from their boulders writhed a welter of blood-spurting, struggling horses, and painted men flopped or lay still where the first clap of the volley had struck them. In one bite the entire center had been taken out of the oncoming array.

Now a strange, wild thing happened. Like an angry wave which hurls itself upon a rock and breaks on its front, the savage ranks divided on either side of the outcropping and roared on down the valley in two separate wings.

Regret watched them swoop past, firing wildly at the defenders as they went, until they circled off to safety under the distant bluffs down the valley. Then slowly they returned at extreme distance from that deadly little "island" outcropping, to the place from which they had begun their charge, and where Iron Shirt sat his horse, coldly awaiting them, with his more seasoned warriors who had not participated in that first unplanned, abortive rush.

Just back of Regret a Ranger dragged a limp leg as he crawled over the rocks, leaving a long scarlet smear of blood where he went. There were other casualties, also. As by instinct the wounded men headed toward the little sheltered basin where Eloise sat, tearing up her petticoat for bandages.

Other Rangers exulted.

"That'll learn 'em!"

"Took the middle out'n 'em like slicin' a watermelon!"

"See 'em scatterin' off over the landscape like a passel of antelopes!"

Regret spoke to his nearest neighbor. "What weight bullets does your gun throw?"

"Twenty to the pound."

"Same as this. Lend me a round or two, will you?"

"Surest thing."

Up the valley Iron Shirt had begun to gather his braves again, the lesser chiefs scurrying about, hurrying up the stragglers.

Wyman Cruze knelt on one knee, his hand shading his eyes.

"What do you think?" Regret called over to him.

"I think that fust rush was only the young bucks, a-thirstin' for glory, an' bustin' away on their own," the frontiersman said. "Ole Iron Shirt never ordered that charge. I bet he's givin' 'em hell right now. See, how he's linin' up the hull outfit? Iron Shirt knows damn well what he's doin'. This time they'll come in two waves—all five hundred of 'em. Fust wave takes our volley. Second carries the charge home—right over these rocks. It'll be— interestin'."

So Wyman Cruze, that master of understatement, expressed his belief in the slimness of their chances.

Iron Shirt himself would come with his warriors this time. Regret pictured them in his mind, sweeping about these rocks, throwing themselves from their horses' backs, clambering over the Ranger position, hacking and stabbing, killing every living thing.

Nothing could stop the weight of such a charge.

With a sick hopelessness he thought of Eloise. She had been so excited by this battle. She probably did not even at this minute suspect that she was doomed. She had never in her life harmed anyone, and even now she was busy ministering to suffering, bleeding men. Yet she must die horribly, as the rest of them must die . . . perhaps more horribly.

He thought of what had happened to Sue Ellen Irvin . . . savage lust and brutality . . .

He shuddered and felt an impulse to crawl over the rocks to Eloise. At least he could die beside her. . . . But that would do no good.

Carefully, with his borrowed ammunition, he began loading the beautiful weapon in his hands. Powder, bullet, patch, copper percussion cap, all in order. One more shot ready.

He glanced at the ferocious Comanche horde half a mile away. Every warrior in the array seemed to be looking at the stark figure with the distant shimmer of chain mail.

Suddenly, as if voices were in his ears, Paul Regret remembered words that had been spoken to him.

Sam Houston's voice: *Iron Shirt might well be called the king of the Comanches. Beware of Iron Shirt. . . .*

Old Musketoon's voice: *They believe him invulnerable and invincible . . . As long as he leads them they cannot be defeated. . . .*

Nobody noticed him as he rolled over the nearer boulder and slid down a slight slope to the ground, carrying with him the rifle. His feet pained him so miserably still that he could not even think of walking, but he wriggled back behind the rocks, to where Amelung's thoroughbred was tethered.

He was a creature of grace and beauty and gentleness. As Regret crawled painfully toward him and unfastened him, he extended his dark velvety muzzle downward and snuffed, for such an approach was strange and new to him. His dainty ears pricked forward, his eyes were soft and luminous, but he stood like a rock as, with the agony of his swollen feet contorting his face, the man drew himself up by the stirrup leathers, slid the rifle into its scabbard, grasped the horn and cantle of the saddle, and almost by the strength of his arms alone, pulled himself across the horse's back.

None of this had been observed. The Rangers were too intent, watching the gathering storm up the valley, where the Indians massed and shifted, forming their charge.

Regret settled himself in the saddle, avoiding the stirrups because of his painful feet, and gripping only with his knees. Then he drew again the rifle from its boot.

Now he was ready. All at once he gave the horse a stinging cut with the ends of the reins, and the spirited creature bounded, at a gallop in two strides, past the Rangers crouched among their rocks.

He heard Cruze's surprised shout, "Regret! Whar ye goin'?"

And did not reply.

Then he was far beyond the outcropping. Behind him the frontiersman called out in a great voice for him to come back, and others were tossing questions back and forth. But the sounds receded as he thundered past the stricken litter of Indians and horses where the first volley had smitten them, and galloped straight toward the center of the widespread Comanche array.

Paul Regret was sure that some of his comrades believed he had gone mad, perhaps was seeking a deliberate suicide, as a man sometimes does when his intellect snaps. But never, in all his life, had he done anything more coldly and deliberately calculated than this thing upon which he was embarking.

He had gambled all his life. Now, however, he was launching on his greatest of all gambles, having first calculated, and knowing full well the desperately long chance he was taking, yet accepting it in his cast for the greatest stakes for which he had ever played.

Herein lay his gamble: How much did Iron Shirt really mean to the Comanche war? If his savage people actually believed him gifted with supernatural powers, and therefore, as long as he was with them, charged with the terrible purpose which only a conviction that they could not be defeated gave them, the great chief meant everything.

Regret's purpose was remorselessly simple: to kill Iron Shirt.

But the odds against him were enormous and varied.

What if he, himself, were shot down before he got close enough for a sure shot? What if he missed? What if, after all, Iron Shirt was not the talismanic figure he was thought to be?

If Regret won, perhaps Eloise—and his friends—would escape the Comanche spears, even if he did not. If he lost . . . a gambler must know how to lose, but the stakes were so heavy this time that he could not think of the consequences of losing.

At long rifle range the savages still maneuvered, some circling their horses, others fidgeting back and forth in the lines which Iron Shirt was forming. They saw the single horseman galloping toward them, and for a few moments they watched him in astonishment, unable to understand foolhardiness so complete.

Then they opened on him.

Regret heard the first sputtering outburst of shots, followed by a continual rising drum roll of rifle fire.

Low in his saddle he whipped the horse, and the magnificent animal responded with everything in him. A sagebrush flat whipped past under them, the thoroughbred

218

buckjumped over some broken rocks, then leaped a narrow arroyo without breaking stride, and galloped on.

About them in the air sounded the keen *phit-phit* of bullets, and here and there leaden slugs kicked up little smoking clouds of dust on the ground.

How long before the inevitable happened? Regret held his breath, set his teeth, counted and gloated over every rod, every yard he gained.

Hardly halfway to the Comanches, he suddenly felt his horse's knees buckle. All limp in the air the gelding went— from a thundering run to a long sliding fall. Twenty feet over his neck the rider was pitched, his face scarred with gravel, half stunned, but still clutching the rifle.

That was Regret's first thought—the precious rifle. Rolling over, he examined it eagerly, fearfully. The copper percussion cap still sat on the nipple under the closed hammer. The muzzle was clean, the stock unbroken. It was undamaged by the fall.

The horse was dead, a bullet through its skull. About Regret a storm of lead beat up the sand. He wriggled behind the carcass, expecting each instant to feel the shock of a slug in his body. But he made it, and was for the moment fairly safe behind the bulwark of flesh.

A full quarter of a mile away were the Comanches. Too far for a sure shot, even if he had not been held down by their stinging bullets. Bitter disappointment swept over him that he had been brought down so soon too soon to do what he had set out to do, at such sacrifice.

The Indian fire suddenly ceased. Cautiously Regret raised his head just enough to peer over the carcass.

Iron Shirt was ready at last. He was about to launch his grand charge. No more bullets were to be wasted on a single man. Perhaps they believed him disabled, or even dead. In any case, the chief was playing a far greater game. He would scoop up fifty Texas Rangers all at once. As for that lone outrider, he could not escape. They would spear him without even slowing down as the charge rode over him.

Regret slid his rifle over the side of the dead horse. Even as he did so, the first of the two divisions of Comanches which Iron Shirt had marshaled, began moving slowly forward, gathering speed as it came.

It was a sight unforgettable. High above the Indian ranks towered the mighty walls of the Palo Duro. On the rim he saw moving black specks: the heads of Comancheros who had recovered from their panic sufficiently to return and watch the wiping out of the Texans.

A clamor of war cries shivered the air. Lances tossed high above spreading war bonnets in menace and defiance. A noble, gallant spectacle; save for its deadly meaning.

Then Regret saw Iron Shirt ride out before the van.

The great chief lifted an arm in a gesture of majesty. Across his lips he struck his open hand, and from his throat pealed the Comanche war scream.

All at once he quirted his horse, and charged. With a yell that outdid anything they had previously uttered, the warriors behind him lashed their ponies toward the doomed handful of white men in a glittering thunderbolt of destruction.

Regret drew back his rifle hammer.

Down upon him roared the Indian horde, gaining momentum with every bound. To him, far out ahead of all his friends, it was a vision of horses—white horses, bay horses, black horses, piebald horses—necks outstretched, nostrils distended, manes whipping, bellies to the ground as their flashing hoofs beat the earth. Low the warriors crouched on their mounts, so that he could see little more of the riders than round bull-hide shields, plume-tufted war bonnets, and lance heads twinkling viciously in front.

Murder was in every one of those hundreds of savage hearts. Yet for Regret they did not exist at all. Save for only one.

The rifle was at his shoulder, and again he marveled at its perfect balance. One shot he had. One only. There would be no time to reload. On that single leaden messenger flying across space depended everything.

He snuggled his cheek against the stock, and his eye glanced down the sights. In them he caught a crinkling web of steel.

No, he must not risk that. The bullet might be deflected by the links of mail, only to increase Iron Shirt's supernatural reputation, making more certain the fate of those among the rocks.

A smaller target. The sights lifted.

So close was the charge now that Regret could see the scowling, twisted Comanche visages, smeared hideously with war paint.

Only one was not scowling. Iron Shirt, twenty yards ahead of all his warriors, rode erect and not crouching, with a strange face of calm, as if he were wondering, planning already his next move, almost aloof from the excitement and turmoil of the battle he was leading.

Regret sucked in a deep breath. The rifle barrel steadied. His finger crooked on the trigger.

The recoil jolted his shoulder at the rifle's report. For an instant a white puff of smoke blotted out everything before his eyes.

In that instant a prayer was in Paul Regret's heart. If he had got Iron Shirt, the Comanches could spear him now.

Smoke drifted aside. Great God! Iron Shirt still rode toward him, erect and calm. He had missed. . . .

In that dreadful moment the fact that he would be the first to be killed did not seem particularly important to Regret. Curiously, he felt at first only annoyance with himself at missing. Then he was sick with disappointment that he had risked the shot at the head, when he was sure he could have struck the chief in the body. Very probably the bullet would have cut through the steel links anyway.

An error in judgment . . . with what fearful consequences.

To be slaughtered, all of them—Eloise to die——

And he lay helpless, his one chance squandered.

Suddenly he blinked. *Iron Shirt's saddle was empty.*

The horse still galloped forward, but the grim rider was gone.

Regret's heart gave a great leap. He had not missed after all. The invincible vitality of the great Comanche had carried him on, erect in his saddle, for yards after he was dead—with the bullet in his brain.

Now, let the savages do their will on Paul Regret. . . .

But warriors were pulling their horses to jolting stops. In a confused trampling of many hoofs, clouds of dust mounted skyward. The charge had disintegrated, shrill cries of alarm, of consternation filled the air. Regret was forgotten—forgotten were those Rangers among the rocks —in the stunning national tragedy which had befallen the Comanche people.

Two braves circled their horses and seized their fallen chief, one by each arm, lifting his body from the ground between them. Thus carrying him, they galloped to the rear. In a disorderly mass every other Comanche followed them.

At the foot of the cliffs they stretched Iron Shirt on the ground. Chiefs huddled about him momentarily, then scattered to their horses again.

Iron Shirt was dead. The legend of invulnerability, of invincibility, was shattered.

Regret heard the Indian voices, voices of fear and mourning, voices of despair, as they disappeared into the throat of the gorge, bearing with them the body of their chief—the body of their hopes, their fighting fame, their pride, their unity.

The voices grew faint, still more faint, faded into the distance. . . .

3

Paul Regret buried his head in his arms. Suddenly he was very weary. All washed out.

Thoughts, confused thoughts, ran through his mind.

They were safe, back there among the rocks . . . Eloise was safe now. An overwhelming relief and thankfulness in that.

The Comanchero roost would be so utterly destroyed by the Rangers that no trace of it would remain in Palo Duro canyon to affront the earth in after years.

Sam Houston would be profoundly pleased. The miracle had taken place. He would have his twelve months of peace on the border, for the Comanches would not take the field again until a full year of ceremonial mourning for Iron Shirt, the greatest leader they had ever produced, had passed. Houston now could be sure of his mighty ambition to bring Texas safely into the Union.

There is majesty in greatness. Remembering Houston's roughhewn face, and the reserve power in it which only men of supreme caliber possess, Regret thought also of Iron Shirt. And in his soul he knew that the lordly Comanche, whom he had done to death, was great also, in his own way, according to his own lights.

He heard a tramping of feet. At last he summoned strength in his weariness to raise his head.

The Rangers were coming to him, some mounted, others afoot. By an untold effort, he sat up.

He saw Eloise and Wyman Cruze walking together, ahead of them all.

She began to run to him. Tears, salt as the sea, were on her cheeks. She was kneeling beside him, her young arms about him, cradling his battered head on her shoulder.

One part of his mind became conscious of sound. Voices beating in his ears. The Rangers . . . a storm of cheering for Paul Regret . . . a wild, frantic tribute from men who had seen him incredibly, singlehandedly, save them all. The cheering made him feel humble, and grateful, and unworthy.

But he was too tired even to lift his eyes. The cool, smooth cheek of the girl against his was for the moment the only verity in life.